THE KILLING SHED

Chrissy Ferguson Mysteries Book 1

C. L. Janet

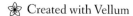

This book is dedicated to my Mum.
You were the strongest person I ever knew. You taught me to believe that I could do anything with some hard work and imagination. Now, I am putting that to the test.
I miss you every day.

Also by C. L. Janet

Cargill's Leap

The Devil's Elbow (Free in ebook at www.
cljanetauthor.com or available in paperback at Amazon)

1

CHRISSY DIDN'T FEEL the need to pull the smart tweed jacket around her skinny frame, the internal warmth of inebriation fending off the chill wind sweeping down Edinburgh's Haymarket. Focusing on putting one foot in front of the other, she kept her head down, not wanting to be noticed by anyone who knew her. The only excuse for Chrissy's drunkenness was that it was Tuesday. Tomorrow's excuse would be that it was Wednesday. But then she only drank to stop a dead girl doing guest spots in her dreams.

The sound of laughter drew her attention. Students tipped out from the red-fronted bar imaginatively named 'Jock's Place', staggering arm in arm across the street to catch the last bus back to the halls of residence. Chrissy quickly averted her eyes, clinging to the shadows cast by the shuttered stores. Running into students that could be in her class tomorrow was not appealing. They paid her no heed, too intent on their flirting to be interested in an *almost* thirty-year-old drunk platting her way home.

The flat was only a few hundred yards away, above a trendy French Bistro that would be closed now leaving the heady stench of garlic hanging in the night air. The aromas from the evening's cooking would find their way upstairs, stubbornly clinging to the cheap soft furnishings no matter what she did to banish them.

Chrissy made slow progress, her legs leaden, whisky sloshing around her otherwise empty stomach. The edge of her vision was blurring, the cracks in the pavement wobbling like they were made of wool. She had overdone it tonight. Screwing up her eyes, she tried to reset the fuzziness. It only made matters worse, her head swimming as soon as her equilibrium lost the landmarks to orient it.

Trying to refocus, her head floated, the lights of Haymarket tracking paths like shooting stars across her retinas. Disoriented, she continued to move forwards, waiting for the world to become stable again. Chrissy caught her foot on something soft yet immobile, the toe of her sensible shoe wedging against it while the rest of her body continued to lurch forwards. The sound of her forehead rattling the shutters of Doozie's Gifts echoed along the emptying street, Chrissy's brain ricocheting off the sides of her skull as bone met metal.

Grabbing at the bars between the shutters, Chrissy broke her fall, halting her rapid descent to the floor. For a moment she let herself hang there, waiting for her consciousness to take control of her limbs. Hauling herself up, she looked down to see what had laid waste to her remaining dignity. It was difficult to make out the person huddled in the doorway, threadbare blankets bundled around every limb to stave off the cold Scottish night.

'I'm so sorry. I . . . I didn't see you,' Chrissy stammered, stepping back to put a respectable distance between herself and the feet that had almost floored her.

The girl was tucked as far back as possible into the recessed doorway, her hooded head obscured by the darkness. Only the eyes peering over the scarf wrapped around her face were visible, the strip light from the window filtering under the shutter to reflect on their watery surface.

She showed no sign of moving. Chrissy took another step back, feeling uneasy under her scrutiny.

'I really am sorry . . .'

The girl leaned forwards, her face emerging from the umbra as she pulled down her hood. The air around Chrissy solidified, capturing the oxygen, rendering it unavailable. Her throat constricted, dry air clawing at her windpipe as she tried to swallow. The sound of the street faded away, leaving behind a deafening void of silence penetrated only by the corporal noises of her own body. She was paralysed, rooted to the spot, unable to do anything except stare. It wasn't possible. It couldn't be her. But unmistakably, it *was* her.

The ground beneath Chrissy's feet seemed to shake, tremors creeping up her body. Still, she could not tear her gaze away. She had fallen over the girl whose deadness had disturbed her sleep for the last twenty years.

The girl raised a black pencilled-in eyebrow, cocking her head as she contemplated Chrissy. Her eyes were too familiar, the smudged winged eyeliner extending out to dyed black hair plastered in sweaty clumps against her forehead. Silver studs pierced through her nose and lips. Details that were more than a coincidence.

The girl began to ferret around in the blankets that swathed her body, retrieving a dirty rag that she held out towards Chrissy. The sleeve of her jacket pulled back revealing inexpertly inked tattoos extending back from the wrist to her forearm.

'You're bleeding,' the girl said, her voice light and girlish, incongruent with the darkness of her appearance.

Chrissy's hand flew up to her forehead, awareness of the warm trickle of blood penetrating her stagnation. Red viscous fluid coated her fingers, incipient pain throbbing in time with the thumping in her chest. The girl wafted the rag again, but she couldn't take it. With a sigh, the girl shuffled out, rising to her feet and moving over to where Chrissy stood her shoes still welded to the pavement.

The girl was short, the top of her head barely reaching shoulder level on Chrissy's five-foot-ten frame. She began to wipe the blood from Chrissy's fingers in a motherly way, vivid red streaks mingling with the dried-in stains from God knows what. Now that she was close, Chrissy became aware of a rancid smell emanating from her, a mix of unwashed clothes, sweat and something sweet and sickly that made her nose crease involuntarily. As the girl moved to dab the rag against her forehead, Chrissy pulled away from her touch.

'You do it then,' she said, holding out the blood-stained cloth.

Chrissy took it, more to halt the ministrations than from a desire to mop her brow. Even in shock, filth touching the open wound on her head seemed foolhardy.

'Thank you.'

The words creaked out of her, finding their way through the inertia to the outside.

'You're welcome, Chrissy.'

The sound of her name reverberated through her muscles like an explosion of energy, waking her from torpor.

'Wait! You know my name.'

The girl didn't answer, turning away to return to the sanctity of the doorway. Chrissy grabbed at her arm. She stopped, turning back, an arcane smile curling her lips.

'How do you know my name?' Chrissy demanded.

Without a word, the girl began to unwind the scarf wrapped around her neck, her dark eyes fixed on Chrissy's face. The sickly stench intensified as the fabric fell away, the jagged hole in the girl's neck belching blood with each beat of her heart. Chrissy staggered back crashing into a parked car. The alarm began to wail shattering the silence like broken glass. Her legs crumbled and she slid to the floor, her breath rasping thick and fast.

'No, no! It isn't possible. You can't be here!'

Chrissy was shaking her head, her voice panicked as the reality of the girl tangled with images from her dreams. She squeezed her eyes tight shut, blocking out the familiarity of the girl's face, the reality of the wound she had seen inflicted night after night.

Someone was kneeling beside her, shaking her, calling her.

'Missy! Missy! Are you OK?'

The unwashed smell drifted across her nostrils again. Chrissy opened her eyes, daring to let the world back in. A woman wrapped in a black scarf was leaning over her, concern etched on her lined face.

'Are you all right dear?' she asked, her grubby hands cold as she pressed her palms to Chrissy's cheeks.

'What happened? The girl . . .'

'What girl?' the woman asked, looking around. 'There's only you and me here love. I was helping you with your cut and you freaked out.'

'It . . . it was you?'

Chrissy focused on the woman, middled aged, grey-haired and completely intact. She didn't know her. Scrabbling to her feet, she leaned against the car still blaring out the violation, the filthy rag balled up in her fist.

'You gave me this?' she asked, holding the cloth out towards the woman who nodded, eyeing her warily.

Chrissy's head was spiralling. Nothing made sense. Pushing the rag into the woman's hand, she walked unsteadily towards the flat, her staggering no longer the fault of too much booze. All traces of alcohol had drained away as her dream crashed unceremoniously into reality.

Fumbling with the keys, she let herself in, collapsing onto the stairs as weakness overwhelmed her. The girl had been a constant presence in Chrissy's life since she was a child, dying over and over again in her nightmares. The dream had come only rarely until four years ago. Then everything changed. Now Chrissy saw the same girl murdered night after night unless she obliterated her consciousness in a bottle.

Running her hands through her dishevelled hair, Chrissy heaved herself up and climbed wearily upstairs. Her head was pulsing, a dull ache settling where she had face-planted the shutter. Without pausing to remove her jacket, she snatched a half-empty bottle of whisky from amongst the melee of shopping channel packaging balancing precariously on the countertop, the image of the girl refusing to leave her mind.

The sagging frame of the sofa creaked as her legs failed to control her descent. Pouring a healthy measure into the used glass on the coffee table, she downed it in one swallow, the neat spirit scalding her throat comfortingly. Resting her head back, Chrissy focused on her breathing, counting it in and out until the rhythm slowed. Her body was shaking uncontrollably, goosebumps prickling her skin. She kicked off her shoes, pulling the red tartan blanket from the back of the sofa and wrapping it around her body as she curled up against the hand-knitted cushion she had brought from her mother's house.

Chrissy had never felt more alone. There was no one to listen. No one to comfort her, tell her it was just a dream. No one to reassure her the girl hadn't really been there, that the knock on the head had probably confused her. Even if there had been someone to offer those words of platitude, Chrissy wouldn't have believed them. The truth was better. She was losing her mind. It wasn't entirely unexpected. Mental unbalance was a family trait.

2

A LOUD BEEPING sound rang through her head, becoming more and more insistent as she tried to drag herself into the land of the living. Something was suffocating her. The hand-knitted cushion was smothering her as she woke face down on the deflated royal blue couch, still wearing her tweed jacket and the smell of stale whisky. Chrissy raised her head with difficulty, trying to get her dry, scratchy eyes to focus on the here and now and the source of the noise.

Struggling to her feet, she stumbled over the tartan blanket that was wrapped, vice-like around her legs. Her shin clattered into the small coffee table, sending her empty glass and a pile of student essays tumbling to the floor.

'Shit, shit, shit!'

Chrissy rubbed at the bruise blooming beneath her jeans as she hobbled stiffly to the bedroom. Banging her hand repeatedly on the shouting clock, she eventually hit the snooze button by chance, restoring relative calm. Sinking onto the unmade bed, she steadied her head on her hands wincing as she pressed the angry welt on her forehead. The dull throb added to the pounding headache already rattling her teeth, blood starting to bead where the cut opened up again.

Her stomach churned, protesting at the lack of anything solid to soak up the alcohol. No time to eat. It was eight o'clock. Time to move. With a momentous effort, she hoisted herself to her feet, the room swimming around her, the urgent need to pee driving her towards the tired bathroom. As she sat down, the clock piped up again.

'For Christ's sake, shut the fuck up!'

The clock did not oblige but picked up the pace and volume of its beeps. Pulling up her pants on the move, she reached the clock just as it took a momentary break from the yelling. Flicking the switch to 'off', she reset it ready for the next day. The bed looked inviting, but she couldn't lie down again. Coffee. Coffee would help.

She walked back into the living room and picked up the glass that thankfully hadn't smashed. Setting it upright on the table, she gathered the essays from the floor, large red letters on the corner rewarding the students' efforts. She leafed through the top paper. There were comments throughout the text in her hand. Comments she had done in the wee small hours while watching late-night repeats on the shopping channel, distracted by a sun-kissed woman in a smart suit demonstrating the essential features of a luggage set that came in a choice of six colours. When she had found herself considering five suitcases in a turquoise palm tree print despite never having travelled further than London, Chrissy had turned down the sound and started marking the essays. Anything to keep the dead girl out of her headspace.

The coffee maker had turned on automatically at the same time as the alarm. Pleased she remembered to set it last night, the smell of fresh coffee lured her across the room. The flat had one main living space that served as both lounge and kitchen. The walls were a shit-brown colour no one would ever choose for their own home. White tiles and kitchen units, doors drooping with neglect, broke up the dour monotony.

When she moved in, Chrissy was excited to have a place of her own in the big city. She had nested, adding splashes of colour with plants soon replaced by vases of fake flowers after their demise at her hand. Most of the furniture had come with the flat and had that 'rented accommodation' look, its cheapness showing in the wear and tear. The walls were mainly obscured with art and bookshelves she had added in the early days, now layered with at least a year's worth of dust.

Chrissy searched for an almost clean mug, finding one teetering on the corner of the desk threatened by a landslide of junk mail offering discount tyres, deals at

Farm Foods and manifestos from at least five years of by-elections. She filled it from the coffee pot, then searched around for last night's whisky bottle. Finding it stuffed behind a sofa cushion, she poured the remaining contents into the mug, the bottle making a clunk as she threw it into the recycling to join its brothers.

The email request was waiting in her inbox when Chrissy switched on the office computer half an hour later. A summons like this was unlikely to be good. In seven years at the University, she had been to the Dean's office only three times. Once, four years ago, as a 'welcome to the faculty' when she had transitioned from post-graduate student to full-time lecturer. Then again about a week later for an awkward conversation about the bereavement policy. Last year, a student accused her of drinking on the job and she had been hauled in again. Little shit. She never drank on the job.

There were no details in the email. Just a 'please come and see me at your earliest convenience' request. She wasn't teaching until ten so there was no reason not to go now. Chrissy spent a few moments trying to find an excuse to delay. Nothing came and there was no use putting it off.

Opening the top drawer, she sprayed her mouth with one of the breath fresheners rolling around in there, then searched the debris in the bottom of her bag for an extra strong mint. Confident she smelled minty fresh, Chrissy made her way out of the office and along the corridor, past numerous office doors with name-plates signifying the occupant or department that lived there.

The stairwell was deserted as she made her way down. The only students on campus at this time of day were ensconced in 9 am classes trying to open their minds to the pearls of wisdom being delivered by learned souls. Or at least trying to feign interest while fighting to stay awake. Chrissy was grateful she didn't see anyone from the faculty either. If she had, she would have been forced to say where she was going and that would have led to questions later in the staff room about what 'Hitler' wanted.

The Dean earned the nickname due to her auto-cratic ruling of the School, with few colleagues both-ering to engage in any discussion knowing the outcome of 'staff consultation' was already decided. The recently polished nameplate came into view all too quickly - 'Dean, School of Philosophy, Psychology and Language Sciences'. Chrissy could hear a one-sided conversation coming in hushed tones from within. Hitler was on the phone. She was about to turn away when she heard the receiver go down and silence fell. No getting away from it.

She knocked tentatively.

'Come in.'

Chrissy took a deep breath, then pushed open the heavy, wood-veneered door.

'Ah Chrissy, yes. Please come in and take a seat.'

Hitler stood up as she entered, indicating one of the upholstered chairs facing the imposing, clutter-free desk that spanned almost the full width of the long, narrow office.

'And close the door behind you.'

Ominous. This was a conversation not to be overheard.

Chrissy did as she was told, her stomach tightening as she took the designated seat. Hitler, real name, Professor Patricia Edgecombe, sat down, clasping her hands over the desk, her small blue eyes peering hard through tortoiseshell, brow line glasses. Her hair was too thin and straggly to suit the shoulder-length cut she favoured, the overall impression made worse by her determination to fight natural curls with straightening irons every day.

The silence stretched awkwardly as Patricia searched for words to start the conversation. Chrissy shifted nervously on the uncomfortable chair.

'What happened to your head?'

Chrissy felt the freshly applied band-aid stuck to her forehead.

'Oh, nothing. I fell.'

A frown passed fleetingly across Patricia's face quickly replaced by a forced smile.

'Do you want some herbal tea?'

Not what Chrissy was expecting, but at least it meant she probably wasn't going to be fired. You didn't make tea for someone about to receive their marching orders.

'Coffee if you've got it.'

Hitler nodded, her insincere politeness exaggerating the simpering sound of her voice.

'I'm sure I can manage that. I don't have any sugar or milk in here, but I can go and get some from Susan if you want it?'

Susan was the hapless, eternally morose secretary that sat in a small office next door, tending to Patricia Edgecombe's needs from Monday to Thursday. On Friday, she had to fend for herself after a recent review of the support services identified money-saving cuts, resulting in the last day of the week becoming self-service for Deans.

'No, it's fine. Black with no sugar's how I like it.'

Patricia came around the desk to where a small kettle was balanced on an empty bookshelf. She was a small woman – only about five foot two – but rather too round for the size twelve pantsuit she had squeezed into. The navy-blue trousers were stretched tightly across her buttocks, the zip barely hanging on as it strained across the evidence of her love of fudge doughnuts. The pinstriped blazer was a nice cut but the days when it fastened and hung flatteringly on her body were long gone. The outfit was finished with a white blouse sporting a blue biro mark on the front, and frumpy court shoes bought for comfort, not style.

It was impossible to put an age on Hitler. Her complexion was pale until something annoyed her. Then she passed from ruddy to puce in the blink of an eye. But her skin was relatively unlined and speculation amongst the faculty put her in her mid-forties.

Patricia passed Chrissy a chipped bone china mug decorated with ugly flowers, containing a brown liquid that barely passed for coffee.

'Thanks.'

Chrissy took a sip and wrinkled her nose, sliding the mug onto the desk hoping the conversation would move on and she wouldn't have to pick it up again.

'So, Chrissy, how've you been?'

This was obviously a diversion. Starting the conversation with some friendly overtures and enquiring about the person's health, were the first lessons in 'Being an Effective Line Manager 101'. The next step was to ask about family. That was null and void in Chrissy's case. She didn't have any family anymore.

Chrissy was eager to get this over, the dance around the real reason she was here becoming quickly tiresome.

'Professor Edgecombe, thank you for enquiring about my well-being, but I'm sure it isn't the reason you asked to see me. Is there something you want to discuss?'

Chrissy crossed her legs, relaxing back into the chair and lacing her fingers in her lap. Her dark eyes stared intently at her boss who flinched almost imperceptibly at her directness. Hitler seemed flustered. She had planned to follow the chapter on having difficult conversations with staff to the letter. But Chrissy had just jumped over a few stages and now she needed to regain her focus.

'My enquiring after your well-being is not entirely unrelated to why you're here Chrissy.'

Now we were getting to it. Hitler started to straighten the already pristine desk, buying some time before she launched into the next sentence. Chrissy watched in silence, preparing herself for what was to come. She felt the familiar knot in her stomach as her muscles braced, ready to fend off any emotion that might threaten to break her.

'You see Chrissy...'

Her name again. Patronising.

'... we, that is me and your colleagues, have been worried about you.'

Bollocks. Her colleagues barely noticed her. Academics spent their days locked away in their offices preparing to teach, marking piles of student work or researching whatever vitally important question was captivating their mind this month. A junior faculty member like Chrissy who actively avoided their company, wouldn't even register in their sphere of awareness. Except for Sarah perhaps. But she wouldn't have come tattling to Hitler. This had come from some-where else.

Chrissy started to jiggle her ankle, her lips pressing together to contain the swear words threatening to escape.

'I'm sorry. Who exactly has been worried about me?'

Despite her best efforts, the question was accusing.

'Well, some people have noticed that you've been struggling recently.'

'Some people?'

'Who doesn't matter now does it? What matters is that people who care about you are worried.'

Spittle sprayed from Chrissy's pursed lips as she sniggered. Her eyes rolled towards the ceiling, settling briefly on a fluorescent tube flickering in the silver reflective light before coming back to Hitler's face. She could see the woman was irritated now, her hands gripped so tightly together the knuckles appeared white.

'OK, so what are these 'people who care about me' worried about?' Chrissy asked with thinly veiled cynicism.

Hitler composed herself, restoring the factitious smile on her face.

'Chrissy, it hasn't gone unnoticed that you're not looking after yourself very well.'

She looked Chrissy up and down as she spoke, making her shift uncomfortably, pulling her smart navy-blue blazer closer around her undernourished frame.

'And the drinking Chrissy. It's clear you haven't got to grips with the drinking yet despite our conversation a few years ago.'

There it was. The real reason she was here. Someone had reported her again for drinking. But she had been careful. She never drank at work and never directly before she taught a class.

'Have I been doing my job?'

Chrissy's voice was clipped, each word articulated clearly.

'What do you mean?'

'Have I ever missed a lecture, a deadline, or failed to turn up to a meeting?'

'Well no. But . . .'

'Have I ever delivered a bad lecture, received poor feedback from the students about my classes, or failed to offer the necessary support when needed?'

'No, not at all. Your classes are highly praised by the students. You know that.'

'Well then, is it any business of the *'people who care about me'* if I chose to have a drink sometimes when the workday is done?'

Hitler couldn't miss the anger in her tone now. Realising this wasn't going well, she changed tack.

'Chrissy, I've no doubt you're a good teacher, and you do your job admirably. It's even more impressive that you cope so well when it is clear to me, and others, that personally, things aren't as they should be.'

Chrissy leaned forward, opening her mouth ready to let go of a tirade about it being no one's business and she just wanted to be left alone. But Hitler raised her hand.

'Just hear me out will you.'

She swallowed back the words and reluctantly settled back into the chair, her jaw set, defiance radiating from every part of her body.

'Since your mother died, you've barely been hanging on Chrissy. It's not surprising. You haven't given yourself any time to grieve. You only took a couple of days off and haven't taken a day of annual leave since. It's not doing you any good.'

Chrissy sat in silence, chewing the inside of her lip.

'I think you should consider taking a leave of absence. Get yourself together. Get a handle on the drinking. Look after yourself for a while.'

Patricia stared over the top of her glasses, tenting her fingers while she waited for Chrissy to respond.

'Are you forcing me to take some time off?'

'No, no of course not. But I think you should. I'm worried about you Chrissy.'

This was a lie and they both knew it. What she was worried about was Chrissy going off the deep end and causing disharmony in her School.

'Is that it then? Can I go? I have a class to teach in ten minutes.'

'Yes. Yes, you can go. But please think about what I've said, Chrissy. Take some time off.'

Chrissy flew out of the chair like it was burning her bony arse, racing to the door that she almost ripped off its hinges in her eagerness to escape. Her head swam, the banging in her chest resonating through her ears as she strode rapidly down the corridor. Taking the stairs two at a time, she reached her office sweaty and out of breath. The plaque on her door read 'Dr Chrissy Ferguson, PhD. Forensic Psychologist', but it lacked the shine of the one on the Dean's door. Fingerprints marked the tarnished brass; staff offices up here were only cleaned once in a blue moon.

When she joined the faculty, that name plaque had been her pride and joy. It meant she had arrived, with a shiny new Doctorate and a permanent job teaching her speciality. It was to be the start of everything. Her career, her life. She lived her perfect life for one whole week. Then her mother walked into Rannoch Loch on a cold January day.

August 1994

Father was still, his life leaching away in the blood blooming across the fetid floor. A calloused hand clutched at the wound in his neck, an inconsequential effort to slow the inevitable. It appealed to the boy's spirit, seeing Father attempting to save himself, watching fear mount at the realisation he was going to die.

The gurgling coming from Father's throat faded to nothing, the hand caked in blood falling to his side. The boy took a few steps forward, kneeling by the dead body of the man he had hated all his life. Father's eyes stared unseeing, his slack mouth revealing the few, yellow-stained teeth that had managed to survive fifty years. It was strange to see someone whose presence had filled every corner of his world reduced to this, a decaying mass of flesh and bone, a pathetic heap of soon-to-be stinking meat.

Leaning over the body, he brought his face close. The smell of tobacco and whisky mixed with the coppery stench of blood and shit as Father's bowels emptied.

'You'll never hurt me again,' he whispered, hawking back a gob of phlegm, the salty taste registering before he spat into Father's vacant eyes.

The sticking knife was still clutched in his hand, Father's blood mingling with gore from the days' slaughtering. Calmly, he replaced it in the leather roll beside other butchery tools, tying it up and leaving it by the shed door. He would keep that. A memento of this day.

He looked back at Father's body. It wasn't right to leave him lying peacefully in death. He didn't deserve peace. The sound of bones breaking underfoot as he stomped on Father's dead fingers was thrilling, the force of his heavy boot smashing down on the face that had tormented him, exhilarating. When his energy was spent, Father's face was unrecognisable, cheekbones shattered, leathery skin torn by the viciousness of his kicks.

The shackles hung from the pulley on the ceiling. He fastened the chain around Father's thick ankle, the iron rattling as it pulled tight. It took every ounce of strength his sixteen-year-old arms possessed to hoist twenty-stone of dead weight. Breath rasping, sweat running from his brow, he secured the chains to stop Father crashing back to the floor.

Wiping his top lip on a shirt sleeve, heart pumping

with exertion and revenge, he staggered back. Father's corpse swung above him, arms hanging down, mouth drooping open, skin sagging as flaccid muscles let go. Death had always disgusted him. The end of life marred by everything wretched the body was capable of. Only the blood was beautiful, scarlet, silky, deserving to be set free before the end came. Before it was imprisoned inside rotting flesh, contaminated by mouldering tissue.

His breathing began to calm, the silence of the shed disturbed only by the creaking of wooden beams as Father swayed back and forth. As he watched the body stilled, the momentum, gone. There was nothing left. Nothing of the man that was Father. Nothing of the boy he had been.

The morning sun assaulted his eyes as he pushed open the door, the brightness of the day contrasting with the darkness inside him. He slid the bar across, padlocking the shed but not knowing why. No one would come looking for Father. There was no one left to care.

3

'Why do people kill?'

Chrissy looked around the class, pacing back and forth in front of the podium. Blank faces stared back at her, no one willing to make the first contribution. She rephrased.

'What evolutionary benefits does murder bring to a killer?'

She waited, a few bodies shifting, steeling themselves to open the discussion. A hand raised on the third row. Taylor Benson, a blond-haired, blue-eyed American, swimming in the arrogance his good looks and family money granted him. None too bright though.

Chrissy stretched out a hand to acknowledge him, her fingers trembling as she pointed.

'Access to a good shag.'

A ripple of laughter passed through the students, Taylor revelling in the attention.

Chrissy smiled. Smart arse. She'd met many Taylor Benson's in her classroom.

'Yes, sex is a strong evolutionary motive for killing, but can you explain why?'

She stared Taylor down until he lost his swagger. As expected, he wasn't planning on elaborating. Chrissy looked around the class when it became obvious he had nothing more to say.

There were about forty bodies in the lecture hall today, two-thirds of those registered. Not bad for a Wednesday morning. She did well with attendance, the controversial topics helping prise students from their beds. Her class was in one of the nicer lecture halls today, raked seating with benches rather than flip-style desks students could hide behind texting their friends two rows back. The room had no windows, giving it a serious place of learning vibe once the lights were dimmed and the PowerPoint slides illuminated the front.

'Well, sex is paramount to Hamilton's theory of genetic fitness.'

Someone had done the reading. Chrissy scanned the rows looking for the source of the voice. Chloe McBride. An enigma. Trowelled on make-up, false eyelashes reaching her tattooed eyebrows, shocking pink false nails too long to facilitate manual dexterity, and bleach-blonde hair. She looked like a porn star but thought like an academic.

'Go on Chloe.'

'Hamilton's theory is all about passing genes on to the next generation either directly to your own kids, or indirectly through your genetic relatives having kids.'

The girl knew her stuff. Chrissy nodded in encouragement, the movement rattling her tender brain against her skull.

'To pass on their genes, men need to compete with other men for limited resources, like for fertile women. One way to do that is to get rid of the competition and make sure they 'get the girl' so to speak.'

'Good. Good. Can anyone add anything to that?'

Chrissy looked around, opening the floor. No one spoke, so she prompted again.

'What about female choice?'

A couple of hands in the middle of the class shot up. Chrissy picked on Janice Williams, a quiet loner from the wrong side of town who rarely spoke but could best them all in smarts. Chrissy noticed a few mean girls roll their eyes as Janice shifted in her seat, immediately regretting raising her hand.

The girl was pale, spotty and unwashed. Her dark hair hung limply around her ashen face, clinging to the sides like a pair of half-drawn curtains. Her clothes were cheap, old and muted, the grey jumper misshapen and threadbare around the elbows. Chrissy couldn't see from here but was certain she'd be wearing the usual unfashionable jeans and black lace-up pumps almost worn through on the soles.

Chrissy liked Janice. She always had a special affinity for students that made it here against the odds. They worked harder, appreciating the opportunity more. The girl began to mumble.

'Say that again Janice. I didn't quite catch it.'

Janice cleared her throat, fidgeted again and took a deep breath in. Chrissy waited, giving her a chance to compose herself. Red blotches appeared down the girl's neck and Chrissy could see the pen shaking as she gripped it for support.

'Women are the limited sex.'

Janice's voice was thin, shaky, but audible.

'Limited how?' Chrissy asked.

'Limited because they can only have so many reproductive events in their lifetime - so many babies. So, they need to make sure every baby they have is the best it can be – I mean genetically –so they're choosy. They chose the best quality male they can.'

'But what has any of that got to do with killing someone?'

The interruption came from Edward Souter in the back row. A know-it-all whose favourite pastime was to ask questions with the sole aim of demonstrating his intellect. Dark-haired, good-looking in a studious way, glasses he probably only wore because they made him look worldly, and bumfluff on his chin that looked ridiculous.

Chrissy was about to step in but Janice, surprisingly, had it covered.

'If you just listen, I'm trying to explain,' she said sharply, wheeling around to give Edward a hard stare.

Chrissy suppressed a smile.

'Go on Janice.'

'If you're a poor-quality man who hasn't got much going for you...'

Janice rolled her eyes and cocked her head in Edward's direction. Chrissy couldn't help her smirk. This girl was not as downtrodden as she seemed.

'...you aren't likely to get picked, are you? That would seriously damage your chance of passing on genes to the next generation. No woman, no sex, no kids, no genes passed on. If you're in that situation, you could improve your chances by reducing the number of good quality males around – bump a few off so your chance of being picked by a woman goes up.'

'But in that case, all murderers would be weak men who couldn't attract a woman and that's clearly not true. A lot of murderers are described as attractive, charismatic. Not the dregs of the gene pool.'

Edward was on a roll. Janice turned round to face him again.

'I'm not saying it's the only reason, just one strategy that could improve someone's chances of fathering kids.'

No sign of Janice's nervousness now. She was eloquent, clear and assertive. Chrissy let them take turns as they debated the point for a few rounds, listening, waiting for the exchange to get too heated or go off-topic. These moments made the job worthwhile. Young minds flexing their academic muscles, developing an argument based on their nascent understanding of the material, empowered by their learning.

Tempers were beginning to fray, voices talking over one another, neither respecting the rules of conversational turn-taking. Time to intervene.

'I think you're both making some good points.'

Chrissy raised her voice to be heard. Edward and Janice quieted, each looking smug, both believing they had won.

'The point here is that understanding how evolution has shaped the human psyche can help us understand the good and bad of human behaviour better. That doesn't mean every human will behave according to the hard-nosed interpretation of evolutionary theory. What evolutionary psychologists are saying is that ultimately, all human behaviour can be better understood in the light of evolutionary theory. That is, if we realise that everyone, whether we like to think of it this way or not, will make decisions that benefit their survival and reproductive success, we can make sense of human actions, even those that seem abnormal or detrimental. Like murder.'

Her monologue was met with interested stares. Chrissy paused to let her words sink in.

'OK. On the handout I passed around, you'll find a

press release about a five-year-old girl who was killed by her father. Working in small groups, I want you to identify the potential evolutionary drivers for this crime.'

There was a rustle of papers and banging of seats as the class rearranged itself into twos and threes. Chrissy was surprised to see Edward clamouring over rows of benches to get to Janice, who looked equally surprised to see him settle into the seat next to her. They immediately picked up where they left off, with lots of agitated handwaving as each tried to make their point more vociferously than the other.

Chrissy leaned back against the podium, enjoying the sound of chatter coming from all parts of the lecture hall, the ugly scene in the Dean's office momentarily forgotten. She walked up each aisle, catching snippets of conversations, most focused on the task she set. Another few minutes, then she'd bring the class back together to collate their thoughts.

Edward and Janice were still going at it. It looked like he may have met his match in the girl from the wrong side of the tracks. Good for her.

'Right, turn back to face me. Let's hear what you came up with.'

More shuffling and some low-level chatter while each group manoeuvred until everyone was facing the front.

Chrissy glanced around, waiting for the hubbub to

settle. Then she saw her. Sitting in the middle of the empty row behind Edward and Janice. The girl.

Chrissy staggered back, catching herself on the podium as she swayed, dizzy, sick. Closing her eyes, she hoped when they opened again, the girl would be gone. But she wasn't. Still, she sat there, eyes no longer cold or dead but fixed on Chrissy, a smile playing on the corners of her lips as if she was pleased to be there. Her skin looked livid, pallid against the gaping wound in her neck, the blood, old now, congealed in brown stains across the ravaged throat.

Chrissy's breath caught in her chest, sweat beading on her top lip.

'Dr Ferguson, Dr Ferguson, are you OK?'

She hadn't noticed Chloe McBride leave the seats and come to her side. The girl was holding her arm, taking some weight to prevent her collapsing in a heap. Chrissy looked around. Everything was blurred, distorted as if behind frosted glass. Everything except her, the girl from the dream who stood out in high definition, smiling benignly from the middle row. Chrissy screwed her eyes more tightly closed. *I'm losing my mind.* She could hear Chloe calling again, her voice drifting in from miles away.

Other students came to the front. Chrissy was vaguely aware of more hands under her armpits, stronger hands, probably male. Letting the image of the lecture hall in again, she tried to focus on where the girl sat, but the view was blocked by more people trying to offer help. Straining, she looked out towards the benches. They were empty now apart from the few students who had stayed in their seats rather than come to her aid. The dead girl was gone.

Chrissy felt strength return to her legs.

'I'm OK. I'm OK,' she murmured, holding her weight and pulling her arms away from the grip of those around her. 'Really, I'm all right. I just went a bit dizzy, that's all. Please, I'm fine.'

All eyes were on her. She straightened herself up and tried to look together. It probably wasn't working because everyone was still looking like she was damaged goods.

'Please, go back to your seats. I'll be fine. But I think we'll call it a day. I probably just need some water and something to eat. I skipped breakfast.'

Her light-hearted tone seemed to reassure the class as they slowly drifted back to their seats to retrieve their belongings. Chrissy scoured the room. Still no sign of the dead girl.

The students filtered out, only Janice pausing to look back, her eyes silently questioning. Chrissy raised her hand in a wave and nodded to the girl, who, satisfied, followed the rest of the class out. The lecture hall was empty now. Completely empty. Only the sound of Chrissy's heart hammering in her chest disturbed the peace. No dead dream girl.

Chrissy pushed open the exit door and tried to walk calmly on jelly legs. She wanted to run back to the sanctuary of her office, close the door on the world and try to get a hold of herself. She wanted a drink. Only the weakness and tremors wracking every inch of her body prevented her from breaking into a sprint.

It seemed to take an age to get back to the fifth floor. She even took the lift for what was probably the second time in her life, not trusting her muscles to make the climb. Fumbling, hands shaking so much the lock seemed impenetrable, Chrissy sighed gratefully when eventually the key found its spot. The office was dark even though it wasn't yet noon, the small window restricting all but the most determined light. Usually, she would flick on the fluorescent lights, but not today. She wanted the dark.

Chrissy locked the door from the inside, leaving the keys dangling to ensure even someone with a master key would be kept out. She needed to be alone, safe in her solitude.

Collapsing down on the office chair behind the desk, Chrissy took a small silver hip flask from the bottom drawer - her emergency stash - downing its contents in one. Her hand shook as she tried to screw the small lid back in place. *What the hell happened?* She knew the girl hadn't been there. Knew the vision was in her mind. The problem was why? What was wrong in her head that was making her dreams pay a visit to the lecture hall?

Chrissy looked down at the silver flask still gripped in her hand, fingerprints making steamy marks on the surface. Maybe Hitler was right? Maybe she should take some time off? Get her shit together.

Throwing the flask into her bag, Chrissy snatched up the pile of essays that still needed grading. She reached Hitler's office determined to take her counsel and knocked quickly, not waiting to be invited in.

'I've decided to take your advice. I'm taking a leave of absence with immediate effect.'

Patricia Edgecombe looked benumbed, her mouth hanging open as she searched for words. Chrissy was in no mood to hear anything she might want to say, slamming the essays down onto the neatly organised desk before Hitler could comment.

'These need marking. The students are expecting them back next Monday.'

Chrissy turned to go, leaving her boss in stunned silence. It wasn't until her hand was on the door handle that Patricia found her voice.

'Chrissy, when will you be back?'

'No idea. I'll be in touch.'

4

Two DAYS. Two days since she walked out of the
Dean's office. Two days since she'd had a drink. The
flat never looked cleaner. No dishes in the sink or old
ready-meal trays on the kitchen side. No dirty laundry
on the bedroom floor. No clean laundry on the
armchair. Even the desk had reappeared from under its
habitual farrago.

No bottles in the recycling.

The newsreader launched into a story about the
latest EuroMillions winners. Not what she wanted to
hear. Chrissy turned off the TV and picked up the
book she'd been trying to read. She read the page with
the turned-down corner. None of it seemed familiar.
Turning back a few pages, she scanned for the gist of
the story. Still, nothing she could remember. Throwing
the book across the room, she buried her head in her
hands.

'What the fuck do normal people do!'

There was no one in the room to answer her.

Flicking the TV back on, she surfed through the channels, not giving anything more than a few seconds to hold her interest before moving on. The remote juddered as she balanced her elbow on her knees which were subconsciously bouncing nervously up and down. The TV went off again and Chrissy started to pace the room. God, she needed a drink.

In the kitchen, she opened every cupboard, searching for anything. Even that crap bottle of wine she got in the department's Secret Santa. Nothing. She'd done a good job. There wasn't a drop of alcohol in the place.

Slamming the last cupboard, she ripped off her jumper, the room feeling suddenly stifling. She tossed it on the chair and went to the bedroom to retrieve a green sleeveless tank top from the drawer, tucking it into her jeans before throwing herself back down on the sofa. In seconds, Chrissy was on her feet again, snatching up the discarded jumper, folding it neatly and returning it to the bedroom.

Collecting the book from the floor, she sat down in the armchair, opening it a few chapters back. At the bottom of the first page, she tried to recall what she had just read. Nothing. Shutting the book, she let her head fall back against the sofa, closing her eyes, trying not to think. Immediately, the vision of the dead girl, bleeding from the neck swam through her mind.

'I can't do this!'

Chrissy was on her feet, crossing the room, snatching up her purse and keys. It was no good. She needed a drink. Not just in a physical way. She needed it to cast the images from her mind.

As she reached the door, a loud chime announced someone was on the other side. Chrissy looked through the peephole and smiled. Saved by the bell quite literally.

'Where the fuck have you been? And why aren't you answering your fucking phone? And what the fuck happened to this place? And what the fuck have you done to your hair?'

Dr Sarah Cohen. Chrissy's only friend in the department. Foul-mouthed sociology lecturer who looked like a throwback to the seventies with flared jeans, a tight, striped turtle-neck sweater and blond pigtails she somehow managed to carry off even in her early thirties.

'Well, hello to you too.'

Chrissy tossed her keys and purse back onto the counter as Sarah plonked down onto the armchair that protested even though the woman weighed next to nothing.

'You had me so fucking worried! Hitler said you were taking some time off but wouldn't tell me why.'

Sarah placed a bottle on the table. The whisky's presence seemed to fill the room.

'Pass me a couple of glasses will you? And an ashtray.'

Chrissy went to the cupboard and pulled out two glasses, put one back, handing a glass and saucer that doubled as an ashtray to her friend.

'What the fuck. . .'

'I've given up.'

'Seriously?'

'Yep. Seriously. Two days now.'

Sarah looked at her in amazement, taking a cigarette paper and some tobacco out of her bag.

'I'm going to make tea. Do you want some?'

'Are you kidding me? You look like shit.'

Sarah pointed at Chrissy.

'If that's sobriety, I'll pass thanks.'

Chrissy turned away, trying not to focus on the sound of the whisky's seal breaking, the glugging of the amber liquid into the glass. Trying not to smell the malty aroma that made a beeline for her nose.

Clutching the mug of tea, Chrissy sat down on the sofa, kicking off her shoes and curling her legs underneath her.

'I don't think in all the years I've been coming here I've ever been able to sit on this chair. It's usually covered in shit. It's really fucking uncomfortable.'

Chrissy laughed. It felt good.

Sarah took a slug of whisky and Chrissy could almost taste it. She slurped her tea, looking anywhere but at the coveted glass.

'So come on. Spill. What's going on with you Chrissy? Start with the hair.'

Sarah settled back, pulling her legs up onto the chair and balancing the ashtray in her lap. Clouds of smoke billowed around her head as she exhaled the drag on her cigarette, trying to blow upwards as if this somehow made it disappear and not catch in Chrissy's throat.

Chrissy felt her hair self-consciously. It had seemed like a good idea at the time. A fresh start, new hair. The visit to the hairdressers had happened on her first day off. She had them cut her long red hair into a chin-length bob with a heavy fringe. She wasn't sure she liked it.

'I fancied a change. You know, new start and all.'

Sarah cocked her head to the side, her large steely-blue eyes fixed intently on Chrissy's head.

'I like it. It suits you.'

'Really?'

'Yes, really. Makes you look like a Scottish Twiggy.'

Chrissy laughed again. It was good to have Sarah here.

'You look like shit though. You haven't been sleep-ing, have you?'

Chrissy shook her head. For a moment, they sat in amicable silence, Sarah puffing on her cigarette, Chrissy staring out of the window.

'So why are you holed up here instead of being at work?'

Sarah took another slug of whisky, then topped up her glass.

'Hitler suggested I take some time off.'

'What? What for?'

'Apparently, 'people' are worried about me.'

'Bollocks!'

'That's what I thought. I wasn't going to oblige her, but then...'

Chrissy tailed off. Sarah was the only person she had talked to about the dreams. But even so, telling her she was hallucinating about the dead dream girl when she was awake, was something else.

'Then what?'

Sarah wouldn't judge and she needed to tell someone.

'But then, I saw the girl from my dreams. Once on the street, then in the lecture hall.'

Sarah leaned forwards, placing the ashtray on the small side table, flicking off the ash balancing precariously on her cigarette before settling back again.

'She's a student?'

'No, not exactly. I saw her sitting in the middle row, like some kind of apparition or hallucination or something.'

Chrissy stood up and walked into the kitchen area. She tipped the mug of undrunk tea down the sink then leaned on the countertop, watching her friend for signs of disbelief.

'Are you saying you saw the ghost of your dead dream girl sitting in your lecture?'

'I know. It's ridiculous, isn't it? But yes, I saw her, gaping neck wound and all.'

'Fuck!'

Chrissy came back to sit down. Sarah stared at her, absently rolling another cigarette.

'What are you going to do? Do you think you should get some help?'

'You mean a psychiatrist?'

'Well, it couldn't hurt, could it?'

'I've tried it before. My mother sent me to see someone when I first had the dreams. They said it was 'suppressed grief' after the accident. Pretty hard to accept that as an explanation for my dream girl making guest appearances in my lecture twenty years later.'

'Good point. But that doesn't mean seeing someone now wouldn't be worth it.'

'Maybe. But I think I need to get off the booze first.'

Sarah slowly lowered the glass that was almost at her lips, sliding it onto the table without taking a drink.

'So, what are you going to do with your time off?'

'I have absolutely no idea.'

'Well, the cleaning's done,' Sarah said glancing around the pristine room. 'You've had a makeover. How about going up North? Sorting out the cottage?'

Chrissy shook her head decisively.

'No way. I'm not ready.'

'Chrissy, it's been four years. Maybe going home will let you get some perspective on all this. Sort out what's going on in your head?'

'Trust me, going home is the last thing I need. There's nothing there for me except bad memories.'

'Look, I'm no expert.'

'You don't say.'

Sarah ignored the sarcastic interruption.

'But you haven't dealt with what happened in Kinloch Rannoch. Maybe if you did, it would help. Might even chase your ghosts away.'

'I know you mean well, but I can't. Not yet.'

Sarah knew she was beaten.

'Well at least think about it, won't you? You're going to go stir crazy sitting in here all day.'

Chrissy nodded.

'I promise I'll think about it,' she lied.

There was no way in hell she was going home.

For the next hour, Chrissy relaxed as Sarah disappeared intermittently behind clouds of cigarette smoke. They gossiped about work, bad-mouthed Hitler and reminisced about how academia used to be before mitigating circumstances policies, 'students as partners' agendas and rights of appeal.

As the light began to fade and the sounds of evening revellers drifted up from the street below, Sarah stretched, then looked at her watch.

'Well, I better get going. Got a lecture to finish for

tomorrow. I'll leave you to your... whatever the hell
this is.'

Sarah placed a cigarette she had rolled but not
smoked into her tobacco tin and stood up.

'You better take that with you,' Chrissy said indicating the whisky bottle.

'You sure?'

'Of course, I'm not, but I've got to try.'

Shrugging, Sarah secured the lid and then dropped
the bottle into her sizable bag. She came across the
room and hugged Chrissy.

'You'll be OK bitch.'

'Thanks Sarah.'

Chrissy felt tears well in her eyes for no reason she
could identify. Her friend held on for a few minutes
then, with an extra squeeze, let go and headed for the
door.

'Try and get some sleep Chrissy.'

She was gone.

Chrissy leaned back on the sofa, tears spilling
softly on her cheeks. What the hell was wrong with her
that a hug rendered her a sopping mess? It must be the
tiredness. Or the withdrawal. She wiped away the tears
with a deep breath and got up.

'Pull yourself together woman!'

She snatched up the glass and overflowing ashtray
Sarah had left and marched purposefully to the kitchen.
Emptying the fag ends into the bin, she washed the

saucer. The glass sat on the drainer, taunting her with the inch of whisky left in the bottom. Picking it up, she raised it to her nose. It smelled good. She put the glass to her lips. A sip wouldn't hurt. The vision of the dead girl sitting in her lecture sauntered through her mind. She lowered the glass and tipped the contents down the drain.

5

EVERYTHING WAS PREPARED. Looking around the white room, he double-checked again. He hadn't forgotten anything. Everything was ready. He just needed her. Where the hell was she? Just one last check, then he would go outside to wait.

The unconscious girl hung from the ceiling, shackled by her wrists and ankles. Her body was hoisted horizontally like a sagging human hammock, head hanging down towards the floor. He stood by her side, measuring the relative height of her throat against his body. Too low. Although his girl was small, she would need the head to be higher than this to get a good angle. And he should lift the feet. Let gravity do the work.

Chains attached to the shackles stretched over a pulley system rigged across the white ceiling. He moved over to where they hung and pulled down hard. The girl's inert form heaved up a few inches, her legs gaining extra height as he pulled down on the chain suspending her feet. Now she looked like she was performing a badly executed dive into a non-existent swimming pool.

Returning to his captive, he bent to stare into her soporose face, careful not to touch her with anything but his gloved hand. Her hair was dark, cropped short enough at the sides for the scalp to be visible, longer on top and gelled into a quiff. She wore skinny jeans on her not-so-skinny legs, and a vintage T-Rex t-shirt, taut across chubby arms and a rotund stomach. Her ample bust was squashed by the too-tight sports bra that flattened her breasts like whoopee cushions against her chest. Her face was clean, bereft of any signs of makeup. Her shoes missing, pudgy sockless feet sticking out from drainpipe tight denim.

The girl was still out of it. That was good. They were so much trouble if they regained consciousness before the end.

'You're an ugly bitch, aren't you?'

Laughing mirthlessly, he pushed at the chains, causing the girl to swing back and forth, like a sado-masochistic plumb line.

Satisfied that everything was well-planned, he climbed the stairs out of the cellar, emerging into an old barn missing its roof and two walls. The light was fading, taking with it any pretence of warmth the earlier weak sun had given. Shadows crept down the dramatic landscape of the glen, the water of Loch Rannoch appearing deep blue in the distance. He shivered as the breeze whipped through his thin shirt, swearing under his breath. Folding his arms around his muscular torso, he tried to ward off the cold evening air.

Where was she? If she didn't get here soon, the girl would wake up and that would complicate things. Tensing his jaw, he thought of the woman he waited for. Maybe she was starting to unravel? He would need to be careful.

About to go back inside, he heard a shuffling coming from a few feet away. Turning, he saw a woman in her late forties stepping out from the shadows. His temper immediately flared, the desire to grab her by the arm and drag her into the cellar, raw.

Taking a deep breath, he steadied himself.

'Ah, my love! So glad you're here. Why didn't you come out when you saw me standing here, waiting for you?'

His voice was sweet, even charming as he suppressed the anger raging within that she was both late and had left him freezing his tits off for no reason. He caressed her face, placing a kiss on her sharp cheekbone. She smiled. Her thin top lip curled in to reveal small teeth, her huge protuberant eyes unblinking.

'Well, come on. We better get downstairs. She's waiting for you.'

The woman let him take her hand to guide her down into the cellar. He locked the door behind them, placing his hand on the small of her back, encouraging her down the stairs. Once inside, she made to run to the suspended girl, but he pulled her back.

'Not yet. You need to get changed first.'

He handed her a white linen dress, neatly folded and wrapped in plastic.

'Here, put this on.'

The woman stripped off where she stood with no signs of modesty. She was skinny and birdlike, every bone in her body prominently displayed through papery flesh.

'Underwear too,' he instructed.

She removed the once-white, old cotton bra that served no purpose across her flat chest, and pink panties that looked new in comparison. Ripping open the plastic, she slipped the dress over her head. It almost buried her, hanging like a sack around her tiny frame.

'Put your clothes on the stairs but fold them neatly mind.'

The woman did as she was told, carefully flattening the blue corduroy skirt, greying white blouse and mishappen beige cardigan into a tidy bundle that she placed with her well-worn shoes on the bottom stair. While she folded, her body twitched, her hazel eyes flicking from him to the comatose girl.

'Good. Now go and stand over there, but no touching until I say.'

He watched the woman shuffle towards the middle of the white room, her head tipped back so she could keep her eyes on the suspended girl. Now and then, she wound her fingers in her limp mousy-brown hair, fanatically twisting until some pulled out. The habit explained the thin, straggly appearance that matched the rest of her so perfectly.

Carefully, he removed his clothes, hanging them on a hook in the wall, replacing them with a white cotton robe that he tied securely around his waist. With his gloved hand, he pushed the woman's clothes to the other side of the stair to make sure they were as far away as possible from his own, then walked out to stand beside her.

She was fidgeting from foot to foot, her whole body bristling with anticipation.

'Are you ready?'

Nodding vigorously, she held out her hands, waiting for his story.

'This girl was sent here to kill you. Your husband sent her because he wants you dead. You need to protect yourself, to make sure she can't hurt you. The only way to do that is to strike the first blow. To get rid of her. Do you understand?'

The fidgeting ratcheted up, the woman trembling as she nodded again.

'Remember, just as I showed you.'

He placed the thick silver knife across her outstretched palms, her bony fingers curling around it. Before he had a chance to make more than a step back, she launched herself at the unconscious girl's throat, screaming like a banshee as she plunged the knife deep into her neck. Blood sprayed across the woman's face as she drew back the knife to strike another blow.

He only just got there in time, grabbing her arm, surprised at the strength of the tiny woman as she struggled against him to push the knife towards the girl again.

'That's enough. Once is enough.'

Her breath was audible as it whistled through clenched teeth, spittle escaping with every exhale. Still, she didn't lower the knife, keeping her muscles tense, fighting against him.

'That's enough my love. You've done what was needed,' he said calmly.

Slowly, she relaxed, letting him relieve her of the knife as he drew her to his chest. He stroked her head, the feel of her in his arms appalling him. He looked over at the dead girl. Blood was still pouring from the wound, draining away her life, splattering like beautiful rain on the white-tiled floor. He needed to get rid of the woman now.

'Come on, let's clean you up and then you can go home.'

Gently, he led her to the far side of the room where shelves of bleach and disinfectant lined the walls above a pristine white sink. He ran the tap until steam enveloped the water, wetting a cloth under the flow and using it to wipe the blood from her face. He was gentle, murmuring soothingly while he tended to her.

When all traces of red were gone, he lifted her face to look into her eyes, his hands sweaty inside the latex gloves.

'Now listen to me. You're to get changed back into your own clothes. Leave the dress here with me. When you've changed, go home and take a long hot shower, then put your clothes into the laundry. Do you understand?'

The woman nodded.

'Right then, off you go.'

Obediently, she followed his instructions, doffing the dress and pulling on her own, tired clothes. She followed him up the stairs where he let her out of the cellar, watching as she ran through the trees and out of sight.

Back behind locked doors, he closed his eyes and drew in a deep breath, slowly exhaling to centre himself. That could have gone badly. She was becoming unstable. But that was something to worry about later. Now was his time.

He removed the repulsiveness of the corpse,

pulling the chains suspending the girl's body, now grey, bloodless and limp and swinging it to the far side of the white room. He released the brake on the pulley and the dead meat landed in a broken heap on the floor, no longer registering as part of his world.

Ripping off the gloves he threw them into the sink, then walked over to the edge of the blood pool, his bare feet making no sound as he padded across the cold floor. Slowly, he untied the robe and let it fall to the ground. Staring at the red viscous fluid, he felt the familiar stirring in his groin. His erection swelled, his cock harder than it ever got between the sheets with some whore.

He fell to his knees, pushing his hands forward until his fingertips felt the blood. It was still warm, slick as it seeped over his hands, congealing in the lines and wrinkles of his skin. The room fell away. Now there was nothing except his naked skin and the blood. He laid down with his chest flattened against the floor, his head turned sideways, submerging his cheek into the red fluid. The coppery smell played around his nostrils as he moved his arms and legs through the viscous liquid, marking out morbid spaces that quickly dissipated as the blood flowed back towards his body.

Rolling over on his back, he ran blood-soaked hands across his face. He let them trail down his body, exhilarated by the feel of the silky liquid coating his chest. His erection stood up like a scarlet flagpole, jerking erratically as it waited for his attention.

It didn't take much. Just a few yanks with his blood-covered hand. The strength of his release drained him. He lay panting, sweat mixing with the blood on his face, his ears filled with the sound of his heart hammering against his sternum. At that moment, he had no strength, no mind. He was nothing, barely existing in this place of death.

Slowly, his body calmed, his breathing returning to normal, his come mingling with the blood on his toned stomach. The quietness of the room was blissful, his sense of peace, paradisal. He remained staring up at the white ceiling, his soul flooded with the euphoria of this perfection.

He didn't know how long he lay there. Maybe he had slept for a while? It was hard to remember. Sitting up, he looked down, surprised to see his naked skin, the blood smears turning brown in the dry air. He lifted his hands to his face. They smelled like old coins, stagnant, rusty. Scrambling to his feet, he slipped on the viscid body fluid surrounding him.

Stepping back, he looked around, seeing the corpse of the dead girl, blood on the floor, all over his body. His insides twisted as he raced to evacuate the contents of his stomach into the sink. Trembling, he turned on the tap to wash away the puke, wiping a hand across his lips to rid his mouth of the sour taste.

Everything seemed surreal, out of body. He closed his eyes, the memories of blood running through his fingers, staining his skin, inflaming his arousal, disgusting him. Grabbing a new bar of medicated soap from the shelf, he lathered up his hands and forearms under the scalding water. As the soap rinsed away, the water turned pink. He watched it circle the plug hole and then disappear before tipping quantities of bleach in its wake.

The desire to scrub the filth from the rest of his body was overwhelming. Dragging the hose pipe from the coil on the wall, he moved to stand over the drain buried into the floor. He depressed the handle, releasing a jet of cold water onto his chest. As the blood began to run down his body, the water began to warm. He lifted the hose above his head, showering his face and hair.

When the water started to run clear, he turned the hose on the white tiles, forcing the blood towards the drain. After twenty minutes of work, the floor had regained its whiteness. He was more comfortable now, the evidence of his depravity removed. Taking two large bottles of bleach from the shelf, he tipped the contents of both across the floor. Pulling on fresh gloves, he scrubbed every inch of the white room, rinsed it with clean water then repeated the process. Next, he took bleach to his skin, scrubbing at his legs and arms until they burned, determined to wash away his vileness.

Satisfied that the first clean was complete, he turned his attention to the dead girl. He looked at her twisted corpse, her face showing the first signs of rigor.

He was numb to the suffering inflicted on her young body, immune to the pain her death would cause those who knew her. To him, she had never been a person. She had been the means to an end. Now, her remains were just a bloody inconvenience.

6

CHRISSY SAT BOLT UPRIGHT, breath catching in her lungs, chest heaving in and out. She fought with the covers, struggling to free her arms in panic. Her newly acquired fringe was plastered to her clammy forehead, her top lip glistening with gathering droplets of sweat. Throwing back the covers, she swung her legs to the ground, feeling for her tatty slippers in the darkness.

As her eyes began to adjust to the light, the shadows in the flat came into focus, an orange glow from the streetlight filtering through the window. She never closed the curtains, an old habit from growing up in the middle of nowhere. Anyway, on the second floor, only the most determined peeping tom would get an eyeful.

Chrissy padded across to the kitchen, her ridiculous cat print pyjamas hanging from her boy-like frame. She filled a glass from the tap and took it back to the bedroom. Her hands trembled as she brought the water to her dry lips, head still light as the terror from her dream flooded through her body.

The digital number on the clock caught her attention as it flicked over, its red illuminated face announcing the third hour of the day. She perched on the edge of the bed, clicking on the lamp and taking another drink. Her heart was more regular now, the dizziness in her head settling. She slipped her legs back under the duvet to protect against the chill, pulling the covers up to her chin. This was the third night in a row, fear had dragged her brutally from an uneasy sleep.

For twenty years, she had dreamt about the same girl. Yet these recent somnambulist excursions were different. Usually, she could only see the victim, the knife as it plunged into her neck, some unknown perpetrator thrusting it through her jugular severing her hold on life. Now, she could see the room, the white tiled walls, the white painted ceiling, the white floor. There were no windows, only a mirror above a white sink and stairs leading upwards as if the room was below ground level. A girl, shackled at the wrists and ankles, hung from chains across the ceiling. Her head was slumped down on her chest, her neck no longer supporting its weight. She was dead.

This wasn't the same girl as before. She was short and stocky with a teddy-boy haircut, the quiff losing its structure as the gel fought against gravity. She was wearing skinny jeans and a t-shirt with something on the front Chrissy couldn't make out, no shoes or socks. There was no one else in the room. Everywhere she looked was abnormally clean, the smell of soap and bleach assaulting her nose. The room was silent, still, eerie.

In her dream, Chrissy walked over to where the girl hung, her feet making no sound on the spotless tiles. She seemed to float towards the greying corpse, her presence making no impression on the white room. Tentatively, she reached out a hand, twisting her fingers through the girl's hair, pulling her head back so she could see into her face. The girl was plain, skin scrubbed clean, her complexion pallid, puffy.

Chrissy guessed she was probably in her late teens or early twenties at most. The hole in her throat was ragged, flaps of skin protruding outwards whatever made it, thrust in and pulled out with force. The wound was dry, clotted blood trapped between torn muscle and tissue. Chrissy couldn't look away, her eyes glued to the gaping flesh.

Her vision had become blurry, tears welling to obscure her view. Who was this girl? How had she got here? Wiping her eyes, the girl came back into focus. Chrissy was still holding onto her hair when she felt the head twitch. Instantly, she let go, drawing in her breath sharply. The head did not drop but stayed in its tilted position, the neck cricked unnaturally. The dead girl opened her lids, blackness where the eyes should be. The sound of her own scream had hurtled her back to the land of wakefulness, trembling, sweaty, fighting with the bedclothes.

Chrissy glanced back at the clock. 3.30 am. Hours before the rest of the world started the day. Slipping back to sleep was not an option. She didn't want to see the dead girl again. Throwing back the covers, she pulled an old, hand-knitted grey cardigan over her nightclothes and went back to the living room.

The half-empty whisky bottle was still on the table, a glass, covered in fingerprints and lip marks, sat by its side. Her sobriety had failed. It was the dead girl's fault. Pouring a hefty measure, she downed it in one, savouring the burning sensation on her tongue, the warm, comforting feeling as it trickled down her throat. It was what she needed.

Chrissy refilled the glass and then curled up on the sofa, wrapping her legs in the red tartan blanket and nestling the laptop on her knees. The screen burst to life on the QVC site, showing her basket that contained three storage bags with flamingos on, a set of kitchen tools and a string of Christmas lights in the shape of angels. The result of last night's insomnia. Thankfully, she hadn't checked out yet.

She closed the browser, feeling only slight regret over the angel lights, and scrolled through her Facebook feed. Pictures of peoples' lunch, smiling faces of kids baking with grandma, news headlines promising the coldest winter in a century, and some celebrity who was the latest to be eliminated from Strictly Come Dancing.

Further down the page was a photograph of Loch Rannoch, posted by an old school friend telling the world they had run the twenty-two-mile route around the Loch in training for the next marathon. Idiot. Who wants to run that far?

Chrissy paused, flicking through the five or six photographs showing different views of the water. There was no denying, the scenery was stunning. She didn't often admit it, but Chrissy missed her home, missed the open spaces, the hills and the green. Maybe Sarah had been right? Going home for a while might be good for her. It might slay some demons if she went back and sorted out the cottage. Feeling more awake and with her mind made up, she typed 'car rentals' into the search engine.

By five o'clock the following afternoon, Chrissy was throwing luggage into the back of a blue Ford Focus.

'You going away love?'

Mrs Something from the flat next door, one of the only residents on the street that wasn't linked to the University.

'Just for a few days. I'm heading up north.'

'That'll be nice dear. Always good to get away for a while. My late husband and I . . .'

'I'm sorry Mrs . . . I'm in a bit of a rush.'

Chrissy felt rude interrupting, but she wasn't in the mood to hear Mrs Something's tales of the past. The woman looked slightly affronted. Chrissy backed away, smiling apologetically, waving as she disappeared through the door leading into the stairwell of her flat. She rushed up the stairs, took one last look around and grabbed her purse and a shopping bag from the counter.

Thankfully, Mrs Something had gone when she got back downstairs. Settling into the car, throwing her bag into the passenger footwell and leaving the shopping bag on the front seat, she fiddled with the Bluetooth until it connected to her phone, then pulled away heading out of the city.

Chrissy left the motorway behind at Perth, relaxing into the drive as the built-up cities and towns dissolved into open countryside. The weather was kind, clear skies letting the autumn sun paint everything with warmth. Everywhere she looked, the acres of woodlands and miles of hedges glowed in the golds and reds of the season. It was a long time since she had made this journey. The beauty of Perthshire took her breath away.

As she began to bear left, past Pitlochry and Blair Athol, Sidh Chailleann, the Munro known in English as Schiehallion, came into view. The majestic mountain kept a watchful guard over Kinloch Rannoch, with legend saying fairies lived in the caves at its base. It towered over a thousand metres, its rocky summit accessible by a well-maintained path, making it a favourite first for many 'Munro baggers'.

The moon had risen by the time she turned down the single-track road winding towards the shores of the Loch, the lone white cottage stark against the dark landscape. The car bumped along the uneven surface, the harshness of the preceding winter taking its toll on the gravelled road. She pulled up by the front door, gripping the steering wheel hard, her knuckles draining of colour.

Her last memory of this place was closing the door on her past the day after her mother's funeral. On that day, she had been running from her childhood, her sadness, from herself. Now, she was back, not ready to face the memories, but here anyway.

Chrissy's legs felt stiff as she got out of the car, her buttocks numb after over two hours of driving. She reached over and pulled the shopping bag across to the driver's seat, pulled out the whisky and took a swig directly from the bottle.

'Dutch courage,' she murmured.

She ferreted around in the centre console for the key to the house, the Highland cow keyring chipped from many years of kicking around in the back of her 'useless stuff' drawer. There were no streetlamps here, but the night was clear, the moon casting a silvery glow that reflected on the Loch to light her way.

Chrissy could see the grass had grown wild, hogweed overthrowing the gentler plants that used to fill the borders around the cottage. The door was faded, the paintwork that was a vibrant blue, peeling to reveal the weathered wood beneath. The white harling was cracked in places, pieces disintegrating to powdery grey snow. She felt guilty. The house looked mournful, unloved. No longer the pride and joy of the Ferguson family.

Taking another mouthful of liquid courage, she pushed open the door that protested at being disturbed. Fumbling around, she found the plastic switch, throwing light into the small kitchen for the first time in four years.

Chrissy blinked, her eyes narrowing at the sudden brightness. The house smelled cold and stale. She placed the bottle on the kitchen worktop and threw the key into a glass bowl by the door. The noise it made seemed abnormally loud in the stillness of the room, making Chrissy think the bowl had smashed. She jerked her head to look, but it was sitting there, just as it always had, completely intact, two other sets of keys laid against its glass base.

The kitchen was full of wooden cabinets, a wooden dresser and a dining table making it look overcrowded. Everything in here had been made by her father, a carpenter by trade, and lover of making things for their home. His passion was in every room, from the built-in wardrobes to the carved fruit bowl on the countertop.

Chrissy used to love the smell of beeswax that permeated the air daily as her mother polished all the furniture and ornaments her father made. There wasn't a week went by when he didn't come out of the workshop with something for the cottage. Consequently, it was overstuffed, bursting at the gunnels with remodelled bits of trees.

Coming back was a mistake. Chrissy felt tears stinging her eyes. They were all still here. Her parents, her sister. Nothing had changed. Everything was as it had been when the house was filled with happiness and love. Even the years of madness that followed hadn't disturbed the homeliness of the house. But they had disturbed Chrissy.

She couldn't stand it. She needed to get out. Grabbing the keys, she headed back out the door. The cold air hit her face, the wind blowing across the Loch bringing bone-numbing cold. Chrissy went to the car and pulled out a thicker coat, a woolly beanie in bottle green and a torch. At least she had come prepared.

7

BETTER DRESSED, Chrissy used the torchlight to guide her footing as she walked up the pot-holed road in the direction of the village. It was fully dark now, the sounds of the night beginning to stir. Chrissy considered cutting through the woodland but thought better of it, turning left a little further along onto the main road.

The moon lit her way now, so she stowed the torch in her pocket, grateful to bury her hands in the depths of her green woollen coat. The Rannoch Arms Hotel came into view as she rounded the bend, the lights from the porch casting an amber glow across the tarmac. The white façade stared down from its elevated position, stairs taking guests from the road to its welcome. Cold now, Chrissy turned into the hotel, suddenly in need of warmth and people.

The Tickled Trout bar in the hotel felt familiar,

comforting with its tartan carpet, blue and brown leather seats, and soft grey panelled walls. The bar was decorated with fishing paraphernalia, the outdoor terrace providing stunning views of the loch and Schei-hallion for those brave enough to admire the vista on an inclement October night.

Chrissy headed over to the bar, scanning the numerous whiskies lining the back shelf. The barmaid was chatting to a regular at the end of the counter, her mild cockney lilt out of place in the very Scottish ambi-ence. She saw Chrissy and came bustling over.

'Well, I never! Chrissy Fergusson as I live and breathe!'

'Hello Mirren.'

Chrissy gave the woman a coy smile, her cheeks tingling as the warm air chased away the cold.

Mirren Doyle came around the bar and gathered Chrissy into her arms. It felt good to be hugged by someone she had genuine affection for.

'How long has it been? Too long, that's how long it's been!' Mirren said, a note of chastisement in her words.

She stood back, staring Chrissy up and down.

'You're too thin girl! You haven't been taking care of yourself down there in the big city.'

Mirren's display had caught the attention of other customers in the bar, many of whom Chrissy knew and who were now staring. She felt the heat rise in her face, wanting the ground to open and swallow her whole.

'So, what brings you back home Chrissy? Not that I'm complaining. It's so good to see you.'

'Oh, you know, I've got some days off work and thought it was about time.'

Mirren raised a perfectly plucked eyebrow but said nothing. She left Chrissy's side and returned behind the bar.

'What can I get you then?'

'I'll take a Glenmorangie. Better make it a double.'

Mirren nodded then fussed around, pouring a hefty measure of whisky and filling a small glass jug with water. Chrissy watched her, amazed that she didn't seem to have aged at all from when she first met her as a child. Her artificially blonde hair was still in the same, shoulder-length style, the front layered flatteringly, the long fringe swept to the side. Her face was angular, perfectly made up, the mouth a little too wide but generous with its smiles. The laughter lines around her brown eyes were the only tell-tale signs of the passing years. Chrissy guessed she must be in her early sixties by now.

She was carrying a little more weight than when she had last seen her, the tartan skirt of her work uniform pulling slightly across the hips. The rest of her outfit still fitted perfectly, the cream blouse and blue waistcoat suiting her inherent class. A gold tag pinned to her chest announced her name, the only other accessories were a pair of pearl earrings and a wedding band she had always worn even though no husband had ever been around.

Mirren's appropriate court shoes clacked along the bar floor as she brought over her drink. Chrissy noticed her perfectly manicured pink nails as she placed the glass in front of her, surreptitiously curling her chewed nails into the palms of her hands. She had always bitten at her fingers, but the recent abstinence from booze had left them more gnawed than usual.

'Tell me then, what have you been up to since you were last here?'

Chrissy didn't want to haul over her life for Mirren. Besides, there wasn't much to tell.

'Not a lot really. I'm still working at the University and that keeps me pretty busy. What about you? Any news from Kinloch Rannoch?'

She hoped the switch of focus would deflect the conversation away from her.

'You know the village. Nothing much changes here. Everyone is still into everyone else's business, the tourists still come and go, and the winters still freeze you to the bone.'

Mirren smiled nonchalantly, as unwilling to talk about her own life as Chrissy was.

'Can I get you another?' Mirren asked noticing Chrissy had already emptied the Glenmorangie.

'Yes please, and are you still doing food?'

Mirren passed her a menu, replenishing her glass while Chrissy perused the choices. The door to the bar opened and Chrissy turned to see Martin Doyle, Mirren's youngest son, come in wearing a hotel uniform. He was in his late thirties now but still as gorgeous as Chrissy remembered, his blond hair showing no sign of grey, his piercing blue eyes as fresh and alive as ever. She felt herself blush as he gave her a wide smile and came over to gather her into an embrace.

'Chrissy Ferguson! What the hell are you doing back here? I thought you escaped!'

He released her from his arms but continued to hold onto both hands. Chrissy had spent her youth crushing on Martin Doyle although he never seemed to notice her.

'I came home to sort out the cottage,' she said, the heat in her face finally subsiding. 'I didn't expect you'd still be here.'

'I just can't seem to stay away. I'm working here at the hotel now, Deputy Manager,' he said proudly. 'I love Kinloch Rannoch and I like to be near mum.'

He left Chrissy and went round the bar, planting a kiss on Mirren's cheek.

'I'm in a rush now, late for my shift. But it would be great to catch up while you're here. Maybe meet for a drink tomorrow?'

'I'd like that.'

'Great. Leave your number with mum and I'll give you a call.'

Chrissy nodded and watched Martin disappear

through the door into the hotel.

'He seems in good form,' she said as Mirren set down her glass.

'Yes, he was working at a hotel in Perth up until about five years ago, but when a spot opened up here, he jumped at it. It's lovely to have him back.'

'Has he got a family?' Chrissy enquired, trying to sound casual.

Mirren smiled knowingly, her eyes twinkling as she watched Chrissy.

'No. He was married, but it didn't work out. No kids. I don't think there's anyone special now. Not that he'd tell me!'

Mirren's eyes followed to where her son had exited through the door.

'What about his brother? Devon, wasn't it?'

Mirren looked back at Chrissy.

'Devon lives down in Dundee. He's a software engineer. Married with a couple of kids. He seems happy. He doesn't come back here very often.'

Chrissy sensed a sadness in Mirren when she spoke of her eldest son, so she didn't push it, turning her attention back to the menu.

'What will it be then?' Mirren asked.

'It all looks good, but I really only wanted a sandwich.'

'We only serve light meals until three, but seen as it's you, I'm sure I can sweet talk the chef.'

Mirren took the full menu from Chrissy, replacing

it with the lunchtime one.

'I'll have a BLT if that's OK?'

'I'm sure it will be. Why don't you go and take a seat and I'll bring it over when it's ready.'

'That would be great. Thanks Mirren.'

Chrissy poured a drop of water into her whisky then left the bar, heading for a vacant table with no near neighbours. She was still receiving interested glances from the other patrons, some who probably knew something of her history in the village, others who were curious about the newcomer. Not keen to engage with either group, she kept her eyes fixed on her destination, acknowledging no one as she passed by.

She removed her coat and folded it on the seat next to her. Gradually, stares fell away and everyone returned to their own business. Satisfied she was no longer the centre of attention, Chrissy looked around the bar.

A middle-aged man with a balding pate, Pringle jumper and beige chinos sat with his sour-faced wife. Chrissy recognised them as Archie and Morag Devlin, a stiff-upper-lipped couple who would be appalled to know some of the things their wild daughter had got up to at school. Charlotte Devlin had been the year above Chrissy and was known to put it about. Last Chrissy heard, she ended up pregnant at sixteen and was quietly shunted off to one of Morag's relatives to have the baby. This hadn't stopped the Devlin's looking down on everyone.

Two men in their late sixties sat at the table closest to her. As she looked across, she caught the eye of one, Brodie Quinn, a nice chap who used to run the post office. He had salt and pepper hair and an open face and was smartly dressed in a long-sleeved blue shirt and jeans.

He was sitting with Reggie Cowie, a retired barrister who had adopted the look of an old salty sea dog now that he no longer needed to suit up. He had an unlit pipe hanging from his lips that were barely visible through the dense grey moustache and beard. A thick woollen hat lay on the table that matched the murky green of his cable-knit sweater. The two men were chatting animatedly and didn't pay Chrissy more than a cursory glance. Everyone else in the bar must have been guests of the hotel, transient visitors to the Tickled Trout.

Absorbed in her people-watching, Chrissy jumped as she felt something cold and wet nudge at her hand. A medium-sized black and white dog with long shaggy hair stood at her feet, its tail going around in circles as it displayed pleasure in catching her attention.

'Hello, who are you then?'

The dog swung its backside against her legs, leaning in as she ran her hand down its soft body. She had never owned a dog but always wanted one. She tickled it just behind the ears, causing it to push its head harder against her as the back leg started to thump on the floor in a sham scratch.

'Is that good?'

The dog's mouth hung open in a happy smile, the tongue lolling out of one side making it look dopey and cute.

'I see you've met Ness?'

Chrissy hadn't noticed Mirren approach the table balancing a crusty BLT on a tray.

'Is she yours?'

'No, but I look after her here while her owner's at work.'

'She's lovely.'

She bent down to stroke the dog again that was now sitting with its head resting across Chrissy's knees, eyes straining to look longingly at the sandwich on the table.

'Yes, she's a sweet thing. No trouble either. I didn't notice her slink out of her basket. She's a crafty one. I'll take her away if she's bothering you?'

'No, not at all. I'm glad of the company.'

'OK then. I'd better get back to the bar. Enjoy your food.'

Mirren walked away and Ness gave her a glance, then focused back on the sandwich. As Chrissy took a bite, a front paw came up and rested on her knee.

'Do you want some?'

The paw patted her knee again and Chrissy fished inside the bread for a piece of bacon, giving it to the dog who spilt a string of drool down her jeans, then returned the paw to her knee.

'I can see I'm going to end up with a lettuce and tomato sandwich here.'

She pulled out more bacon, posted it into Ness's open mouth, and then ruffled the dog's fur. Once the sandwich was gone Ness trotted off, introducing herself to a family of four who just had food delivered.

'Cupboard love,' Chrissy murmured as she watched Mirren haul the dog by the collar towards her basket at the end of the bar.

Chrissy relaxed back, not eager to return to the memories in the cottage. The Devlin's had gone now and some of the hotel guests had either ventured out to another pub or retreated to the sanctity of their rooms. Brodie and Reggie were still chewing the fat, their glasses replenished as they settled in for another hour of freedom from their wives.

With the bar emptier, snippets of their conversation drifted towards Chrissy.

'They still haven't found her then?'

Reggie's pipe bounced between his lips as he spoke. Brodie shook his head, gulping his real ale, leaving a foam moustache that he licked away.

'That copper doesn't seem to know his arse from his elbow,' he chimed in. 'Jackie says they haven't got any leads even though the girl's been missing for over a week.'

Chrissy remembered Jackie was Brodie's youngest daughter who worked as a civilian at Pitlochry Police station.

'Sounds to me like she doesn't want to be found. There's probably something going on in that family that she wanted to escape from. I always thought the father was a bit odd.'

Brodie was nodding in affirmation of Reggie's pearls of wisdom.

Their conversation moved away from the missing girl, meandering through the reasons why the father was odd, which seemed to include no more heinous crimes than not wanting to jump on the Kinloch Rannoch gossip wagon and working away three nights a week, and then to the chances of Aberfeldy winning the bowling league.

Chrissy downed the last of her drink and went back to the bar. Mirren took the glass and poured her another measure without asking what she wanted.

'Is there a local girl missing Mirren?'

Mirren put the refilled glass in front of her.

'You heard about that then?'

'Well not really. I just overheard Reggie and Brodie saying something about the police not finding her yet.'

Mirren leaned in conspiratorially.

'She went missing about a week ago. She left her girlfriend in the bar at the Dunalastair Hotel, saying she was heading home, but she never made it. She hasn't been seen since. The family are distraught. She's the oldest of three girls and apparently, it's very out of character for her to just disappear without telling anyone where she was going. They live over the river but only moved in a couple of years ago, so I don't think you'll know them. Her name is Sonja, Sonja McBride.'

'And the police are looking for her?'

'Yes, they've been swarming all over the village since she went missing but I don't think they've come up with anything yet.'

Mirren reached under the bar and withdrew a folded copy of the Daily Record, passing it to Chrissy. She unfolded it to see the girl from her recent dreams smiling from the front page, her head leaning on a pretty blonde girl beaming at her side, both toasting the world with bottles of cider.

The newspaper began to shake, everything but the girl's face fading into oblivion. Chrissy felt the blood drain from her head, sending the room spinning.

'Chrissy! Chrissy! Are you all right?'

She felt Mirren's hand on her arm, but she couldn't acknowledge it. Her mouth was dry, her throat constricted. Slowly, she folded the paper, pushing it back across the bar towards Mirren, then turned and ran. The cold made her gasp as she raced through the exit, the icy wind cooling her sweaty skin. She paced back and forth, hands on her hips, her mind reeling.

A wave of nausea swelled inside her, knocking her off balance. She braced herself against the wall of the hotel and vomited up semi-digested BLT doing back-stroke in Glenmorangie. Two young men heading into the hotel couldn't help but heckle.

'Too much of the good stuff eh lassie?'

Chrissy feigned a good-natured smile, willing them to move on quickly. Luckily, they weren't gallant types and carried on their way after a cheap laugh at her expense. Feeling better, she wiped her hand across her mouth, searching in the pocket of her jeans for a tissue. She found one that had seen better days, dabbing at the tears leaking from her eyes with the least soiled corner. She stuffed it back in her pocket, smoothed her hair and went back into the bar.

Worry lines furrowed Mirren's brow as she hurried across to take Chrissy's hands.

'Thank goodness. I thought you might have left. And without your coat. What happened?'

'Sorry Mirren. I just started to feel a bit sick. I needed some air. I'm fine now.'

'Well, you don't look fine. You're the colour of ash! Come and sit down.'

Chrissy didn't want to be delayed. In the few minutes since she had been back in the bar, she had decided what to do.

'No, I won't actually. It's been a long day. I think I just need to go home and rest.'

She extracted her hands from Mirren's and went to retrieve her coat from where she had left it. Her untouched whisky still sat on the bar. She was probably going to need a drink to get through this. Downing the Glenmorangie in one, she shrugged into her coat, pulling the hat from the pocket, tugging it over her dark red hair.

'How much do I owe you?' she asked, pulling some notes from her jeans.

'Don't worry about it. It's on me.'

'Oh Mirren, I couldn't.'

'Yes, you can. You are staying a while?'

'At least a few days.'

'That's good. Glad to hear it. You can repay me with a coffee at the café before you leave.'

Chrissy nodded, eager to be away.

'Thanks Mirren.'

She was about to leave when something occurred to her.

'I meant to ask, is it the police in Pitlochry that are dealing with the missing girl?'

Mirren looked suspicious.

'Why do you want to know?'

'No reason. I was just curious that's all.'

Her answer didn't sound convincing and judging by the stare Mirren was giving her, it wasn't. Nonetheless, she answered.

'They've sent someone up from Tayside Major Incident Team. A DCI by the name of Ross Fraser. He's leading the investigation. Quite a nice guy for a policeman. They've set up an incident room at the fire station. They're working out of there.'

Major Incident Team. That meant they weren't expecting to find Sonja McBride alive.

August 1984

Blood splattered across the floor, the mortal wound belching red with each beat of the dying beast's heart. He could hear the other animals jostling and banging against the wooden killing shed, their terrified squeals piercing the air as they sensed impending death.

The boy fixed his eyes on his worn-out shoes, not wanting to witness the last breaths of the animal hoisted unceremoniously by its back legs to allow gravity to do its work. His toes were pushing uncomfortably against the leather, his nails bruised from a day incarcerated in shoes two sizes too small. He hummed to himself, blocking out the sounds of slaughter, trying to halt the tears stinging his eyes.

The grip around his arm startled him, dirty finger-nails digging painfully into his skin, the smell of tobacco, whisky and sweat telling him Father was nearby.

'Don't just stand there. Get over here.'

His legs buckled as Father dragged him forwards, his feet slipping on the blood-soaked floor as he tried to keep pace. He wanted to cry, to run back to his gentle mother propped upright in the saggy armchair, her faded housecoat clutched around her frail body, her breath shallow to protect the two broken ribs.

Father shoved him forward. He banged into the bleeding carcass, the pig's blood splashing across his face, its body swinging back and forth like a baleful pendulum. The boy caught his breath, shoulders tensed, Father's callous laughter ringing in his ears.

Scrabbling away, he wiped the smears of red from his face with the arm of his threadbare jumper. The boy pressed his back against bales of clean straw stacked along the wall, praying to disappear into the prickly grass.

Father laid down the sticking knife, thrusting a butchering blade into the animal's belly, ripping its flesh until everything from inside was laid in a heap at his feet. The boy watched him, the muscular forearms soaked in blood, the plastic apron doing a poor job of keeping him clean.

The stench was unbearable. The metallic smell of blood mingled with shit and piss from many animals emptying their bowels in fear. The boy gagged, ammonia stinging his eyes and throat. Father seemed oblivious.

The eviscerated pig was lowered into the trolley, its

skin greying, tiny eyes, glassy. It didn't quite fit, its head and forelimbs hanging over the edge. Father wheeled it into the cold room, the boy remaining frozen to the spot. He listened as the lifeless body was heaved onto a meat hook before the empty trolley was wheeled back into the killing shed.

Father wiped his face, leaving pink streaks where the blood from his hands mixed with sweat. He moved towards the other pigs, arms outstretched, growling menacingly. The animals shuffled away until they were cowering, huddled tightly together in the corner of the pen. Now, the pigs became eerily silent, their eyes watching as the gate clunked shut trapping them in the waiting room of death. It was an unexpected moment of calm. The calm before the storm.

'Come here boy.'

The sound of Father's voice made him jump. The boy didn't move, shaking his head, pushing his back harder against the straw. He saw the twitch in Father's cheek, a sure sign of the rising tide of anger. Still, he couldn't make his too-small shoes step forward.

In seconds, Father was on him, the stinging pain from the slap across his face accompanied by a sharp pounding in his head. He felt strong fingers twisting through his hair and winced as Father dragged him towards the empty shackles hanging from the ceiling. Thick chains wrapped around the pulley before coiling on the blood-stained floor like an angry iron serpent languishing in a river of red.

Father grabbed his hands, forcing him to grip the solid links of the chain.

'When I tell you, pull.'

The boy didn't look at Father. He didn't look at the pigs. He kept his eyes focused on his own small hands holding tightly to the chain, not daring to let go.

Father moved away, the sound of a blade being dragged across a sharpening stone echoing in the silent shed. The boy's knees began to buckle, only his grip on the chain holding him up.

'You ready boy?'

Ready for what? He didn't know. But he nodded, eyes still fixed on the chain in his hands, face throbbing as the bruise began to discolour the pale skin of his cheek.

Father moved towards the penned pigs, the sticking blade glinting as a shard of light penetrated a gap in the wooden walls of the shed. The boy glanced towards the animals, his panic matching theirs.

Father was at the pen, the squealing of the pigs swelling again. The boy wanted to cover his ears, to block out their noise, but he was too afraid. Afraid to let go of the chain still gripped in his ineffectual hands.

The gate jarred as it opened, the pigs pushing further into the corner, each bullying their way into the centre, selfishly ensuring they were not easy pickings on the edge of the group. In panic, one pig ran towards the open gate, the temptation of possible freedom too great. Father knew this would happen and he was ready for it.

In seconds, the big man was on the terrified animal, one muscular arm wrapped around its neck, the other plunging the blade expertly into its jugular. The pig fell to the ground, it screams piercing the air. The boy cast a glance at the dying animal, its legs jerking in a futile effort to get up and run away.

Father moved quickly, shackling the animal by its hind leg. Then he was by his side, blood-stained hands gripping the chain with him.

'Pull.'

The order came ferociously and he dared not disobey. He pulled with all his might, muscles burning as he added his feeble strength to that of Father.

The weight of the animal tautened the chain and it slipped back from his hands.

'Pull you idiot!'

Father's glare forced him to wrap his fingers more tightly around the chain. His feet were barely touching the floor as he put all his weight behind the task. Tears escaped down his cheeks, mixing with the sweat glistening on his small, red face.

Then it was over. Father braced the chain and the boy let go, collapsing to his knees as all the strength left his weakened body. Tears flowed freely now, Father's tobacco-stained teeth barely visible through blurred vision as he threw back his head and laughed at his broken son.

The boy's eyes closed, blocking out the shed as he

buried his face in his knees, hugging them to his aching body.

'Get up.'

He couldn't. There was no strength left in him. Fingers dug into the boy's shoulder, pulling him roughly to his feet. He didn't open his eyes but screwed them up more tightly, waiting for the weight of Father's fist to come again.

8

DCI Ross Fraser pulled off the Tupperware lid and
took out a blueberry muffin, baked by his own fair hand
last night. Peeling off the tissue case he sank his teeth
into the soft, crumbly bun, closing his eyes as he
savoured the sweetness. He sauntered over to the case
board scanning each picture, each piece of illegible
scrawl, most followed by a question mark. Seven days
and still nothing of use in finding Sonja McBride. How
could someone disappear in a small place like this
without someone knowing something?

Refusing to give up, he walked through each
element on the board, dropping blueberry muffin
crumbs on the fire station floor. There was nothing.
Nothing to grab onto. No leads to follow.

Screwing up the cake wrapper, he threw it back
into the Tupperware box and pulled out another.

'I don't know how you can eat cake continuously and still look like a whippet.'

Ross turned to see his partner, Detective Inspector Hugh McCann, coming out of the makeshift interview room, a pile of papers in his hand, the buttons on his grey shirt stretching precariously across his gut. Ross swallowed a mouthful of sponge, waving the muffin in the direction Hugh had appeared from.

'Who was that?'

'Sonja's girlfriend. She remembered someone Sonja had been talking to at the pub before she left. I don't think it's anything, just some bloke making a play for a threesome probably. But I'll check it out.'

Hugh wiped the back of his hand across his glistening brow, pushing back grey hair and taking the weight off tired feet by leaning against the desk. He looked worn out. They all were. They had been burning the midnight oil for a week now and were still no nearer to finding out what happened to the missing girl.

'Sounds like it can wait until tomorrow. You should get back to the hotel. It's getting late,' Ross said, patting his DI on the shoulder. Hugh looked relieved, heaving himself upright, tucking his shirt more securely in his taut pants.

'What about you? You coming?'

'I'm just going to look over the notes once more. Maybe something'll jump out.'

Hugh seriously doubted it but nodded, his kind blue eyes skimming the board behind Ross.

'Jason's out back, manning the phone. He said he'd stay another hour and then call it a night.'

'OK. Great. I'll see you at the hotel later.'

Hugh shrugged on his suit jacket, the elbows and back creased from two days' wear and took a muffin from the box.

'One for the road,' he said, picking up the rucksack that contained the wizened salad he hadn't eaten for lunch.

Ross smiled, picking up the file marked 'Sonja McBride' as Hugh doddered out. Sitting at his temporary desk, he screwed up his second empty muffin case, launching it towards the bin across the room. It missed, the yellow polka dot paper joining another five littered around the base.

He had only scanned down the first page when the uniformed officer down from Pitlochry to help with the investigation stuck his head around the door.

'Sorry to bother you DCI Fraser, but there's a woman at the front desk who is saying she saw a murder in her dreams.'

Ross screwed up his face.

'Seriously? Get rid of her.'

'Well, I would. It's just that the girl she's describing sounds a lot like Sonja McBride.'

Ross sighed. He wasn't in the mood for crackpots. He was tired, irritable and annoyed. He just wanted to look through the case notes and then head back to the hotel for a nightcap. The uniformed officer loitered in the doorway, waiting for some instruction. Ross supposed he better talk to her, otherwise, she would likely just keep coming back. Her sort always did.

'What's her name?'

The sound of a thick wadge of paper hitting a desk drew Ross's attention. Detective Sergeant Jason Moore had come in from the back office, his temper fraying after listening to numerous erroneous leads from members of the public. Jason was the looker on the team. Mid-forties, tall, muscular, with dark hair, dark eyes and perpetual stubble, brought on to the case because of his local knowledge. Ross was annoyed to see that even after a sixteen-hour shift, he still looked impeccable.

The uniformed officer took a notepad out of his pocket and flicked back a few pages.

'She says her name is Dr Chrissy Ferguson.'

A doctor. That made her more interesting.

'Chrissy? Did you say Chrissy's here?'

DS Moore sauntered over to Ross.

'Do you know her?'

'Not really. I didn't know her personally, but I remember her living in the village. She left about four years ago after her mum died. Came back for the funeral, but that was it. Never been here since.'

'She died? How?'

'Drowned in the Loch. She was a drinker, and it

seems she got plastered and decided to go for a midnight swim in January.'

Ross hmphed.

'It seems the daughter's as crazy as her mother. She's here claiming to see murders in her sleep.'

'That doesn't sound like Chrissy. She always struck me as sensible. She got out of Kinloch Rannoch. Moved to Edinburgh I think. You should talk to her.'

'Can't see a way out of it.'

'Well let me know if anything interesting comes of it. Unless you need anything else, I'm going home.'

'Who's the lucky lady tonight?' Ross asked with a wry smile.

'No-one. I'm beat. Just me and re-runs of George and Mildred.'

'I bet!'.

Jason winked and headed out of the station, squeezing his bulk past the uniformed officer still standing irritably at the door.

'You'd better show Dr Ferguson through.'

The uniform nodded and followed in Jason's foot-steps. Ross brushed the cake crumbs off his wrinkled blue shirt, looking around for his tie. It was thrown casually over the back of the chair. He picked it up and threaded it under the collar, then pulled it out and threw it back on the desk.

'Fuck it. She'll have to take me as she finds me at this time of night.'

He tucked the shirt more tidily into the slim-cut,

dark blue, pinstriped pants, scooped up the rest of the muffins and went into the interview room. If he was going to do this, he was going to do it with snacks.

The uniformed officer was back within minutes catching Ross picking cake from his teeth, Dr Chrissy Ferguson trailing in his wake. She wasn't what he expected. The young woman was probably in her late twenties, tall and a bit too skinny. She was deathly pale, dark rings making her face look hollow. Her hair was only just visible below a green beanie hat, but Ross could see it was a dark reddish brown, cut into a chin-length bob, the fringe framing her heart-shaped face.

She looked frail, her large brown eyes almost child-like. But Ross suspected there was hidden steel beneath the willowy demeanour if she had coped with an alcoholic mother who killed herself and still managed to get out of here to become a doctor.

He wiped his hands down his trousers, making sure no blueberry muffin crumbs were sticking to his fingers.

'Dr Ferguson. Thank you for coming in.'

Ross extended a hand, and she took it tentatively. Her hand was cold, the long slender fingers would have been elegant had the nails not been chewed within an inch of their life.

'Please, sit down. Can I get you a coffee, or tea?'

Chrissy took the seat opposite where he had placed the muffins and notebook.

'No, nothing thanks.'

Ross took his seat, picked up the pen and tried to look interested.

'So, Dr Ferguson...'

'Please call me Chrissy.'

'Right, Chrissy. I understand you have some information that might be relevant to our case.'

'Sonja McBride is dead.'

Straight to the point. Chrissy was picking at her nails, bits of skin collecting on the green woollen coat.

'How do you know that?'

'I saw her, dead.'

'Saw her where?'

'I know you're going to think I'm crazy. Maybe I am. Even I'm not sure.'

She was rambling, her large eyes darting around the barren room. Ross waited, pen poised as Chrissy took a deep breath, closing her eyes as if she couldn't believe what she was about to say.

'I saw it in a dream.'

Ross nodded, trying to maintain a serious face. Chrissy couldn't hold his gaze, bowing her head, almost in shame.

'Tell me what you saw?'

Chrissy raised her eyes, surprise obvious on her face. She must have expected him to laugh, tease or dismiss her as a mad woman. He wasn't sure why he hadn't.

'I . . . I saw Sonja. She was hanging from the ceiling of this place. It was white . . . all white.'

'Sonja was white?'

'No, no. The room. Everything was white. Sonja was hanging from chains around her ankles and wrists. She didn't have any shoes on . . .'

Chrissy's eyes glazed over as she became lost in her memory. Ross let her muse for a moment.

'And she was dead?' he prompted, bringing Chrissy back to the present. She blinked her large, doleful eyes a couple of times.

'Yes, she was dead. There was a ragged wound in her neck like she'd been stabbed with a javelin or something. But there was no blood. Everywhere was clean. Really clean.'

'And did you see anyone else in your dream?'

Chrissy looked down at her lap again, twisting her fingers together.

'No. There was no one else there.'

Ross sat back on the chair, tapping his pen absently on the notepad. Chrissy stared at him, waiting for a reaction. He wasn't sure what his reaction was going to be. She didn't seem crazy. But seeing murders in your dreams was borderline insane. Taking another muffin out of the box, more to kill time than because he wanted one, he pushed the Tupperware over to Chrissy.

'Blueberry muffin? I made them and they're good even if I say so myself.'

Chrissy frowned, shaking her head with a confused stare. Not surprising really. Offering someone cake who had just been talking about the murder of his missing girl was definitely odd.

'No, thank you. I don't have a sweet tooth.'

Ross put his muffin back in the box, rubbing his hands together to get rid of the sugary residue.

'Look Chrissy, I understand what you saw seemed very real to you, but it was only a dream. We haven't got any reason to think harm has come to Sonja. At the moment, she's just missing.'

'Then why are the Major Investigation Team being sent here? You're not expecting to find her alive, are you?'

Clever girl. She knew how this went.

'I can see there's no point trying to sugarcoat things for you. We're concerned that something may have happened to Sonja. Her disappearance is out of character and there have been absolutely no sightings of her since she left the pub last weekend, which is worrying.'

'So, you're treating this as a murder inquiry?'

'Not officially.'

They sat in silence for a moment, neither sure where to go from here.

'I know she's dead. I'm sure of it.'

There was a note of pleading in her voice, those puppy dog eyes, begging him to understand. He felt himself weaken. There was something about this woman that made him want to believe her.

'Look, Chrissy, let's suppose what you saw is true, there's nothing in what you've told me so far that could

help us find her. Can you tell me anything else?
Anything that might help us find this white room?'

Chrissy started chewing her lips, her teeth digging
in so hard they lost their rosy colour.

'There were stairs leading up and no windows. I
think the room was below ground level. A cellar or
something. I don't know why, but I don't think it was in
a house. It seemed remote, isolated. There was no
sound at all. But I wouldn't trust that. The soundtracks
to my dreams are often kooky.'

'You dream a lot then?'

Chrissy's cheeks flushed. She hadn't meant to open
a line of questioning that went beyond her dream of
Sonja.

'Not really. No more than you I suspect. It's just
that when I dream, the images often come like a silent
movie show, or sound like someone playing a record at
the wrong speed.'

'I see. I rarely dream. Or at least if I do, I can't
remember them.'

'You're lucky.'

Sadness filled her eyes and she looked dog-tired.
She seemed to shrink before his eyes.

'Well, thank you for coming in. We'll look into it.
Now if you just give me a minute to leave a note for my
colleague, I'll drop you off at home.'

'There's really no need. I can walk.'

'I don't think so. In case you've forgotten, we have a
missing girl who might be dead. I'm not about to let

you wander the streets at this time . . .' He glanced at his watch. '. . . at nine o'clock at night, on our own. You'll do as you're told and wait for a lift.'

For the first time, Chrissy smiled. It lit up her whole face, chasing away the demons and making her look almost carefree.

'Wait here and have a muffin.'

He pushed the muffin box towards her again, a glint in his eye this time. She took one and he left her pulling bits off the top and stuffing them into her mouth like she hadn't eaten in days.

Quickly, he scribbled a note for Hugh who would be at the station before him in the morning. His hand-writing was atrocious. Luckily, they had been working together long enough that Hugh had become a dab hand at deciphering his scrawl.

Start checking outbuildings with cellars in the surrounding area. Will explain when I get in. We'll need a background check on Dr Chrissy Ferguson as well.

They might as well start looking into what Chrissy had said. They had bugger-all else.

Back in the interview room, he gave a wry smile as he noticed the last muffin had also gone. He put the lid on the empty box, tucking it under his arm as he collected his jacket and tie.

'Come on then. Where can I drop you?'

'Just at the Rannoch Arms Hotel will be fine.'

'That's where I'm staying. Are you there too?'

'No, but the cottage is just down a lane almost opposite the hotel.'

'I'll take you to your door.'

'Really, there's no need.'

'No arguments. I'm not leaving you until I know you're safe and sound behind your own front door.'

9

'I'VE GOT the information you asked for on Chrissy Ferguson.'

Hugh McCann was waving a file at Ross as he entered the office the following afternoon. He was still wearing the crumpled grey suit and a tie with the remains of his lunch down it.

'It's interesting stuff. Who is she anyway?'

Ross shook off his jacket, taking the file from his partner. He had been out all day dealing with his boss, the press and the family of Sonja McBride. He was exhausted.

'She came in here last night claiming our girl was dead.'

Hugh raised his wiry grey eyebrows.

'And how did she know that?'

'Wait for it. She said she saw it in a dream.'

If Ross was expecting ridicule from Hugh, he didn't get it.

'I see. Her file makes for interesting reading.'

Ross perched on the edge of the desk, opening the file and flicking through the neatly typed details. You had to love Hugh. He wasn't going to be physically chasing down criminals any time soon, and he always looked like he needed the care of a good woman despite being married for thirty years. But he was a stickler for detail, and his reports were thorough beyond reasonable expectations.

'What are the main headlines?'

Ross leaned over and retrieved a Mars bar from his jacket pocket that would serve as dinner tonight, peeling off the wrapper and taking a huge bite while Hugh, perpetually failing on a diet, coveted it wordlessly.

'Chrissy Ferguson, twenty-nine years old, originally from Kinloch Rannoch, now living and working in Edinburgh.'

'What's she doing in Edinburgh?' Ross interrupted.

'She went to university there straight after school. She stayed on when she finished her degree to study for a Doctorate. Got a job as a lecturer after that in the School of Philosophy, Psychology and Language Sciences that she's had for four years. Basically, she never came back here to live once she left.'

'What does she teach?'

'She's a Forensic Psychologist.'

'Ah, that explains it.'

'Explains what?' Hugh asked, looking up from his notes.

'She seemed pretty knowledgeable about how missing investigations like this work.' Ross took another bite of his chocolate. 'Go on.'

'She's had a pretty unhappy past. Used to have a sister. She was a few years older than Chrissy. Name was Eleanor Ferguson. She drowned in a swimming accident, along with her father, Charley Ferguson, a local carpenter. Seems the sister got in trouble swimming out to the folly.'

'The folly?'

'Building on a small island out in the Loch.'

Ross nodded, encouraging Hugh to go on.

'Anyway, Charley went in after his daughter and the Loch took them both. The kid was only ten years old.'

Ross looked at the newspaper clipping Hugh had found that was in the file. A young girl with her arms wrapped around her father, staring out from under the headline announcing their death. He could see traits of Chrissy in both faces. She had obviously got her colouring from her father, red hair, pale, freckled skin and those large brown eyes. Her sister was blonde but had the same eyes and a smile that opened up her face as he had seen Chrissy's do last night

'Didn't her mother die as well?'

'Yes. It seems Neve Ferguson, Chrissy's mother,

never really got over the loss of her husband and daughter. She was sectioned about a year after. Chrissy was shipped off to Edinburgh to live with Charley Ferguson's mother, a widow who lives in Morningside. She was there for about five years until her mother was well. Then she came back here to live.'

Ross fidgeted uneasily. Fate had not treated the Ferguson family well.

'And then the mother killed herself?'

'It seems so. From what I can gather, Neve Ferguson never really pulled it together. She started drinking heavily when she came back to Kinloch Rannoch. Chrissy looked after her until she was eighteen then left to go to university. One morning, soon after Chrissy graduated with her PhD, Neve walked into the Loch on a freezing January morning. There's not much detail about her death. Never even made the press and I haven't tracked down the police report yet.'

'Bloody hell. How does anyone cope with all that?'

Hugh shrugged, closing his notebook. Ross was overwhelmed with admiration for Dr Chrissy Ferguson. Despite everything, she had got out, done well for herself. He knew he'd detected strength under the outward vulnerability.

'I couldn't find any criminal convictions on any of the family. All clean as a whistle.'

Hugh disappeared out of the room and came back a few minutes later holding two Styrofoam cups filled with appalling black coffee. He handed one to Ross who was still leafing through Chrissy's file.

'What was she like then? This Chrissy Ferguson?'

'I hate to say it, but she seemed completely sane and believable.'

Ross threw the file across the desk and folded his arms. He took a gulp of coffee, his face screwing up as he looked at it questioningly.

'Do you think she might be involved?' Hugh asked.

This was a question Ross had been mulling over all night.

'My gut tells me no. But if the girl does turn up dead and the details fit what she told me, it's going to be hard to convince anyone else she didn't have insider knowledge.'

'Your gut's usually right though Ross. And who knows, maybe she really did see it in her dreams. The minds a bloody funny thing.'

The door crashed open, and DC Jason Moore hurried in looking his usual suave, debonair self. Hugh shot him a resentful look as he took off his leather jacket to reveal a perfectly pressed black shirt, taut over rippling muscles. Noticing the egg mayonnaise down his tie, Hugh tried to scratch it off unobtrusively.

'I've just got off the phone with a Professor Patricia Edgecombe. She's the Dean of Chrissy Ferguson's department at Edinburgh University.'

Jason pulled a crumpled piece of paper from his shirt pocket, straightened it out and read from it.

'She's the Dean of the School of Philosophy, Psychology and Language Sciences – crap, what a bloody mouthful. Anyway, she confirmed that Chrissy Ferguson was in Edinburgh until yesterday morning. She was a weird one though. All she wanted to know was whether Chrissy's name was going to be in the paper and if so, could we make sure she wasn't linked to the University.'

He screwed up the paper and tossed it into the bin. Ross rolled his eyes as the paper landed neatly inside, all his muffin wrappers from yesterday still rolling around the floor.

'She did say that Chrissy had been advised to take some time off. Didn't say why, just that everyone thought it 'for the best' if she took some time to look after herself. Chrissy went by the office yesterday morning to tell Patricia she was heading up North and didn't know when she'd be back.'

Jason shrugged to signify his lack of understanding of what that meant. Ross felt irrationally angry at Jason's flippancy.

'I'm not surprised she needed to take a break with a history like hers,' he snapped.

Jason's handsome face was temporarily marred with frown lines.

'What do you mean?'

Ross turned away as Hugh launched into a potted history of Chrissy Ferguson, his mind wandering back to the night before. Despite the improbability of it, he couldn't shake the possibility that Chrissy was right. After all, she had only said what he had been thinking. Sonja McBride was probably dead.

Needing some air, he pushed open the door and went out into the dark night. The cold caught in his lungs, goosebumps prickling his skin. It felt good. Reminded him he was alive. It really was beautiful here.

Working in Dundee, he rarely saw the wildness of the Scottish landscape these days. He had grown up by the shores of the Firth of Clyde, living an idyllic childhood with his parents and younger brother on the isle of Bute. Thinking about his family, he was suddenly overwhelmed by the urge to go home. To see the hotel his parents had run since he was a boy, the rolling hills and heather-covered moorlands, to visit a place that was for him, untouched by death and murder.

He stared out across Weller Poley Park, the small playground area that hosted the Rannoch Highland Games every September, to Scheihallion in the distance, its silhouette visible in the moonlight. Maybe he would run out that way tomorrow. Running was his solace. Pounding the pavements cleared his head, pushing the death he dealt with every day out of his mind. At least for a while. Not to mention it limited the cake damage.

The ringing of the phone drifted through the glass door, its trilling seeming to get more irate when no one made a move to answer it. He could hear the muted voices of Jason and Hugh who were still deep in conversation about Chrissy Ferguson, neither showing any signs of picking up the phone. Annoyed, he stalked back inside and snatched up the receiver, the sudden silence of the ringing finally capturing his partner's attention. Ross listened to the voice on the other end, nodding, adding in the occasional 'uh huh'.

'OK. Thanks. We'll be there as soon as we can,' he said, returning the receiver to its cradle.

Hugh and Jason were looking at him now, waiting for him to share.

Ross slid his arms into the pinstripe jacket, gathering his mobile phone and keys from the desk.

'Come on. They've found Sonja McBride.'

10

Black bags full to bursting lined the walls all the way down the hall. Cardboard boxes were stacked against the stairs, Chrissy's neat handwriting marking each one as 'charity shop', 'recycling' or 'keep'.

There was only one box with the third label. It contained a few photographs, her father's wedding band, diaries, all covered in glittery butterflies and hearts that her sister had written in religiously every day, and some books her father bought for her that she read and re-read while sitting on his lap. The only thing of her mother's in the 'keep' pile was a gold cross and chain that was currently hanging around her neck. It had no religious significance to Chrissy as it had for her mother. But somehow, she couldn't discard it.

It was only eight o'clock and Chrissy had already been up for hours. When DCI Fraser dropped her off last night she had gone straight to bed, only to wake four hours later with the images of Sonja McBride's corpse buzzing around her head. Afraid to go back to sleep and trying desperately not to seek solace in the bottle, she had begun the gargantuan task of emptying the cottage.

Her mother hadn't moved anything after her sister and father died. All their belongings were just as they had been the day they left to swim in the loch. She wanted to be angry about it, but that would be hypocritical. She'd left all her mother's things exactly as they were on the day she killed herself.

So far, she had emptied two bedrooms upstairs, still to tackle her old bedroom that had been kept the same for when she came back from university for holidays. She never had. She spent eight days here after her mother died, just long enough to arrange the funeral and play the role of bereaved daughter.

The day after she had laid her mother to rest, Chrissy had got the hell out of Kinloch Rannoch and hadn't been back since. She wasn't sure why she had come back now. Something had drawn her here. The ghost of Sonja McBride? That was stupid. She didn't believe in the afterlife any more than she believed in heaven and hell.

A knock on the door made her jump. Who the hell was calling at this time of day? It wasn't someone who knew the cottage because they were at the front door that no one ever used.

Chrissy started to clamber over the black bags

blocking the route to the front. She caught sight of herself in the mirror. She looked terrible. Pale and skinny, her eyes sunken with tiredness. She pulled on the old paisley headscarf keeping the hair out of her eyes, hoping it would lie flat and not stick out in defiance of not receiving the grooming it needed to fall in the new style.

Whoever it was knocked again.

'I'm coming, I'm coming!'

By the time she heaved all the black bags out of the way so she could open the door, she was sweaty and out of breath. DCI Ross Fraser was standing on the doorstep, looking like he had just stepped off Saville Row.

'DCI Fraser. This is a surprise.'

'Sorry to call on you so early Dr Ferguson...'

'Chrissy.'

'Yes, sorry, Chrissy. I hope I'm not disturbing anything.'

Ross was looking around her at the general chaos of bin liners and boxes.

'No, not at all. I've been up for hours. Did you want to come in?

'If you don't mind.'

Chrissy stood back to let him pass. Something covered in fur and moving very fast sped past them both.'

'Oh God. I'm so sorry.'

Ross was trying to catch hold of a black and white

dog hurtling around the hall, tail wagging, barking loudly. He caught hold of the collar just as the dog launched itself at Chrissy.

'I told you to wait in the car,' he said reprimanding the creature who seemed completely indifferent to the stern note in his voice. Chrissy suspected DCI Ross Fraser was a pushover when it came to his dog.

'I'm so sorry. She must have jumped out the window. I'll just go and put her back.'

'No need. Ness and I go way back,' Chrissy said, bending to tickle the dog behind her ears.

'You two have met then?'

'In the Tickled Trout yesterday. We bonded over the bacon in my sandwich.'

'Sounds about right. Mirren looks after her for me when I'm working. Up here, I haven't got a dog sitter and I couldn't face putting her in kennels. Thankfully, Mirren stepped in.'

He was a soft touch with his dog. This thought made Chrissy like DCI Fraser a little bit more.

'Mirren also lets me use her kitchen,' he said, handing Chrissy the box he was holding that contained another lot of muffins.

'They're chocolate chip.'

'You'd better bring them through, and I'll put the kettle on. I must warn you though I only have coffee and don't have milk or sugar.'

'That's fine. Black and bitter is how I like it,' he lied.

Chrissy headed down the hall, kicking bin bags out of the way as she went.

'You having a clear out?' Ross asked as they made it through to the kitchen.

'Something like that. Most of it's my mother's. She died about four years ago. But I'm sure you already know that. I would imagine you've done a background check and know more about me than I do myself.'

Ness rushed ahead of them and started doing circuits of the kitchen, nose to the ground.

'Shall I give her some water?'

'If you don't mind. She'll probably make a mess and drip everywhere though.'

'That's OK. As you can see, I'm not house-proud. Please, take a seat.'

She indicated the chairs positioned around a casual dining table, hearing one scrape along the slate tiles as she searched for something to fill with water.

The kitchen was the tidiest room in the house because she hadn't started clearing it yet. But the wooden countertops were layered with four years of dust, the cups still standing upturned on the drainer from when she closed the door on the cottage after her mother's death, all wearing a skin of grime.

Chrissy opened a couple of the pine cupboards, finding a bowl that she rinsed and filled with water for Ness. Immediately, she put it on the floor, the dog started to gulp, her whiskers dripping copious amounts of drool and water on the floor when she finished.

'What kind of dog is she?' Chrissy asked.

'A bearded collie. Lovely nature but takes some exercising.'

Sensing Ross was talking about her, Ness wandered over, sat at his feet and leaned against his besuited legs. He dropped his hand to stroke her head.

'She's already run five miles with me this morning, but she'd go again at the drop of a hat.'

So, Ross Fraser ran. That explained the toned but lithe body despite his love of muffins.

'Right, coffee.'

Chrissy busied herself searching the cupboards for clean cups and coffee filters. She wasn't familiar with the kitchen layout anymore. Last night, she had opened the first cupboard she came to and stowed three bottles of whisky, but that was as far as she had got. Before she found the coffee, she had opened and closed two-thirds of the units and drawers.

'Sorry, it's been a while since I was last here. I can't remember where everything is. I hope the coffee's still good. It hadn't been opened so it should be.'

She could feel Ross's eyes on her as she moved around the kitchen. It made her nervous. Why was he here? When she left the station last night, it had occurred to her that providing details only the murderer would know could make her a suspect. But if he was here to arrest her, he was being very familiar.

Whenever she dared, Chrissy cast a look in Ross's direction. He was a good-looking man. Not a drop-dead gorgeous type, but he had the look of someone you could trust. His light-brown hair swept over to the side and was brushed back, held with some type of hair product. The first smatterings of grey were visible above the ears. His face was chiselled with prominent brows sitting above his hazel eyes with a square chin. For some reason, he had grown a ridiculous moustache that looked like a hairy caterpillar having a snooze on his top lip.

DCI Fraser was well dressed, the good cut of his pinstripe suit obvious even to her untrained eye. The white shirt still had faint creases where it had been removed from the packaging, his sensible blue tie fastened loosely around his neck. His feet were huge, exaggerated by pointed lace-up black shoes. The look was finished off with an expensive-looking watch and plain gold wedding band he wore on his right hand rather than the usual left.

Chrissy handed him a mug and joined him at the table.

'So, to what do I owe the pleasure of this visit? Have you decided whether I'm a crackpot?'

Ross smiled.

'I'm not sure what you are yet. But I came to tell you that we've found Sonja McBride.'

'Alive?'

'No.'

Chrissy felt the colour drain from her face. She didn't want to be right.

'Where did you find her?'

'In an old farm shed about five miles north of the village. Some hikers looking for a place to spend the night found the body.'

'Do you know what happened to her?'

'Forensics are still at the scene but it's pretty obvious the girl bled out from a wound in her neck.'

Chrissy felt a stone settle in the pit of her stomach. She looked at Ross, searching for some indication of what was going through his mind.

'I know what you're thinking Chrissy, but the scene doesn't bear any other resemblance to your dream. The body was found stripped, wrapped in plastic and laid on the floor of an old barn, not suspended from chains in a white room.'

Chrissy nodded, pondering what he said.

'Do you think she was killed there? In the shed?'

'We don't know yet, but it's unlikely. There's no sign of blood at the scene and a wound like that would bleed like a bitch. The girl also seems to have been cleaned up. There's no blood on her skin.'

'So, if she was killed somewhere else and moved to the shed, the white room could be where the murder was committed?'

'In theory, I suppose so. I've had my partner collate a list of all the cellars in the area, but we haven't had the time to look at any of them yet.'

Chrissy was still clutching the untouched coffee, her mind reeling. What the hell was going on with her?

Was she having some kind of premonition? If her dream about Sonja McBride had come true, what did that mean about her other dreams?

The feel of Ness's furry head resting on her knees brought her back to the moment. Ross was staring at her, one leg crossed across the other, his ridiculous long shoe jiggling as he waited for her to process.

'I don't know whether it would be too much for you, but we haven't disturbed the scene yet. I'm heading over there now and thought you might want to come. See if anything surfaces that might be useful? The forensic team should have almost finished processing and we'll be able to move the body soon.'

See the girl from her dreams? Did she want that? It wasn't a question of what she wanted. She needed to see her. Chrissy pushed the lukewarm coffee away, looking at Ross from across the table.

'Are you asking me to come because I'm a mad woman who sees murders in her dreams, or because I'm a Forensic Psychologist who knows something about human behaviour?'

The edges of Ross's lips curled, his eyes twinkling like a mischievous schoolboy.

'Can it be both?'

Chrissy laughed, feeling the tension that had coiled in her stomach since she heard Sonja was dead, relax a little. She couldn't help it. She liked DCI Ross Fraser even if he was still on the fence about her sanity. To be fair, so was she.

'I'll come,' she said. 'I'll just nip upstairs and get changed.'

She returned a few minutes later wearing jeans, a burgundy turtleneck sweater and sensible boots. Ross had cleared away the coffee cups that were now sparkling on the drainer along with the two mugs that had stood there for four years, and Ness's water bowl.

'Have you got a tea towel to dry these?' he asked as she came back into the kitchen.

Chrissy smirked. She couldn't remember ever drying a pot in her life.

'Just leave them to air dry.'

Ross looked uneasy, as if she had asked him to streak naked across the glen. Reluctantly, he stepped away from the dishes and followed Chrissy out the back door.

'Come on Ness.'

While they were talking, the dog had curled up under the table, snoozing until the next adventure began. At the sound of her name, she came trotting out the door, tail swinging lazily from side to side. Outside, she shook, her long fur swishing through the air like she was doing a shampoo advert.

Ross opened the rear door of his silver Freelander and she jumped in.

'I'll just have to drop Ness off at Mirren's on the way.'

Chrissy threw her coat in next to the dog then climbed into the passenger seat.

'Oh, wait a minute.'

She was out the car again, heading back into the house. Within seconds, she was back, clutching the box of chocolate chip muffins.

'For the journey,' she said smiling, climbing back into the car.

11

THEY DROVE out of the village towards the west end of
the loch, the windscreen wipers clattering as they
reached full speed in the sudden downpour. They
hadn't spoken since they left Mirren's, Ross concen-
trating on navigating the water-covered roads.

Chrissy looked out of the window as they turned
right, heading away from the loch into the wilder, hilly
landscape. Mist hung heavy in the air blurring all but
the closest trees into ghostly outlines, an ethereal forest
crossing the patchworked farmland in intermittent
swathes. They drove on in silence until Ross turned off
the tarmacked road onto a dirt track, new tyre treads
pressed into the mud indicating numerous vehicles had
recently skidded their way up the hill.

The Freelander lurched across the overgrown
grass, pulling easily through the slippery ridges.

'It's just up there,' he said, indicating where the

land flattened out. 'You can't see it from the road because it's behind the treeline.'

Chrissy looked towards the spot he indicated seeing a dense patch of woodland emerge from the mist. As they passed the ancient trees, numerous cars came into view parked away to the side of a decrepit, wood-built barn. Ross pulled up beside them, silencing the engine, then turning to Chrissy.

'Are you sure about this? The body has been there for a few days.'

She nodded, her throat too dry to speak.

'OK then. You'll need to suit up – put on some overalls – before we go in.'

Chrissy got out of the car, the smell of wet grass and the rotting detritus of fallen leaves carrying to her nostrils on the breeze. The rain had eased now to a grey drizzle, giving everything a grainy look. Ross was already talking to a uniformed officer who had come forward to meet him. He stood with his hands on his slender hips, nodding as he listened to what the man had to say.

Chrissy pulled on her coat and looked around. The barn stood with its back to the trees, gaping holes where the front doors would once have been. Its walls were ash coloured, the wood heavily weathered by harsh Scottish winters. The reddish-brown corrugated roof seemed too heavy, the whole building sagging under the weight of time. It was a forlorn place, forgotten, never expecting to be the centre of attention again.

Chrissy buried her hands deep in the pockets of her coat and walked over to join Ross. Her shoulders crept up towards her ears, in part from cold, and part from apprehension. Ross acknowledged her with a quick smile, letting the uniformed officer finish his sentence before he introduced her.

'Thanks Ollie. This is Dr Chrissy Ferguson, a forensic psychologist from Edinburgh University who's helping us with the investigation. She has local knowledge that might be useful. Chrissy, this is PC Ollie Buchan who has come over from Pitlochry to assist.'

The PC nodded curtly in Chrissy's direction.

'If that's all Ross, I'd better get back inside. There are some suits in the back of the area car if you're going in.'

He pointed swiftly towards the parked cars and then, was gone.

'Thanks for not introducing me as the crazy woman who saw a murder in her dreams.'

'Coppers talk, so that reputation may have proceeded you,' Ross said smiling. 'Come on, let's get suited up and then we can go inside.'

He led Chrissy over to the white and neon Vauxhall Insignia, opening the back door and pulling two paper suits and pairs of shoe covers from the seat. Chrissy, reluctant to relinquish the warmth of her coat, tried to pull the overalls on over it. Ross laughed as she got wedged, her arms flailing like an upturned turtle, the thick wool fabric bunching up around her waist.

'Do you want some help with that?'

He stepped towards her, perfectly ensconced in his own paper bag.

'You'll have to take off your coat or it won't go on.'

She let him pull her arms out of the suit and helped her take off the coat. Shivering, she quickly pushed her arms into the rustling sleeves and pulled up the zip.

'Leave the shoe covers off until we get to where the tape is,' he instructed.

Chrissy padded after him, her boots slipping every now and again on the sodden grass. They stopped at the yellow crime scene tape and pulled the blue booties over their now muddy shoes. Ross took a pair of latex gloves out of the pocket of his suit and handed them the Chrissy.

'You need to put these on.'

Doing as she was told, she took a deep breath before pulling the hood up over her hair.

'I look like an anaemic smurf.'

'Welcome to the clan,' he said, opening his arms wide in a welcoming gesture.

She grinned, looking through the barn door to see a whole tribe of anaemic smurfs trooping around inside.

'Are you ready?' he asked, and the smile fell away from her face.

She nodded tentatively then tracked in his wake as he crossed the crime scene tape.

A rotund man, head to toe in white paper, came trundling over as soon as he spotted Ross. His complexion was ruddy, sweat beading on his brow and top lip. Chrissy put him in his fifties given the lined face and tendrils of grey hair sneaking out from under the hood.

'Chrissy, this is DI Hugh McCann, my partner. Hugh, this is Dr Chrissy Ferguson.'

A knowing look fled across Hugh's face before he pinned a wide smile on his lips and shook her gloved hand enthusiastically.

'Nice to meet you Dr Ferguson.'

'Chrissy, please call me Chrissy.'

'Nice to meet you then Chrissy.'

Hugh was everything Chrissy imagined a grandfather should be, kind-faced, cuddly with a deep voice and a ready smile. She liked him instantly.

'So, anything new?' Ross asked once the introductions were done.

'They've almost finished examining the scene. Heather Stone is the Scene Investigator in charge.'

'Where's Diane?'

'She's not made it yet but they're expecting her any minute.'

'Who's Diane?' Chrissy asked.

Ross turned to look at her.

'The pathologist assigned to the case. She works out of Glasgow University but is coming up to look at the body in situ before it's moved.'

A jolt of reality shot through Chrissy. Sonja McBride had been diminished to 'the body', everything she was snuffed out, only a pile of flesh and bone remaining. It hit her unexpectedly, the reality that this wasn't just a troubling dream. A young woman had lost her life. A mother had lost a daughter. People would be grieving for Sonja McBride, shocked at the brutality of her death. Blaming themselves for not saving her. Tears stung the back of Chrissy's eyes. She cleared her throat quickly, trying to swallow them away.

Ross turned his attention back to Hugh.

'I'm going to let Chrissy look around, see if anything stands out to her.'

'You've decided she isn't crazy then?'

Hugh gave Chrissy a furtive wink as Ross's cheeks coloured up.

'I just . . . I thought . . . I thought that her knowledge of behaviour might be of use.'

As Ross stumbled over his words, Chrissy and Hugh burst out laughing. Realising she wasn't offended, he cracked a smile. It seemed to hit all of them at once that frivolity was inappropriate, sombre expressions settling back on all three faces.

'Ready?' Ross asked, offering his hand to Chrissy.

It seemed a familiar gesture, but she was grateful for it. Her legs had suddenly turned to jelly, her heart thumping like a bass drum in her chest. She took his hand and let him lead her towards a mound hidden under a white sheet in the centre of the floor. As they moved away from the open barn door, the cloying, sickening smell of death played around her nostrils, getting stronger with every step.

Chrissy couldn't take her eyes away from the shrouded lump that was Sonja McBride. She tried to look around, to take in the surroundings, but nothing could keep her gaze from the concealed body for long.

'I warn you, it's not a pretty sight.'

Ross was kneeling down, his gloved hand on the corner of the sheet.

'Are you sure you want to do this?'

She nodded, and Ross drew back the cover.

The wall of stink hit the back of her throat, the smell of rotting meat triggering the gag reflex. Spontaneously, her hand flew over her nose and mouth, as if hoping to catch the vomit if it made an appearance. She instantly regretted the two chocolate chip muffins she had eaten on the way here.

'You OK?'

Ross looked over at her, concern clouding his face. She lowered her hand, letting the foulness in. With the sheet drawn back, the smell thinned, dissipating in the air and making it more tolerable.

'Yes, I'm fine. The smell . . . it just caught me off guard.'

Slowly, she took a few steps closer to the body of Sonja McBride. The girl's head was sticking out above a plastic sheet that had been used to wrap the corpse. She was on her back, her skin sagging, the relaxed muscles of her face beginning to wither. Her eyes were gone, a seething mass of maggots in the hollowed-out sockets, her mouth hanging limply to one side. Insects had also moved into the wound on her neck, squirming larvae destroying what was left of Sonja's throat. Chrissy couldn't see the rest of the body, the plastic wrapped tightly around her torso and legs. Her pudgy bare feet were pressed against the polythene, shoeless and grey.

'Hi, I'm Heather Stone. And you are?'

Chrissy jumped as another paper-clad investigator announced her presence.

'Hi Heather,' Ross said, covering Sonja with the sheet and getting to his feet. 'This is Dr Chrissy Ferguson, a Forensic Psychologist who's helping us with the case.'

'Oh. I didn't see you there DCI Fraser. I thought she might be from the press,' Heather said, cocking her hooded head in Chrissy's direction. 'They've been sniffing around here all morning.'

Heather didn't look particularly pleased to hear Chrissy wasn't a journalist. In fact, she looked positively disappointed not to be able to turf her out, continuing to eye her suspiciously in case she morphed into a reporter before her eyes. Chrissy felt uncomfortable under the dour woman's scrutiny, glancing up at Ross, silently pleading with him to get the attention off her. He seemed to get the message.

'What can you tell me Heather? Anything new?'

'Well, she's been dead at least five days – minimal

rigor and she's in the active decay stage – but we'll need the entomologists and path to confirm time of death. The plastic probably slowed the insect infestation on the body, but not to the head, and we don't know whether she's been kept inside since she died, or not.'

Heather said all this without any trace of emotion or empathy. It was like she was reading a weather report.

'Any trace evidence on the body?'

'Nothing so far. Diane wants to move it to the lab before we take off the rest of the plastic.'

'Her name was Sonja. She's not an 'it'.'

Chrissy had spoken before she could stop herself. Heather shot her a look, her face as deadpan as ever, then carried on as if she hadn't interrupted.

'We've taken some skin swabs from around the wound. It looks like the girl's neck was cleaned after she bled out. I'm pretty sure she didn't die here. No fresh blood or signs of a cleaning agent.'

'Anything else? Hugh mentioned you'd found some biologicals?'

'Yes, I'm not sure they're going to be very helpful though. We found traces of blood on the floor, but it looks like it might have been there for years. Jason was here earlier and said this place could have been an old killing shed. I think that might be a good call.'

'Killing shed?' Ross asked.

'Somewhere they used for slaughtering livestock.'

Heather rolled her eyes towards the roof and Chrissy and Ross followed her line of sight. A rusted pulley system spanned the ceiling, shackles hanging from old iron chains that coiled like tarnished vipers where they reached the floor. Chrissy met Ross's gaze, the details of her dream crossing both their minds. Heather seemed oblivious to their silent exchange.

'Apparently, farmers with small herds who live a long way from an abattoir sometimes slaughter and butcher their own stock. It's cheaper to move carcasses than live animals. If that's what this is, some type of abandoned slaughterhouse, then the blood might not be human.'

'OK. Thanks Heather. Tell Diane I'll talk to her later.'

'I'm not your messenger,' Heather spat as she stalked away.

'She's a real ray of sunshine,' Chrissy said once sure Heather was out of earshot.

'She's a miserable bugger. Bloody good Scene Investigator though. Come on, let's get out of here. You look green.'

Ross guided her by the arm towards the barn doors. Past the crime tape, Chrissy ripped off the paper suit, gloves and shoe covers that seemed impregnated with the fetid smell of rotting flesh. Ross put both suits in the waste bag, waiting until they had put some distance between themselves and the crime scene and some colour had returned to Chrissy's face before he spoke.

'The body – sorry, Sonja – will be moved to the pathology lab at Glasgow University as soon as Diane has had a look around. It will probably be a few days before we get her report.'

'Can you ask her to look for bruising around Sonja's wrists and ankles?'

'I know what you're thinking but those chains didn't look like they'd been moved in years.'

'Maybe not, but Heather said she probably wasn't killed here. The primary murder scene is still to be discovered.'

'Diane's good, one of the best. If there's bruising anywhere, she'll find it.'

12

Forty-eight hours. Forty-eight hours since she had looked upon the decaying remains of Sonja McBride. Two whole days since she had heard anything from DCI Ross Fraser. Two days of being bored out of her skin. Two days with no dreams. Two days, sober as a judge.

Chrissy threw three more black bags into the bin in the backyard, full even though it was only emptied that morning. She went back into the house where at least forty more sat looking at her, some for trashing, some for recycling. It would take six months to get rid of these by filling the bins.

As well as the bags, boxes for the charity shop were stacked in every available space. The woman in the Cancer Research shop in Pitlochry had been very helpful, and annoyingly sympathetic when Chrissy explained why she had so much stuff to get rid of.

They were sending a van to collect them all tomorrow. Maybe she could find someone to pick up the rubbish and recycling too?

The 'keep' pile hadn't grown by much. A few childhood trinkets from her own bedroom, a threadbare teddy and a silver-backed hairbrush her grandmother had given her. A pile of artists' canvases loitered between the 'keep' and 'bin' sections as if they couldn't make up their minds about where they wanted to be.

The phone vibrated in her pocket. She expected a text full of expletives from Sarah Cohen, asking when she was coming back to work. But it wasn't. The message was from a number with no name. Someone not on her contacts list.

She opened the text that was straightforward and to the point.

'*Come down to the station when you have time. I'll be here all day. Ross.*'

Chrissy felt a thrill of excitement, remembered that a girl had been murdered, felt guilty for being momentarily happy that Ross wanted to see her and then raced upstairs to shower.

She trotted down the stairs twenty minutes later, hair freshly washed, dressed in dark grey cords and a denim shirt. She had even swept a layer of mascara over her eyelashes although didn't really know why. She felt good, fresh for the first time in months.

Chrissy looked around for her keys, pushed the

phone into her pocket and grabbed her green coat from the hook by the door as she left. The heavy rain of the last few days had finally stopped, leaving the landscape bathed in autumnal sunshine. Steam rose from the damp hillsides as the warmth of the sun dried the ground, making the hills look like they had a forty-a-day habit. The loch was calm, the surface shimmering in the brightness. The edges gently lapped high on the bank, the water's volume swelled by the recent rains.

Chrissy took a moment to appreciate the view, memories of standing here with her family vivid and raw. She missed them. Despite everything, she missed her mother. The loch had taken everything and left her an orphan. Left her alone.

A tear escaped down her cheek. Impatiently, she swept it away. She shouldn't wallow. Life was good. Sonja McBride would never get the chance to live. Chrissy got into the car, checked her mascara hadn't run in the rear-view mirror, then headed off to Rannoch Fire station.

Ross was in reception when she arrived, photocopying pages from a file.

'Chrissy! Thanks for coming down.'

The broad smile on his face made her think he was genuinely pleased to see her. It was a nice feeling. He came round the counter, dropping the file on top of the copier. For a moment, she thought he was going to hug her and felt disappointed when he stopped short, placing his hands on his hips.

'You look well,' he said. 'Much better than when I last saw you anyway.'

'That wouldn't be hard. I spent the whole time swallowing down bile and trying not to vomit all over your crime scene.'

'I was impressed you managed to keep it together. Not many hold on to the contents of their stomach at the sight of their first decaying body. Especially with a bellyful of chocolate chip muffins.'

'What can I say? I'm a tough nut to crack.'

'That you are.'

He was looking at her, his expression unfathomable. He seemed confused by something, by her. Aware he had been staring for too long, he cleared his throat, dropping his gaze.

'You'd better come through to the back. I've got the pathologist report back on Sonja McBride.'

His words brought her back to the here and now with a bang. A girl was dead. This was not the time to try and get into the head of DCI Ross Fraser.

Ross stood aside and let her pass behind the counter. He scooped up the file and escorted her through the door into the make-shift incident room.

'Can I get you some coffee? It's crap but wet?'

'I'll risk a cup,' she said, shrugging out of her coat.

Ross disappeared into the back of the station, returning within a minute holding two mugs of black coffee. He handed one to Chrissy that had an image of Loch Rannoch on the front with the words 'The Most Beautiful Place in Scotland' emblazened underneath. His mug depicted a Highland cow wearing a tartan Tam O' Shanter and playing the bagpipes.

'Souvenirs?' Chrissy asked, nodding towards the mugs.

'Sort of. I couldn't stand drinking coffee from plastic cups anymore, so I bought these from the newsagents. It was slim pickings.'

Chrissy took a slurp from her Loch Rannoch mug. He was right. The coffee was awful.

'Here, have one of these. It'll take the taste of the coffee away.'

He passed her a plastic box containing eight apple turnovers.

'More of your home-baking?'

'Yes. Mirren's gone away for a few days and so she's letting me stay at the house. I hate hotels. I made these last night.'

Chrissy sat down and took one of the flaky pastries as Ross handed her a serviette.

'If Mirren's away, who's looking after Ness?'

'No-one. She's being a pain around the station. Hugh has just gone out to get some lunch. He took Ness with him to get her out of here for a while. She'll be back soon.'

Chrissy took a huge bite of the pastry, crumbs flying everywhere.

'Oh my God! These are good,' she mumbled through a mouthful of sugary goodness.

Ross looked pleased, taking a turnover himself and tucking in.

'So,' he said, placing his cake on the desk and wiping crumbs from his crisp, dark blue shirt, 'the pathology report confirms a few things we already suspected.'

Ross rubbed his hands together to dislodge a few sugar granules stuck there, taking a seat opposite Chrissy and opening the cardboard sleeve on his desk that contained the report.

Before he could tell her anything, the back door to the station burst open and two officers came in preceded by the black and white fur ball that was Ness. The dog spotted Chrissy and almost knocked the apple turnover out of her hand as she jumped up, placing front paws on her lap and wagging furiously.

'Whoa, Ness! It's good to see you too.'

Chrissy lifted the cake over her head to keep it out of the wet nose's reach and managed to push it onto the edge of the desk without losing it to the eager pooch. Her hands free, she put her arms around Ness who wriggled in appreciation as Chrissy kissed and cuddled her.

'You've made a real friend there.'

Hugh McCann was strolling across to her, fronted by his lavender-clad belly, the shirt buttons straining across the widest part. He was carrying a bulging bag from the Waterside Café that must have contained lunch. He tossed the bag on the other desk in the room, then placed a hand paternally on Chrissy's shoulder. Ness raised her nose in the air and moseyed over to sniff at lunch.

'If I'd known you were here, I'd have got you something to eat.'

'That's fine Hugh. I'm managing with Ross's apple turnovers.'

She felt his fingers squeeze her shoulder before he went over to unpack his bag.

Chrissy didn't know the other officer. He was tall, probably about Ross's height, but a much bigger build. It looked like he worked out, his biceps bulging below the sleeves of his white t-shirt. He was the typical Mr Tall, Dark and Handsome, his black hair showing some signs of salt and pepper grey that only made him more attractive.

He was staring at Chrissy, dark eyes scanning her up and down, his appreciation unguarded.

'Chrissy, this is DS Jason Moore, a detective stationed in Pitlochry who's helping us with the Sonja McBride investigation.'

'So, you're Dr Chrissy Ferguson,' Jason said, coming to perch on Ross's desk, his long muscular thighs almost touching Chrissy's arm as he crossed his ankles and relaxed back.

Ross pulled his file from under Jason's arse, shooting him an angry look. Chrissy gave a giggle that shocked her with its girlishness. She felt Ross's eyes boring into her and dipped her chin to avoid looking at him or the hunk of a man at her side.

'I was just about to tell Chrissy about the pathology report,' Ross said, a note of irritation in his voice.

Jason stood up, his crotch now at Chrissy's eye level. She cast a furtive look at the bulge in his black jeans, feeling her cheeks burn at her brazenness.

'So, as I was saying . . .'

Ross stopped as Jason leaned in towards Chrissy.

'Hold still, you've got pastry crumbs . . .'

Jason reached out and pulled bits of apple turnover from Chrissy's hair, his fingers purposefully grazing her cheek as he did so.

'There you go. All gone.'

She looked up coyly, meeting his gaze, the heat from her cheeks sliding all the way down her neck.

'Thank you,' she said weakly.

The sound of Ross slamming the file down on the desk made her jump. Jason, sensing his boss's annoyance, stepped back from Chrissy and had the good sense to immediately cool his obvious flirtation. The atmosphere was awkward as Ross stared Jason down.

Hugh sensing the tension, gathered up the paper bags containing two sets of lunches and stuffed them back in the carrier bag.

'Come on Jason. We better get going. We can eat this on the way.'

Hugh threw the remaining lunch bag on Ross's desk, then hustled Jason out of the station.

'Where are they going?' Chrissy asked, regaining her senses now Jason had left.

Ross was still tense, picking up the pathology report again, but not meeting her gaze.

'To see Sonja McBride's family. Hugh is acting as family liaison on this case and needs to keep them updated. Not that there's much to tell them yet.'

'The pathology report doesn't help then?'

'It helps some. Just doesn't give us anything concrete about the killer.'

Now they were talking about the case, Ross seemed more his usual self and Chrissy was relieved. Jason Moore had unsettled her for a moment with his manliness, but she had no interest in a guy like him. She had been flattered by his flirtation. It was a long time since anyone had noticed her, a long time since she wanted to be noticed. But he was a player. Not what she needed in her life. And it bothered her that Ross seemed annoyed.

'So, what does the report say?'

Now that the lunch bags had gone, Ness was back, parking her bottom on Chrissy's feet.

'Pathology confirmed the time of death as some-time on Wednesday evening, so about twenty-four hours after she was taken. Her jugular and carotid were severed by the force of the stab wound. She would have bled out in minutes.'

'I guess that's something to be grateful for. She died quickly.'

'It doesn't look like he held her for long either before killing her. No sign of sexual assault, so the motive wasn't rape.'

'You think the killer is a man?'

'Probably. Sonja wasn't a small woman, and it would have taken a certain level of physical strength to overpower her. Plus, we found a needle mark on the back of her neck. It looks like whoever did this might have drugged her, rendered her unconscious. We're waiting on the tox report to confirm if drugs were found in her system. It would take some muscle to lift any unconscious body, but especially one carrying a bit of extra weight.'

'Was there any bruising?'

Ross shifted in his seat, crossing, then uncrossing his legs.

'Yes. Bruising on the ankles and wrists, consistent with being suspended before death by shackles like those found at the scene. However, forensics tested the ones in the shed and there was no evidence they were used in the murder.'

'So, she definitely wasn't killed where we found her?'

Chrissy screwed her head around, trying to read the pathology report upside down.

'It doesn't look like it. There was a small amount of her blood found on the plastic she was wrapped in, but none in the shed. There would have been a lot of blood at the kill site. The pathology report says she was pretty much drained. Even though there was evidence of cleaning products being used around Sonja's neck, there was no evidence of cleaning in the barn. Signs of blood would still have been there if she was killed at the scene.'

Chrissy took another sip of coffee, wrinkling her nose. The taste hadn't got any better. She noticed Ross smirk at her disgust.

'What about the weapon? Anything there?'

'It's hard to get anything definitive. Best guess is that it was a long blade, about eight inches and pretty thick. The problem is that when the weapon was pulled out, it destroyed most of the surrounding tissue, tore through everything, leaving no clear imprint.'

'And there was no other evidence on the body? No body fluids, hair, fibres?'

'No, nothing.'

Ross's lips were pressed tightly together, his frustration at the lack of leads obvious.

'Didn't that Heather woman say they had found blood in the shed?'

'Yes. It was all old though. Looks like Jason might have been right about it being some kind of killing shed. Most of the blood was from pigs.'

'Most?'

'We did find some human blood. We managed to get a DNA profile, but no hits. Whoever it belonged to isn't in the database. It's probably just from the person doing the slaughtering. I would imagine injuries are common in that line of work.'

'So, what now?' Chrissy asked, finishing off the remains of her apple turnover.

Ross ran his hands through his carefully quaffed hair, leaving it appealingly rumpled.

'God, I wish I knew. We're no closer to finding out who did this with no leads to follow.'

He looked disheartened and Chrissy fought the urge to reach out and touch him.

'What about the cellars? Have you had any luck with that?'

'I've had the team on it. We've identified forty-six buildings with cellars in a ten-mile radius of Kinloch Rannoch. We've looked at a few but none match your description so far. To be honest, it's a bit of a long shot, isn't it? I mean, you saw the place in a dream!'

She could see why he thought it was a weak lead. There was absolutely no proof that the cellar existed, let alone it being the place where Sonja was killed. Ross dealt in proof. But she couldn't shake off the belief that the place she had seen in her dreams was where Sonja McBride had met her end.

There didn't seem to be anything else to say. She was disappointed, the buzz of excitement she had felt on the way here was gone.

'Well, I suppose I better get going, leave you to it,'

she said, standing up and brushing the pastry crumbs off her trousers. Ness quickly hoovered them up.

'I'll let you out the back door, save trailing through reception.'

He stood up and indicated the way with his arm. Chrissy grabbed her coat and followed his lead. A large whiteboard stood facing away from them. As she walked past, images of Sonja McBride blue tacked down the side caught her attention. She slowed down to look at the evidence board, scrawled with comments, most followed by question marks to indicate their meaning was still to be confirmed. Ross came to stand behind her, the smell of him surrounding her. He smelled clean, like laundry fresh off the washing line on a windy day.

'It makes sad reading, doesn't it? Everything a question, nothing certain except Sonja McBride is dead.'

His voice was tarnished with sadness, the words dripping with frustration. Chrissy scanned the board, her eyes coming to rest on two images stuck side by side in the top right-hand corner, two names below them followed by the obligatory question marks. Bonnie Harrison and Ciara Campbell.

Her heart skipped then began to thump so loudly she was sure Ross could hear it. She felt the colour drain from her face, glad Ross was behind her. Staring out from the photograph labelled 'Bonnie Harrison' was the dark-haired goth girl who had been doing guest spots in Chrissy's dreams since she was a child, the girl she had seen murdered over and over again.

'Who are these?' she asked, her finger trembling as she pointed to the images.

Ross came round to stand by the side of the board.

'They're cold cases. This one...' he pointed to Chrissy's dream girl, '... is from about twenty years ago. Her name was Bonnie Harrison. The other is from just over four years ago. Ciara Campbell. They came up because they share some similarities with the Sonja McBride case.'

'Similar how?' Chrissy asked, her temple pulsing as blood rushed through her head.

'Both were found within ten miles of Kinloch Rannoch, both with wounds to the neck similar to that of our recent victim. Cause of death for all of them was exsanguination. Both were teenage girls, abducted from a night out with friends. Both had bruising on their wrists and ankles. What's confusing though is that there's also a tonne of differences.'

Ross pulled the picture of Ciara Campbell down from the board.

'This girl was found in an abandoned farm building, the body wrapped in plastic. Like Sonja McBride.'

He pointed to the image of Bonnie Harrison.

'But this one, she was also found in a barn, but her body wasn't wrapped. She was laid out like she was sleeping, the body covered by a blanket.'

'Are you thinking these were all killed by the same

person?'

'Honestly Chrissy, I don't know. In all cases, there was no sign of sexual assault and absolutely no trace evidence or body fluids other than those belonging to the victims found on the bodies, or at the crime scenes. Ciara had a needle mark on her neck, like Sonja, but there was no mention of a puncture wound on Bonnie in the report. That could be because pathology didn't find it, or because it wasn't there.'

Ross was rubbing his chin, his mind mulling over the details of the cases as he explained them to Chrissy. He reached up and stuck the picture of Ciara Campbell back onto the board.

'The other consistency with our case is that in all these cases, the girls were found without their clothes. We never recovered any items they were wearing. It seems too unlikely that the cases are unrelated, but the differences are making it more difficult to connect the dots.'

Chrissy nodded, pushing her trembling hands into her pockets. She needed to get out of here. Needed to think. Ross was still staring at the board, his mind somewhere else.

'Well, I better get going. Thanks for keeping me updated and for the pastry.'

Ross nodded absently, his hand rubbing the back of his neck. He still didn't take his eyes off the board as Chrissy turned towards the door. She was about to push it open when she remembered something. There had been files on Ross's desk, one with the name Bonnie Harrison written in black Sharpie.

She turned back towards Ross who seemed momentarily surprised to see her there.

'I think I left my bag by your desk,' she said, pointing in the general direction of Ross's spot. 'I'll just go and get it.'

She hurried past him, relieved he was still preoccupied with his thoughts. Three files were spread across the desk, one for each victim, the pathology report Ross had been reading from still open on the top. Ness was curled up on a green tartan bed when Chrissy entered the office, her tail hitting the cushion with a dull thud at the potential of some attention.

'Not now Ness.'

The dog knew these words, her head settling back down between her paws.

Chrissy slid the pathology report out of the way. Bonnie's file was on the top. Quickly, she stuffed it down the front of her coat, buttoned it up and hurried back out.

Ross turned in her direction as she approached.

'Stupid me. I don't think I actually brought my bag.'

Chrissy didn't slow down as she spoke, almost running towards the back door and out into the carpark. As she got into the car, she saw Ross staring out of the window after her, a look of confusion on his face.

August 1991

His muscles burned as he hauled the last animal of the day towards the ceiling. Blood caked every inch of him, running into his eyes as it mingled with sweat from his brow. The heat in the killing shed was unbearable, the stink of blood, guts and shit, gagging to anyone else but him. He was used to it after years of slaughter.

At least it was quiet now. Twelve carcasses swinging from meat hooks in the cold room, their blood and entrails gathered around his feet. Soon, there would be thirteen. With a final effort, he pulled down on the chain. His hands slippery with pig gore lost traction, the corpse crashing to the floor, twisted, leaden.

'You idiot!'

Too weak to move, he stood no chance as Father cleared the distance between them in three easy strides, pulled back a bucket-sized fist and laid him out with *one punch. He hadn't heard him come back in. Father stood over him, wiping down the sticking knife with a filthy cloth, his overalls as blood-soaked as his son's.*

'Fucking moron! Get up and finish the job.'

With his head ringing from the force of the blow, he tried to push up on his hands, the messages to his brain sluggish, the world out of focus. Shaking his head, he blinked, trying to get the shed to stop blurring in front of his eyes.

When he didn't move, Father moved towards him, fist raised again. The threat of another hit brought a moment of clarity. Everything stopped spinning and he scrabbled on the bloody floor to get to his feet. He was almost as tall as Father now, his muscles burgeoning as adulthood beckoned, his temper volatile as the hormones of puberty ebbed and flowed.

Father halted his attack, the ferocity of his son's stare stalling him. Without thinking, the boy threw himself forward, thrusting both arms into Father's chest. Taken off guard by his outburst, Father lost his footing, backside slapping down to the floor, blood and guts squashed under his bulk. For a moment he sat in the squalor, staring at the floor, surprised to find himself there.

The exertion had left him shaking, his breath coming thick and fast as he watched Father come to his senses to stand tall and strong before him. He knew what was coming now and was ready for it. He wouldn't take it anymore.

He met Father's fist head-on, turning his shoulder, deflecting the blow from his face. Fury fuelled his limbs as he lashed out, catching Father across the face with a back-handed slap.

Father was laughing, barely flinching as his son used all his strength to pummel his stomach. It didn't take long for his arms to tire, Father swotting him away like an annoying fly. He had nothing left. He would have to take it now. But he wasn't going to cry. He would look Father in the eye as he administered his punishment.

He saw the arm draw back, fighting the urge to screw up his eyes, waiting for the pain. He saw the glint of metal too late. Father was still holding the sticking knife. He felt the tip pierce the skin above his jaw, tearing through the flesh as Father swiped the weapon across his face.

Falling to his knees, he clutched at the tattered remains of his cheek, trying to stem the blood with filthy hands.

'Here.'

Father was holding out the grimy cloth he used to clean up the butchery tools, looking down with his usual emotionless stare. He took it with a trembling hand, finding the cleanest corner and pressing it to his ravaged face.

'Now get back to work.'

The wound wasn't pretty, but it wasn't deep. The blood began to slow as he clambered to his feet. Swaying *precariously, he waited for the dizziness to subside. Father smirked then walked away, his son's immense hatred following in his wake.*

13

CHRISSY SAT cross-legged on the floor leaning over the coffee table her father made, pouring over Bonnie Harrison's file. Her eyes stuck to the images of the girl's face that felt so familiar. She was younger in the school photo, maybe fifteen or sixteen. Her hair was already dyed black, but there were no signs of the gothic eye makeup or tattoos she would adopt when free from the authoritarian dress codes imposed by the establishment.

The fire started to spit, sap igniting as it leaked from the hot logs. The heat felt good on her back, the orange glow flooding the cottage with homeliness. Chrissy shuffled around to face the fire, the flames heating her cheeks as she threw another log into the grate. It was too cold tonight to let it die down.

Turning back to the coffee table, Chrissy drained

her glass, savouring the malty taste. She had been drinking since she returned from seeing Ross. Pouring another healthy measure, she turned the school photograph face down. The next set of pictures displayed Bonnie's dead body illuminated white in the camera flash, her insides on show through the gaping hole in her neck.

The images showed different angles, different close-ups and Chrissy examined them all. The girl's body had been laid out in an old shed, a single door latched from the outside concealing it for two days. The building was small, no bigger than the average 'man shed' in a domestic garden, its rectangular walls painted with wood preservative in recent years.

In one photograph, Bonnie was laid on her back, her legs pressed tightly together, a blanket tucked down each side and under her chin concealing the devastation of her death. In another, the blanket had been removed, her arms folded across her bare chest, hair brushed away from her cold, dead face. It would have looked like she was sleeping if it wasn't for the jagged wound ripped through her neck, and the secondary flaccidity making her skin look like it was sliding from her bones.

A knock on the back door made Chrissy slop whisky down her chin. Quickly, she shuffled the pictures back into the cardboard file and slid it under the cushions of the armchair. Staggering slightly, she got to her feet, bouncing off the kitchen wall as she raced to open the door.

DCI Ross Fraser was standing outside, the chill wind blowing his hair across his face. He tried to hold it down with one hand, the other stuffed deeply into his jacket pocket.

'DCI Fraser! What are you doing here?'

Ross pulled a file from inside his blazer.

'I thought you might like to look at this one as well?'

He was holding out Ciara Campbell's file, the pages catching in the wind and threatening to blow away.

'You'd better come in.'

Chrissy stepped aside to let Ross in, but he didn't move.

'I've got Ness in the car. I can't leave her outside in this. She's not good when it clouds over and goes dark. She panics because she thinks it's going to thunder.'

'Bring her in then.'

'Are you sure you don't mind?'

'Just go and get her will you. It's bloody freezing.'

Ross stuffed the file into Chrissy's hand and sprinted back to the car. He opened the door and a mass of black and white hair shot out and into the house.

'Come on. I've got the fire on in the living room. It's cosy in there.'

By the time Chrissy and Ross got into the lounge,

Ness was curled up against a hand-knitted cushion on the sofa.

'Sorry, she's no sense of propriety. I let her on the furniture at home so she assumes it's a given that she can climb on anywhere.'

He moved towards the dog to pull her to the floor.

'Leave her. It's fine. Besides, she looks comfy.'

Ross tickled Ness behind the ear, then took off his jacket, throwing it over the back of the sofa and sitting down next to her.

'Do you want a drink?'

Chrissy waved the whisky bottle in the air.

'Or I could make coffee?'

'Actually, I'd love a whisky.'

Chrissy took another glass from the dresser and poured one for Ross, handing it to him before topping up her own. She returned to sitting on the floor, folding her legs beneath her and retrieving Bonnie's file from under the chair cushion. She added it to the coffee table with a guilty smile.

Ross took a slug of his drink, his shoulders relaxing as the heat of the room warmed him through. He leaned back against the sofa cushions, crossing his long legs – settling in.

'So, why did you steal my file?'

'I'm really sorry DCI Fraser . . .'

'Will you please call me Ross? I'm off duty.'

He smiled and she was relieved that he didn't seem angry about the file.

'It's difficult to explain,' she said, lowering her eyes and letting her finger trail around the rim of her glass. 'I don't know where to start.'

'How about the beginning?'

Chrissy looked at him, sitting on her mother's sofa, the top button of his dark blue shirt undone, his black trousers creeping up his legs to reveal striped yellow and blue socks above his long, pointy shoes. There was something about him. Something easy. He made her feel comfortable, almost normal.

She stood up and took a silver-framed picture from the mantelpiece and passed it to Ross. The glass was dusty, the colours in the image beginning to fade. Two little girls, one about ten, the other no more than six or seven, were sitting on their father's lap giggling in delight as he tickled them.

'That's me, my father and sister. I'm sure you already know that they were killed in an accident in the loch. It happened shortly after this picture was taken. My sister, Eleanor was a real daredevil, always wanting to go faster, go higher, go farther. She and my father were very close, very much alike.'

Ross handed back the photograph and Chrissy ran her finger tenderly across the people she had lost. She stood the frame on the coffee table, looking at the faces staring back at her as she continued.

'Eleanor was very different to me. I was quiet, bookish. My father didn't really know how to be with me. It was my mother that I was closer to. Until after the accident anyway.'

'Your sister and father drowned, didn't they?'

'Yes, Eleanor showing off as usual. She got into trouble trying to swim to the folly on the island. My father went in after her and they were both lost.'

'I'm sorry Chrissy. If this is too painful . . .'

'No. No, it's not. To be honest, I don't remember much. I have some memories of reading on my father's lap, of watching my sister write endlessly in her diary, but not much else. And I don't remember the accident at all. I was only six.'

Chrissy reached out for the whisky and topped up her glass before offering it to Ross.

'After the accident, my mother changed. It was like she couldn't stand to be in the same room as me, but at the same time was paranoid about everything I did, never letting me go anywhere or see anyone. She even kept me out of school for almost two years, afraid she would lose me if I left the house.'

'That must have been difficult.'

'I guess so. It was just as it was. Everything was so screwed up after the accident that it was just one more thing.'

She shuffled round and leaned back against the armchair, stretching her feet out under the coffee table and crossing her ankles. The fire started to warm her bare feet and she screwed up her toes, enjoying the heat.

'When I was about nine, my mother finally lost it. She had a complete breakdown and was found lying on the shores of the Loch, rocking and mute. It was Mirren who found her, helped her home and encouraged her to get some professional help. She wouldn't at first, but things got so bad she didn't have a choice. She was sectioned and I was taken to live in Morningside with my grandmother.'

Ness's back legs stretched out and kicked Ross as she strived for more sofa space. He shuffled along to give the dog more room.

'I can see who's the boss in that relationship,' Chrissy said smiling, glad for a moment's reprieve from her family history.

Ross stroked the dog's exposed belly, the expression as he looked at Ness telling Chrissy everything she needed to know. This was a man who loved his canine sidekick unconditionally.

'You must have come back to Kinloch Rannoch though?' he said, hand still resting comfortingly on the furry body beside him.

'I came back once mum was released. She was in the care of the hospital for almost four years. It probably should have been longer because she wasn't well when they discharged her. She started drinking a lot and I suppose I became the parent then, taking care of her.'

Ross leaned forward, his brow furrowed. She looked away, not wanting to see pity in his eyes.

'I used to paint then. It was my release, my way of coping.'

'Really? Do you still have your paintings?'

'At the moment. They're piled up by the back door ready to go out to the trash.'

Ross stood up and went into the kitchen. He came back carrying two canvases depicting moody images of Loch Rannoch.

'These are good Chrissy! You can't throw them out.'

She shrugged nonchalantly.

'I haven't picked up a paintbrush since the day I left Kinloch Rannoch.'

Ross propped the paintings against the sideboard.

'Shall I put more wood on the fire?' he asked, already heading towards the log basket.

She nodded, watching him move around the living room. It was nice to have him here. It made the house feel full of life rather than full of ghosts.

'Why did you leave Kinloch Rannoch?' he asked, taking his seat next to Ness who had stretched out even further.

Chrissy reached for the whisky bottle and tipped the last of it into her glass. She tottered to her feet, her head swimming slightly as she pulled herself up.

'I'll just get another bottle.'

She waited for the room to stop spinning, then platted her way into the kitchen. Once there, she splashed some water on her face before retrieving the last bottle of whisky from the cupboard. Ross took it from her as she reached the coffee table. The floor seemed a long way down now, so she dropped into the armchair.

'Sorry, what was the question?'

'I just wondered why you left the village?'

'I wanted to go to university. My grandmother convinced me I should get out of Kinloch Rannoch as soon as I could, stretch my wings, see the world. University seemed like an important first step in making that happen. I got my place and when I told my mother, she threatened to kill herself. I went anyway. After I graduated with my PhD, she carried out her threat. She drowned herself in the same spot my father and sister died.'

Chrissy felt an unexpected swell of emotion as she spoke, chasing it down with a large mouthful of whisky.

'I expect you're wondering why I'm telling you all this. I'm sure you're not interested in my life story,' Chrissy said, trying to sound light-hearted.

'I am interested. You interest me.'

She felt her cheeks flush and was satisfied to see a similar glow on Ross's face. For a moment, their eyes held until Chrissy looked away, unsure of what had happened.

'Well, there is a reason,' she said, letting the moment fade.

'About two years after my father and sister died, I

started to have vivid dreams, dark dreams about murder. Well not about murder in general – about one specific murder.'

Chrissy reached forward and pulled the school photograph of Bonnie Harrison out of the file. She turned it to face Ross.

'I started to dream about this girl, Bonnie Harrison. Although I didn't know her name until I saw her image pinned to your evidence board today.'

She threw the picture onto the table, the face staring up at the ceiling. Ross looked stunned, his bottom lip dropping open slightly as he tried to form a word, a thought.

'I know. Crazy isn't it? At first, I didn't have the dream very often. My grandmother took me to see a psychiatrist who said it was 'repressed grief' which was a load of bollocks because it has never gone away. I stopped talking about it though so everyone would think it had. But it has always been with me. After my mother's suicide, the dreams got worse and worse. Now, the only way I can stop them is this.'

Chrissy held her glass up, toasting to her saviour. Her eyes were stinging and taking a few seconds to catch up with the movements of her head. Ross was sliding in and out of focus, his face just a flesh-coloured blur above a blue shirt.

She heard his glass go down on the table, felt his hands on her knees. He must have perched on the coffee table to be able to reach her. Squinting, she managed to bring him back into view.

'What happened in the dream Chrissy?'

'It's the same as Sonja, only with Bonnie, I see her die. There are people in the room with her. I see her hanging from the shackles, unconscious, but alive. Then someone drives a knife through her neck and there is so much blood . . .'

She started to cry, Ross wiping away her tears with his thumb.

'That's enough Chrissy. You can tell me the rest tomorrow. Now, it's time you went to bed.'

He took the glass out of her hand and pulled her to her feet. Spontaneously, he gathered her into his chest, his steady heartbeat calming her. After a moment, he pulled back, holding her at arm's length.

'Are you OK?'

She nodded.

'I'll be fine.'

'Good. I'll get going so you can get some sleep.'

He gathered up his coat and tried unsuccessfully to rouse Ness from the sofa. He put a hand under her back end and gave it a nudge. Reluctantly, she raised her head, sliding off the sofa until her front paws touched the floor. Keeping her back legs on the seat, she stretched her back, yawning and licking her lips, a small fart escaping from her bum. Then she slithered to a standing position and shook.

'Come on you,' Ross said, walking towards the kitchen door.

Chrissy took two steps forward, intending to see them out before her legs gave way and she staggered into the coffee table. Ross managed to catch her before she went down, hauling her upright.

'I think perhaps I better help you upstairs.'

She clung to him as he half carried her up the narrow, wooden staircase and into the front bedroom that used to belong to her parents. He sat her on the edge of the bed, and she hung her head to try and stop the room reeling.

'Lay down,' he instructed, and she flopped back onto the pillows.

She felt him lift her legs and scoot them up onto the bed. The throw that was usually folded up on the ottoman landed on her, spread out until she was neatly tucked under its warmth.

His weight on the bed made her open her eyes. He was looking down at her, his face half amused, half concerned.

'You need to get some sleep.'

He pushed the hair back from her face and kissed her gently on the forehead. Embarrassed by his forthrightness, he went to move away but she held him fast, sliding an arm around his neck in a surprising moment of muscle control.

'Stay,' she whispered, trying to pull his lips towards her.

He resisted, sitting up and pulling her hand from around him. He tucked it under the blanket, patting it in a fatherly gesture that sobered Chrissy.

'I will stay, to make sure you are OK. But I'm going to sleep downstairs.'

With that, he stood up and backed out of the room, leaving Chrissy alone in the dark feeling mortified.

14

THE WAVE of nausea roused her violently from her coma-like sleep. She sat up with a start as her stomach contorted, vomit spraying across the bedclothes. Quickly, she tried to disentangle herself from the throw, staggering noisily into the small bathroom, just in time for a second stream of sick to hit the toilet bowl.

Chrissy fell to her knees clutching the white porcelain, clammy and shaking. Her head was pounding, the sour taste of regurgitated whisky repulsing her. Through her haze, she heard the bathroom door push open.

'Are you OK?'

Oh God. Ross! She had forgotten he was here.

'I'm fine. Please go.'

She rested her forehead on the cool toilet basin, reaching for the flush. Her insides were not done with her yet. A hand settled on her back, and she turned sharply to see Ross in crumpled trousers and shirt, holding a towel out to her. Tears welled in her eyes as embarrassment mixed with her wretchedness.

'Thank you.'

She took the towel and managed a weak smile. Then her stomach somersaulted, a third bout of vomit hitting the bathroom floor and Ross's socks.

'Oh hell. I'm so sorry,' she murmured. 'Please leave. I'm revolting.'

'You're speaking to a man who has seen more decaying corpses than anyone should. A hungover woman vomiting into a toilet isn't going to scare me away.'

He wiped the hair stuck to her sweaty forehead back, then went to the sink, rinsed a washcloth under the cold tap, and pressed it to Chrissy's face. The tears began to run in earnest now, his kindness breaking her.

'Are you done now?' he asked. 'Is it all up?'

'I think so,' she said timidly, snot starting to run down her nose to add to her overall allure.

'Come on then. Up you get.'

He helped her up, then turned on the shower.

'Get out of those stinky clothes and into the shower. You'll feel better then.'

Chrissy stood there, waiting for him to leave. He didn't. Rooting in the cupboard under the sink, he pulled out a cloth and some disinfectant. On his hands and knees, he started to wipe up her sick.

'Please Ross, don't.'

163

'Just get on with what you're doing and leave me to do this. I promise I won't look.'

The desire to get out of her vomit-stinking clothes won. She knew she couldn't face bending down just now to clean up after herself anyway, so she slowly peeled off last night's jeans and t-shirt and stepped into the shower cubicle. The water felt good, washing away her nausea, if not her humiliation.

She heard the door close as Ross gave her the privacy she yearned for. Turning off the taps, she stepped out into a clean bathroom, her sick-covered clothes, gone. Wrapping a towel around her body, she padded into the bedroom to see the bed stripped, the pillows and duvet folded and piled neatly on the ottoman.

'How am I ever going to look him in the face!'

Tears threatened again and she wished the floor would open and swallow her whole.

Chrissy pulled on some underwear, a sweatshirt and jogging bottoms, then went downstairs, determined to apologise for the third time and then get rid of Ross as quickly as possible. The rest of the day would be spent wallowing in self-pity and maudlin over her self-abasement. Ness trotted over when she entered the kitchen and Chrissy used the act of greeting the dog to avoid Ross's gaze.

'Feeling better?' he asked a note of amusement in his tone.

'Yes, thank you.'

Ross handed her a glass of water and a large mug of black coffee.

'Water first, coffee second.'

She obeyed, downing the water in two goes. He took the glass from her and put it in the washing-up bowl that was already filled with steaming water and bubbles. Chrissy noticed the washing machine was on, her bedclothes spinning around in a bath of suds.

'Ross, you really don't have to do all this. I'm so sorry for everything. But you can go now. I'm fine, really.'

She knew she sounded almost pleading, desperate for him to leave.

'I'm not going anywhere until you've had a decent breakfast.'

He threw two empty whisky bottles into the recycling bin, no sign of judgement on his face.

'You've no food in this house so I'm going into the village. But I'll be back.'

Chrissy's heart sank.

'Really, you don't have to.'

'I know I don't have to, but I'm going to do it anyway.'

She watched him helplessly as he sat on the kitchen chair, pulling shoes onto his sockless feet. Chrissy felt her cheeks colour.

Ross went to the back door and called Ness to come with him. The dog took a few steps forwards, then looked back at Chrissy before trotting back and jumping up on the kitchen window seat. He tried to call her again, but she laid her head between her paws in defiance.

'I don't think she wants to go,' Chrissy said, smiling at the dog's stubbornness. 'You can leave her here.'

'Are you sure?'

'Yes. It's fine. I'll enjoy the company.'

Ross nodded and then was gone. Chrissy sat down beside Ness, stroking the warm furry side.

'Well Ness, it doesn't look like I'm getting rid of either of you for a while.'

Chrissy wasn't sure how she felt about that. She wanted to be alone, serious wallowing to be done. Yet there was comfort in knowing Ross would be back. Taking her coffee, she went back upstairs, dragging clean bedding from the cupboard on the landing to remake the bed in excessively floral sheets.

She dried her hair, attempting to blow-dry it like the hairdresser did, failing miserably and ending up with kinks and waves where they shouldn't have been and a few bits of frizz that she had completely missed. She didn't own any hair straighteners that could fix the damage, so she dragged it back into a clip at the base of her neck, the short length only just staying put.

Starting to feel more human, Chrissy went downstairs to pour herself another coffee. Ross had placed the police files for the two cold cases on the kitchen table. She sat down on one of the wooden chairs and pulled them towards her. Opening the top file, she stared down into the face of Bonnie Harrison. It was hard to reconcile the innocent-looking girl in the school photograph with the cold dead flesh in the crime scene images.

Chrissy laid the pictures of Bonnie's corpse in a line across the table, then did the same with those of Ciara Campbell. With Ciara, it was easy to see the similarities with the Sonja McBride case. The girl was around the same age, her body wrapped in plastic sheeting, lying in an abandoned barn. Ciara's body was found less than twelve hours after her murder. There were minimal signs of decomposition, the muscles of the face still contorted by rigor mortis.

Chrissy looked along the lines of images. There was something different about the two crimes. Not just in the details of the deaths, but in the feel of the scenes. One was clinical, organised and clean. The other, empathetic, remorseful and even tender.

Ness started to bark and wag her tail at the knock on the door. Ross pushed it open without waiting for an invite, a brown paper bag in his arms bulging with more shopping than was necessary for making breakfast. He had obviously called back to Mirren's place, the shirt and trousers replaced with jeans and a jumper. He was also wearing socks now with sneakers. Much better than the ridiculously pointed shoes he always seemed to wear when he was working.

'I got you a few bits for the cupboard,' he said, unpacking bread, porridge, some pasta and sauces, storing them away like he owned the kitchen. Milk, chicken and butter went into the fridge, the ingredients for a full Scottish breakfast remaining on the side by the cooker.

He started opening cupboards and drawers, pulling out a frying pan and some knives.

'I went for traditional breakfast stuff. Do you like haggis?'

'I haven't had a full breakfast for years,' Chrissy said, looking at the spread across the countertop. 'More of a 'bagel-on-the-go-girl' these days if I even bother with breakfast.'

'You should always eat a good breakfast,' he chastised, waving the knife he was using to open a pack of lorne sausage.

'You sound like my grandmother.'

They both laughed. God, he was easy to be around.

'Haggis or black pudding? Or both?'

Chrissy screwed up her nose.

'I hate black pudding.'

'Haggis it is.'

Ross threw the roll of Stornoway black pudding back into the bag.

'I'll take that for Hugh. It's his favourite. That's if his wife will let him have it. She's got him on some kind of low-carb diet this week, not that he's sticking to it.'

Ross went back to chopping tomatoes and mushrooms, lighting the grill and adding oil to the frying pan. The kitchen was soon filled with the tantalising aromas of frying bacon and grilled sausage.

'I've been looking at the files again,' Chrissy said, turning her attention to the photographs. 'There's something different about the Bonnie Harrison murder . . .'

Ross was by her side, gathering up the photographs and pushing them back into their cardboard files.

'No more shop talk until you've got a full stomach.'

'But . . .'

He shushed her, wagging his finger when she opened her mouth again. Beaten, she let him take the files away. Watching in silence as he bustled around the kitchen, Chrissy wondered about the wedding ring on his finger. There had been no mention of a wife, but it was hard to imagine someone so domesticated hadn't got a very lucky woman waiting in the wings. Someone had got themselves quite a catch.

Ross delivered her breakfast, complete with tattie scones and two slices of toast.

'I'll never eat all this,' she said, looking at the huge pile of sausage and bacon, a healthy portion of haggis, plus all the trimmings.

Twenty minutes later, her plate was empty.

Ross handed her another cup of coffee, coming to sit at the table opposite her. The kitchen was spotless, the dishes all returned to their rightful place. He had made her sit and watch, refusing all offers of help, demanding she stay put and relax. Chrissy felt good despite her earlier hurling events. Her stomach was revelling in the full feeling after a good meal, the water Ross had insisted she drank before, during and after breakfast, clearing her head.

'So, you were going to tell me something about the cases.'

Chrissy got up to get the files from the sideboard where Ross had stowed them before breakfast. She laid out the crime scene photographs in two lines, Bonnie on the top, Ciara below. Pulling out two images taken when the forensic teams first arrived on site, she placed them side by side in front of Ross. One of each victim.

'When you look at these, what do you see?'

Ross stared at the pictures.

'Two victims, both dead with similar neck wounds.'

'No, that's not what you can see. You're relying on what you know from the case files. In these images, you can't see their wounds. What do you see in *these* images?'

Ross looked again. The image of Bonnie Harrison showed a girl that looked like she was sleeping under a blanket. Only the pallid complexion gave away the lack of blood flowing through her veins. He couldn't see Ciara's face, her body wrapped in a plastic cocoon, no part of her visible.

'The way they're wrapped is different.'

'Yes, very different.'

Chrissy took a gulp of coffee, stroking Ness's head absently as she pushed her nose onto her knees.

'It's reasonable to assume that whoever moved these bodies from the primary kill site to these farm buildings must have used a vehicle of some kind. Ciara,' she said, pointing to her image, 'has been disposed of, wrapped in a material of convenience that would ensure no trace evidence could transfer from the body to whatever she was moved in, or to the person who moved her. She's been dumped in the shed, like a piece of garbage.'

Ross was nodding, listening intently.

'Bonnie on the other hand, she's been laid out, her hair smoothed over, hands laid across her chest. Then someone took the time to cover her with a fluffy blanket, tucked it under her bare feet, like someone putting a child to bed.'

'OK. What's your point?'

'Whoever put Bonnie in that shed cared about her, wanted to make sure she was comfortable, warm, even in death. Ciara and Sonja weren't shown any such compassion. They were just left, like sacks of meat.'

'Do you think the killer knew Bonnie then? Had some kind of relationship with her?'

'I don't know. Maybe . . .'

Chrissy placed the photographs back in the line-up.

'I can't help thinking someone different dumped Bonnie's body.'

Ross stared at her.

'You think we might be looking for two murderers?'

'Perhaps. Or maybe just someone else did the moving. I know you think the killer is male, but the way Bonnie was laid out, it's kind of maternal. It makes me think a woman did this.'

Chrissy pointed at Bonnie's picture, her hand loitering on the image as she waited for his response. He leaned back against the chair, tapping his fingers absently on the table.

'A female killer?'

'Maybe.'

Ross ran two fingers across his moustache, his brows drawn in as he looked at the pictures.

'It was sixteen years between Bonnie's murder and Ciara Campbell's. That's a long time. It could easily be two different murderers and we could just be connecting dots that aren't there. But the victim profiles are similar and the wounds on the neck. And they were all disposed of in abandoned farm buildings near here . . .'

Ross's voice tailed away. He leaned forward, resting his elbows on the table and rubbing his forehead.

'It's a theory, that's all. What I am saying is whoever laid out Bonnie Harrison seems to have shown empathy, remorse even. With Sonja and Ciara, none of these emotions played any part in their disposal. It could be the same killer. Maybe they felt differently when they got rid of Bonnie. Maybe someone else moved Bonnie's body. Or maybe an entirely different person killed the first victim.'

Ross leaned forward and glared at the images again.

'Too many maybes. The later killings do seem to be more clinical.'

He picked up a couple of photos, staring at their gruesome depictions.

'Ross, there's something I need to tell you about my dreams of Bonnie's murder.'

Ross brought his focus back to her face.

'I told you last night that I see people in the room with Bonnie. I'm pretty sure there are two people, someone with a deep voice – maybe a man – and a woman.'

'That's why you're saying a woman could be involved with Bonnie's murder?'

'No, no. That's what the crime scene photos say. I'm not even sure my dreams can be trusted. They could just be an artefact of my disturbed mind. But I thought I should mention it.'

'I'd love to dismiss it as nonsense from your psyche, but you did dream about two girls who are both dead.'

Ross sighed, leaning back against the chair. Ness changed allegiance and went to stand in front of him, wagging her tail and woofing insistently. He ran a hand over her soft ears, and she stepped away indicating that was not what she wanted.

'I know girl. I'll take you for a walk soon,' Ross said, looking into the amber eyes fixed on his every move.

Ness curled up on his feet, throwing her head down in what resembled a sulk. Ross smiled at her indignation, then looked up at Chrissy.

'Maybe we just keep all these details from your dreams in the background and work with what the evidence says for now.'

Chrissy nodded, feeling relieved she had told him even if she wasn't sure he took any of it seriously.

'If you're right and a woman was involved in Bonnie's murder, what would make her do something like that?' Ross asked, draining his coffee and taking his empty mug to the sink.

'The main driver for killing is usually self-preservation. We kill to protect ourselves or our genetic investment in the future.'

'That sounds like academic-speak.'

Chrissy laughed, realising she had slipped into lecturer mode.

'What I mean is that a powerful motivation for killing another person is to help yourself do better. According to Charles Darwin, one way to 'do better' is to live longer. So, we might kill if someone was threatening our own survival. Another way we can do better is by protecting our genetic investment in the future – in other words, by making sure our children survive and pass on our genes to the next generation and the next. It kind of makes us immortal. With every surviving generation of our offspring, part of us lives on. So, evolutionary theory suggests we would kill to protect our kids if their survival was being threatened in some way.'

Ross looked like his head was hurting.

'It seems like a very hard-nosed way of thinking about human behaviour, and besides, it's difficult to believe Bonnie Harrison was posing a serious threat of harm to anyone's children.'

Chrissy ran a thumb over her lips as she considered.

'Unless you think about it as an outcome of an evolutionary-derived behaviour that manifests maladaptively. Sorry, that was academic again. Evolution has equipped us with a strong desire to survive and protect our children. Sometimes, that evolutionary drive can be problematic. The need to protect your child might become so overpowering that you see threat where there is none. You might act to save your kid because, for some reason, you *believe* they are in danger.'

Ross's mobile phone started to ring.

'But surely, rational thinking would play some part? Killing someone is a pretty extreme thing to do just because you *think* your kid is in danger.'

'It is. But I guess it would depend on what other circumstances were at play.'

'Well, you might be able to convince me that a woman would kill to protect her children, but you still need to convince me how evolution can explain serial killers and psychopaths. I think Darwin had blinkers on when it came to explaining some of the things I've witnessed in my line of work.'

Chrissy smirked and shook her head.

'I look forward to the challenge of convincing you Darwin was on to something.'

The phone continued to ring, and Ross answered it, the broad grin sliding off his face. He hung up, rubbing the top of his nose, taking a blink that seemed to last forever. Chrissy leaned in, waiting for him to speak.

'There's another body.'

15

THE SOUND of voices and trampled branches announced their presence, just in time for him to conceal himself between the trees. Two people shouting someone's name came into view, their expressions a mixture of annoyance and panic. He crouched further down, making sure they were unaware of him.

'Where the bloody hell is he? We've missed the train now! I'll kill him when we find him,' one of them said, his bottom lip pouting sulkily.

The boys were almost men, on the verge of adulthood but still wearing the faces of adolescence. The annoyed one was striding purposefully through the trees, anger seeping through his body language.

The other boy hung back, his brow furrowed, eyes scanning the forest as he walked.

'It's bloody freezing,' the angry boy said. 'If we don't find him soon, I'm going home!'

They will find him. Just a few more steps forward and they would find the boy's body lying in a twisted heap amongst the trees.

He waited, watching, heart pounding on the walls of his chest. Then it happened. Angry boy stopped, his intake of breath audible even at this distance. The colour drained from his face, its whiteness stark against the tenebrous light. The other boy reached his side, legs visibly buckling as his stomach gave way to regurgitate the morning's breakfast.

'Oh God! Oh God! Calvin!'

Angry boy had found his voice. He took a step forward towards the corpse.

'No! No! Stay there.'

The sick boy regained some control.

'You can't touch him. You can't disturb the crime scene. The police. We need to call the police.'

Angry boy fumbled in his pocket to pull out a mobile phone.

'No signal.'

'Me neither. We need to get out of the trees. Come on.'

The two boys started to run back towards the edge of the forest. This was his chance. He needed to leave the scene now, get as far away as possible.

Sure they had gone, he placed a hand on the rock and heaved himself to standing. His legs were leaden from being crumpled beneath him. It took a few steps to get the blood circulating enough for his muscles to move. Walking lightly at first, he made as little sound as possible. He didn't want to bring the boys back here. Only when there was sufficient distance between himself and the body did his pace quicken, breaking into a sprint once the forest was behind him.

The breath heaved in his chest by the time the front door came into view. No one had seen him. The weather was so dreich anyone with sense was closeted in the warm. Reaching out for the door handle he noticed the blood on his hands. He must have touched the body but couldn't remember doing it.

Fumbling with his key, he pushed into the house, going straight for the kitchen and reaching under the sink for a bottle of bleach. Tipping some onto his hands, he lathered it like soap, the red blood stains turning pink. Once the water was steaming, he rinsed his hands, feeling calmer as the evidence swirled away down the plug hole.

Taking two neatly folded cloths from the drawer, he rinsed one under the tap, spilling bleach onto the other. Back at the door, everything was wiped down, the areas stained with blood paid particular attention. The cleaning complete, he tossed both cloths into the washing machine, followed by everything he was wearing. Naked, he switched on the machine, dialling up the temperature and dosing with copious amounts of detergent.

The contents began to spin, the sound of water pumping into the machine reassuring. Nothing could link him to the crime scene. His shoes were at the front door. Even in haste to be rid of the blood, he couldn't bring himself to wear shoes inside the house. There was no way they could get a clear footprint from the forest floor, he was sure. But there was no point taking the risk. Collecting the shoes, he tied them into a plastic bag planning to get rid of them far from Kinloch Rannoch.

The shower was scalding hot, but the tingling as the searing jets lashed his skin was exhilarating. Satisfied with his cleanliness, he switched the dial to cold, his breath catching as the streams turned icy. He stood under the freezing water for as long as he could take before turning off the taps to let his body drip while he unhooked the squeegee from its holder on the pristine white tiles and cleaned down all the glass.

Stepping out, he wrapped a white fluffy towel around his waist, bending under the bathroom sink to pull out four cloths folded into neat squares. The first was used to wipe down the inside of the shower, the second mopping up water droplets loitering in the shower tray and the final two cleaning down the area around the shower cubicle. When he had finished, the shower looked like it was in a bathroom showroom.

He launched the cloths into the laundry basket hidden inside a bathroom cupboard and went into the bedroom. All the surfaces were clear of clutter, the bed with its white bedcovers, freshly made. The clothes in the closet hung with military precision, all on matching coat hangers, each item with a designated amount of space. Pulling out a grey shirt and darker matching chinos, he threw them onto the bed.

The shower had cleared his head. There was only one thing to do now. She had overstepped, gone out on her own. Wasted an opportunity. He needed to get rid of her. She hadn't even been careful! There could be evidence on the body that could be linked to her and consequently, to him. If the police got to her, she would squeal. She was too unstable to face interrogation and not give them away. There was no choice. He had to find her.

16

THE CAR GROUND to a halt in a lay-by on the south side of the loch, about four miles outside of Kinloch Rannoch. Ross climbed out and zipped himself into a dark green Barbour jacket.

'You better wrap up. It's bloody freezing out here and it's a bit of a hike up the hill.'

Chrissy got out of the car, buttoning up her woollen coat and pulling her green beanie down over her ears. She shivered as the wind gusted, its chill finding every pore in everything she was wearing. Burying her hands deep in her pockets, she ran a few steps to catch up with Ross whose long legs were making easy work of the overgrown grass.

'Do we know anything about the victim?'

'Not yet but forensics are on scene so they should have something to tell us when we get there.'

'How far is it?' Chrissy asked, her breath coming thick and fast as she tried to keep pace across the field.

'Just into the treeline.'

Ross pointed about two-hundred yards ahead to the ancient beeches, their shadowy forms rising ominously towards the grayscale sky. Angry clouds dimmed the light, cold rain hitting their skin like shards of glass making them hasten towards the shelter of the trees. Talking wasn't possible now, speed of movement taking every shred of air passing through Chrissy's lungs.

Once under the tangled canopy, Ross slowed his pace. Chrissy was annoyed to see his breathing slow and even, as if he had just taken a gentle country stroll. She could feel her cheeks burning, sweat on her skin chilling with every second, goosebumps standing to attention on her arms and legs. Her breath was raspy, her heartbeat beating a *vivace* rhythm on her ear drums.

Chrissy bent over, a stitch ripping through her side. 'You OK?'

Ross had stopped and backtracked to her side. She nodded, still unable to find enough breath to form a controlled word.

'Sorry, I know I walk quickly. I just wanted to get out of the rain.'

'Quickly!' she managed through the rasps. 'That was a bloody sprint!'

Ross laughed and took her arm as she straightened up.

'It's just up ahead. You set the pace.'

By the time they reached an area of the forest teaming with people in white paper suits, Chrissy had regained some of her composure. The crime scene tape cordoned off an area the size of two football pitches surrounding a white tent erected in the centre. Floodlights illuminated the immediate area, Scene Investigators combing through the forest detritus in all directions.

Heather Stone raised a hand in Ross's direction, coming over to where he and Chrissy waited behind the yellow tape, her face as sour as usual.

'What do we know?' Ross asked as soon as she was in earshot.

Heather pulled down her hood, taking off a mask and balling it in her hand.

'Male, about seventeen years of age, dead.'

'Really? Dead. Fancy that. Dead how?'

Heather glared at Ross stoically, his sarcasm lost on her.

'Stabbed through the neck, bled out. Diane's with the body now.'

'Who found him?'

'His friends. Hugh and Jason are talking to them over there.'

Heather pointed hastily to two young men clustered around Hugh McCann a few feet away. There was a lot of arm waving, one talking so fast Hugh raised his palm in the universal sign for 'slow down', the other standing wide-eyed, shock draining all colour from his face.

Chrissy saw Jason further along the perimeter line chatting to a paper-suited girl who was giggling and batting her eyelids at every word. She laughed to herself remembering how easily she had been flattered by him at the station. Not now though. She had his card marked.

'I'll send Diane over. We've almost finished processing the scene and we're about to move the body.'

'Thanks Heather.'

Sourpuss walked away without a by-your-leave.

'She doesn't get any cheerier,' Chrissy said, watching Heather stalk back towards the tent hiding the body away from view.

'Nope,' Ross said, his mind not on Heather or Chrissy. 'This feels different, doesn't it? I mean, here, out in the open. It's not the same as the others.'

He looked at Chrissy, not really seeing her.

'Were you expecting it to be the same? The same killer?' she asked.

'I suppose I was. It seems too unlikely that there would be two killers roaming around Kinloch Rannoch at the same time. I just assumed it would be the same person. But maybe . . .'

Ross waved towards a woman emerging from the

tent. She waved back before stopping to speak to
Heather Stone. Chrissy leaned out to see around Ross.
The woman was small – no more than 5ft 4 inches tall,
obviously slender underneath the voluminous paper
bag. She came towards them, stripping off her mask
and hood as she walked.

Chrissy was mesmerised. Her skin was rich, dark
brown and perfect. She had black hair, tightly braided
against her scalp, amber beads rattling at the end of
each long plait as she moved. Her deep brown eyes
were large, heavily lashed and full of life. She was the
most stunning woman Chrissy had ever seen.

As she reached Ross, she leaned over the crime
scene tape and placed a kiss on his cheek. His arms
went around her as he hugged her briefly. Their intimacy made Chrissy feel like an outsider, awkward and
alone.

'Diane, this is Dr Chrissy Ferguson. She's the
Forensic Psychologist who has been helping us with a
case.'

Diane gave Chrissy a look up and down, then
smiled, her full lips parting to reveal perfect white
teeth. Chrissy felt unbelievably inadequate, knowing
that her face was probably still blotchy and red from
practically running up the hill after Ross and her hair
was likely going frizzy in the rain.

'Pleased to meet you Dr Ferguson,' Diane said,
extending her hand.

Chrissy took it. It was smooth, warm.

'Please call me Chrissy,' she said, smiling some-what manically.

'Chrissy, this is Dr Diane Fraser, the pathologist on the case.'

'Fraser?'

Chrissy was looking from Ross to Diane, her eyes saucer wide. Diane laughed.

'Yes, I'm his wife,' she said, cocking her head towards Ross.

'Ex-wife,' he chipped in a little too fast.

'You always were one for detail,' she said, nudging Ross on the arm.

Diane's voice was as perfect as everything else about her, a smooth Scottish accent tripping elegantly from her tongue.

'You're Scottish,' Chrissy said, her mouth opening before her brain was engaged.

'You seem shocked? Because I'm not pale-skinned, covered in freckles and red-haired like you?' Diane said, picking up a stray lock of Chrissy's hair peeking out from under her hat. 'Stereotypes are a bitch.'

'I . . . I'm so sorry. I didn't mean . . .'

Chrissy felt heat creeping up her neck as she lurched around trying to find something to say. Nothing useful came.

'I really am sorry.'

Diane's face broke into a broad grin followed by contagious laughter that spread to Ross and then to Chrissy herself.

'OK Diane, you've had your fun. Can you tell me about the victim?'

'I will as soon as you tell me what the hell that thing is languishing across your top lip?'

Ross's fingers went to smooth his absurd moustache.

'You don't like it?'

'It looks like a ferret died on your face.'

'Well, it's a good thing you can't have an opinion on my facial hair anymore, isn't it?'

'Touchy! Shave it off. It makes you look like a porn star.'

Chrissy smirked and Ross looked annoyed.

'Can we please get back to the case?'

Diane gave Chrissy a warm smile before her face set into a more serious expression.

'Young male by the name of Calvin Parks, found by his friends about one o'clock this afternoon. I think Hugh's got more information about what they were doing out here. Current estimate is he's been dead for about three hours and judging by the amount of blood on the ground, the cause of death was exsanguination.'

'There's blood at the scene?' Ross asked, his eyebrows raised.

'Yes. He was most likely killed here. There's no evidence to suggest the body was moved or any attempt at concealing it. He's got his clothes on too.'

'It doesn't sound like this is the same killer, does it?'

'I thought that too until I saw this.'

Diane beckoned Chrissy and Ross across the crime tape, throwing two pairs of shoe covers at them. They hastily pulled them on, then followed her into the tent where bright lights were illuminating the zipped-up body bag containing the corpse of Calvin Parks. Diane fell to her knees and unzipped the bag. With her gloved hand, she turned Calvin's lifeless face to the side revealing a deep penetrating wound in the side of his neck. His skin was torn, the shredded portions hanging outward as if the weapon had been withdrawn at force leaving his severed jugular to belch out the blood that had seeped into the forest floor.

'Look familiar?' Diane asked, staring up at Chrissy and Ross.

'It looks the same as the wound on our other victims,' Ross said, turning his head to get a better view.

'Is it the same weapon then?' Chrissy asked as Diane zipped Calvin back into the privacy of his body bag.

'It looks like it. I won't know for sure until I've compared it to the other victim back at the lab, but if I was a betting woman, I'd say it was.'

'That doesn't necessarily mean it was the same killer though. Someone could have found the weapon discarded by Sonja's killer and used it on Calvin. This looks more like an opportunistic killing than the planned murders we've seen before.'

Ross stood back as he spoke, giving room to two

Scene Investigators who were heaving Calvin's body from the floor. Diane held up a finger to Ross, silently telling him to hold that thought before turning to the men walking away with the body bag.

'Make sure you wait for me. I'm travelling back with you,' Diane shouted, waiting until one of them carrying Calvin nodded.

'You're not staying overnight?' Ross asked.

'No, I want to get back to Glasgow. This case isn't making any sense. There must be something these bodies can tell us, and I want to find it.'

'Well, if anyone can, it's you.'

Diane grinned at Ross, the dazzle from her smile excluding everyone from the conversation except its recipient.

'Thank you for your confidence husband.'

'Ex-husband.'

Ross put his hands on his hips, vaguely annoyed at her insistence in referring to him as if they were still married. His show of irritation amused her, a snicker escaping through her perfect lips.

'Anyway, I'm not sure that it's a different killer. It seems too much of a coincidence for the wound to be inflicted in the same position on Calvin as it was on Sonja McBride and those cold cases you pulled.'

'Was there any evidence of bruising on Calvin's body? Round the wrists or ankles?' Chrissy asked.

Diane turned her deep brown eyes on her and

Chrissy couldn't help the flush that bloomed on her skin.

'Not that I could see. I'll know more once I've had some quality time with Calvin at the lab. We did find evidence suggesting someone ran their hands through the spilt blood, and Heather recovered a partial fingerprint in blood from a rock about three metres from the body. I don't know whether it'll be enough to get a hit in IDENT, but it could be something.'

'OK, thanks Diane. Let me know if you find anything else,' Ross said.

'Will do. I'm going to shoot off now but I'll be in touch tomorrow,'

She stood on her tiptoes and kissed Ross again on the cheek. A spontaneous smile curled his lips giving away his affection for his ex.

'Lovely to meet you Chrissy. Hope to see you again soon. And keep nagging him to shave off that bloody moustache!'

The bloom in Chrissy's cheeks deepened to become a furnace as Diane gave her a conspiratorial smile. Not managing to find words, she offered up a single wave of the hand by way of a goodbye. She felt Ross's eyes on her and turned to see him looking smugly at her.

Chrissy was saved a response by the arrival of Hugh McCann with Jason Moore hanging sheepishly back, Ross's irritation about his flirtation with Chrissy not forgotten. This time, he didn't even look at her, but she didn't feel any disappointment.

'Hi Boss,' Hugh said, flicking through his notebook. 'I've spoken to Calvin Parks' friends. Seems they were staying at the campsite less than a mile from here. Brave lads in October. They said Calvin was an early riser, always got up before they did. Apparently, he fancied himself a bit of a poet and liked the solitude of an early morning hike to inspire his creativity. They think he left the tent about eight this morning.'

'And they didn't hear from him again after that?'

'They got up about ten o'clock. They were supposed to be going home today so they just got on with packing up the tent. When Calvin hadn't come back by eleven, they started to worry. Went looking for him. Found the body at about one o'clock.'

'Can we confirm any of this?'

Jason Moore stepped forward.

'I've been to the campsite and several witnesses confirm that both boys were there until just after eleven. They left their rucksacks in the campsite office when they went looking for Calvin.'

Chrissy noticed that Jason kept his eyes firmly fixed on his notebook as he spoke to Ross who seemed to have completely forgotten that he had been annoyed with him.

'What do you think Hugh?' Ross asked. 'Are they involved?'

'I don't think so. They're both really shaken up.

One of them has only spoken about three words since they found the body. The other can't shut up. But I think they're on the level.'

Ross was nodding, his thoughts occupied.

'If it's all right DCI Fraser, I'd like to take the boys home. Uniform has been dispatched to talk to the families, to tell them what's happened. But if you don't need them for anything else, I think they need to go home.'

Ross seemed surprised to hear the formality of his rank but said nothing.

'Where do they live?'

'Just down in the Borders. It'll take me about five hours to get there and back.'

'OK. Just make sure you tell them we might need to speak to them again.'

Jason nodded, shot Chrissy a coy smile and was gone.

'What's going on with him?' Ross asked Hugh once Jason disappeared out of sight.

'He's panicking that he offended you and it might prevent him from getting assigned to the Major Incident Team permanently.'

'Is that what he wants?'

'Desperately. He's worked a few cases now but only ever on secondment. He wants to make the move full-time.'

Ross looked thoughtful.

'He's good at his job Ross. Great with the female witnesses. Really gets them to open up.'

'I'll bet.'

Hugh shook his head.

'Do him a favour Ross, put in a good word.'

'I'll think about it.'

Hugh sidled off, leaving Chrissy and Ross alone.

'Did you recognise the victim Chrissy? Someone from your dreams?'

'No. Never seen him before in my life. This doesn't fit with anything I've seen.'

He looked disappointed and she felt inadequate on a different level.

'Come on, let's get you home.'

The rain had stopped but the hike back to the car was still freezing as the wind charged them down the hill. Chrissy was grateful when the engine sprung into life and faint traces of heat escaped through the vents. Ross reached for the gear stick to shift into reverse, the gold wedding band catching Chrissy's eye.

'Why do you still wear your wedding ring if you and Diane aren't married anymore?'

Ross looked down at his hand.

'We've been divorced for two years now but I guess I'm still not ready to be single again.'

She was dying to ask him why they had divorced, but as the car pulled off, the subject seemed closed.

August 1994

The midday sun beat down as he marched across the yard, augmenting the stale stench of sweat and pig shit emanating from his rarely-washed overalls. His useless idiot of a son had disappeared again, but he wasn't going to get away with it this time.

Pushing open the kitchen door, the sound of hushed voices coming from the living room caught his attention. His first instinct was to call his wife's name, but something stopped him. Something about the mumbled voices kept him silent.

Carefully, he closed the door, trying to muffle the sound of the catch clicking into the frame with his large hands. It wasn't easy to creep silently across the kitchen. He was the size of a barge and stealthy was not a natural mode for him.

The door to the main living area was ajar. Girlish

giggling wafted through the crack as he approached. He could see the arm of the chair, his wife's hand thrown casually across the faded upholstery, half-moon welts from his fingernails purple against her pale skin.

Slowly, he placed the palm of his hand on the centre of the wooden panelled door, testing for creaks by pushing lightly until it shifted a fraction. No sound. He pushed again, making sure he was concealed behind the door jamb as the view inside the room opened to him.

His wife was reclining on the chair, her summer dress gaping at the neck revealing the slight swell of her breasts. Her head was thrown back, long, mousey hair splayed over the back of the cushions, her green eyes closed. A smile played at the corners of her lips as she ran a hand over the soft hair of her teenage son laid between her legs, his lips latched on to her dark brown nipple.

His fingers slipped inside the wrap of her dress, inexperienced hands fumbling with his mother's soft skin. She didn't stop him as he cupped her breast, squeezing and kneading like she was a loaf of bread.

'Softer son. No girl likes to be treated like a piece of meat. Be gentle, loving,' she murmured, grasping his wrist to lighten his touch.

In seconds, the door smashed fully open. Grabbing his son by the hair, he dragged him to his feet, burying a fist deep into his guts over and over again. The boy's legs collapsed, tears welling in his eyes. His wife was on her *feet, hanging on his arm, trying to stop the beating. She had no chance. She didn't even reach his shoulder.*

Oblivious to her screams, he continued to pummel the boy until his face was nothing more than a bloody pulp. Letting him go, he threw him into the chair, stepping forward to go in with the boot.

His wife threw herself down on top of the boy. It didn't matter to him. She deserved what she got. He kicked relentlessly at his family huddled on the floor, his wife taking the brunt of the force, screams for him to stop only inflaming his anger more.

With her body broken, she collapsed on top of their son, no longer able to hold her own weight. The boy pushed his mother's frail body away, scrambling out from underneath and running towards the door.

Let him go. There would be time to deal with him later. Pulling his wife to her feet, he wedged her against the wall, holding her upright with one arm while the other punched her wretched face. Her head lolled to one side, her eyes swelled shut, blood pouring from every orifice.

'You repulse me!' he yelled, spittle landing on her cheek.

With a final blow, he threw her to the floor, her head making a sickening thump as it contacted the slate hearth. She lay there, staring up at her husband, the rattle of death bubbling in her chest.

Looking down on her, he was disgusted with himself

for letting this whore into his life. Her voice was thready, faint as she begged for his help. It was a waste of time. He would not help. She deserved to die here. She had contaminated his life and he was glad to be rid of her.

17

THE TICKLED TROUT bar was empty except for a middle-aged couple in hiking gear pouring over a map at a table in the corner, and Martin Doyle leaning against the bar nursing a half-drunk pint of larger, reading the paper. Chrissy sidled up towards him, poking him gently in the ribs to catch his attention.

'Chrissy!'

He smiled broadly, its effect on her undiminished despite the intervening years.

'Hi Martin. Is your mother working today?'

'Yeah, she's out back. Did you need to see her?'

'Not especially,' she said. 'I could murder a drink though.'

Martin got up, stepping behind the bar with a decorous bow.

'What can I get you M' Lady?'

'Is it too early for whisky?'

'It can never be too early for whisky says the man with a pint on at 11 am.'

He winked at her and pulled a glass from the shelf. 'Ice?'

'No thanks. I'll take a Glenmorangie. Better make it a large one.'

'Bad morning?' Martin asked as he poured what looked like a triple measure and passed it to Chrissy.

'A frustrating one.'

Martin came back around the bar and took a swallow of his pint. Chrissy noticed his tartan waistcoat neatly folded over a stool. His shirt collar was undone, the sleeves rolled up in even turns to the elbow revealing muscular forearms that she couldn't help but imagine wrapped around her.

'I'm guessing you're not on duty today?'

'Just came off nights. Grabbing a pint and a sandwich before heading home for some well-earned sleep.'

He paused, turning his baby blues on her, a mock look of annoyance on his face.

'You've been ignoring me, Chrissy Ferguson. I've rung you twice now and you still haven't made time to meet me for a drink.'

Chrissy grinned sheepishly.

'Sorry Martin. Things have been a bit crazy with the investigation.'

'Mum mentioned you were helping the police.'

He pulled the paper he was reading forwards. A picture of Sonja McBride and Calvin Parks looked out from the front page under the headline '*Kinloch Rannoch Murders – Police still no nearer catching a killer.*'

'It's terrible, isn't it? I can't believe something like this is happening here, in Kinloch Rannoch!'

His eyes scanned over the journalist's report.

'Is this why you're in here drinking whisky before noon?'

'Partly. Partly because I can't stand being in the cottage. Too many memories.'

Mirren Doyle came back into the bar, loaded down with a full crate of bottles rattling as she walked. Martin was on his feet in seconds, relieving his mother of her burden and setting it down in front of the fridge behind the bar.

'Chrissy! Lovely to see you. You in for some lunch?'

'No, no thanks Mirren. Not today. Just a quick break from clearing the house.'

Martin didn't come back to his seat. He leaned over the bar, downed the rest of his pint and kissed his mother swiftly on the cheek.

'Well, I'm going to leave you two lovely ladies to it and head home. I'm knackered. I'll see you later mum. And Chrissy, I won't give up until you've met me for a drink.'

He grabbed his waistcoat and keys, then with a flirtatious wink, he was gone.

'I think Martin still has a soft spot for you Chrissy,'

Mirren said, watching the door swing shut after her son before starting to unload the bottles from the crate.

'What do you mean 'still'?

'You never noticed? You must have done! How he always came with me when I came to see your mother? How he walked past the cottage every day on the way home even though it's completely out of his way?'

Chrissy looked blank and Mirren shook her head.

'Funny, I always thought you had a bit of a crush on him too.'

'I... well I did. When I was a kid.'

'You're not a kid anymore and neither is he. He's a good man. You could do worse.'

Chrissy dropped her eyes, not wanting to get drawn into where Mirren was going. She drained her glass and didn't protest when Mirren took it to refill. Martin had left his paper. She picked it up and flicked over the page for something to do, wanting to deflect the conversation from childhood crushes. Mirren sensed a losing battle and crouched down to fill up the fridge.

The next page continued the report on the murders, the words in columns around two further images of Bonnie Harrison and Ciara Campbell. The press had obviously got hold of information about the cold cases now. Chrissy folded the paper so just Bonnie's image was visible.

'Mirren, do you remember anything about this girl's disappearance?'

Chrissy pushed the paper across the bar as Mirren stood up, wiping her hands on a tea towel. She picked up the paper and squinted her eyes as she looked at the page.

'Not really. It was a long time ago, wasn't it?'

'Twenty years.'

'I remember it happening, Bonnie something?'

'Bonnie Harrison. Her body was found in an old barn on the edge of the village.'

'Sorry, I hadn't been here long then. I didn't know the girl or her family.'

She passed the paper back to Chrissy and returned to the bottles.

'What about this one?'

Chrissy turned over the paper so that Ciara Campbell was staring out of the page and held it out. Mirren sighed, her brows drawn together, lips pursed. She took the paper reluctantly, stared at it for a minute and then passed it back.

'That one was a few years ago. I can't remember the name.'

'Ciara Campbell. Four years ago. No one was ever caught for either killing.'

'Why are you asking Chrissy? Is there a connection between these cases and that girl who was found recently?'

Mirren folded the tea towel and lined it up neatly with the edge of the bar, looking at Chrissy with her head to one side.

'I don't know. Probably not. They just came up because there are a few similarities with Sonja McBride's death.'

'And the boy? What about him?'

'Calvin Parks? I don't know. I'm not sure the police have had any of the forensic reports back yet.'

Mirren nodded, picking up her cloth again, absently wiping the rims of clean glasses.

'Well, I hope they catch someone soon. People are starting to feel unsafe and that's not good for business.'

Chrissy started to read the report. The details were remarkably accurate. Someone was feeding them information. Maybe the police, hoping to shake out some leads.

The door to the Tickled Trout opened, catching everyone's attention in the quiet. Diane Fraser stood in the doorway, her long black trench coat dripping puddles of water onto the wooden floor.

'Bloody weather. It never stops bloody raining here!'

She cast off her coat, throwing it over the back of a chair.

'Diane!' What are you doing here?'

Chrissy's voice came out three tones higher than normal.

'Well, that's a nice welcome! And I came all this way to see you.'

Diane came over to the bar, wiping her hands over

the front of her hair to dislodge the raindrops clinging there.

'Me? Why did you want to see me?'

Chrissy felt herself tense, her throat constricting as she tried to swallow. Diane smiled.

'Relax. I came to give Ross the results from Calvin Parks' autopsy. But while I was here, I thought I'd drop by and see you.'

'How did you know I was here?'

'I met a handsome blond guy while I was on the way to your cottage. He told me you were in the pub and that made my day.'

Diane beckoned to Mirren who looked annoyed at being summoned. She stared, waiting for an introduction, but Chrissy didn't oblige.

'I'll have a bottle of Budweiser. Don't bother with a glass.'

Mirren's jaw was set, her lips losing some colour as she pressed them together. This wasn't the kind of place where people swigged beer from the bottle. She stropped away to get the Budweiser, placing it down on the bar with a bang.

'Thanks,' Diane said, completely ignoring Mirren's obvious disapproval.

Chrissy noticed Mirren's nostrils flare, the corners of her mouth turning down before she turned away. She snatched up the tea towel and with one last reproachful glower, went back to her cleaning.

'What was the news on Calvin Parks?'

Diane put the bottle to her lips and drank deeply, sighing with pleasure as the cold liquid went down her throat.

'Daytime drinking. You can't beat it. Why does alcohol always taste better when you know you shouldn't be drinking it?'

Chrissy stared at her, waiting for her to answer the question.

'Calvin bled out from the wound on his neck, same as Sonja McBride.'

Diane's eyes flicked over to where Mirren was still cleaning the same glass, the strain showing on her face as she tried to listen in.

'Come on,' Diane said picking up her beer and heading to the farthest table from the bar.

Chrissy followed on, noticing the couple in the corner's eyes tracking them across the floor. It wasn't surprising. Diane was unlike anything that usually frequented the Tickled Trout. Out of her paper suit, she was even more spectacular. Today, she was wearing black and grey striped trousers that clung to her perfect round bottom, with Doc Martins, a white satin shirt open to reveal a glimpse of white push-up bra, and a black leather waistcoat fastened to show off her slim waist. Her beaded hair rattled as she walked, her confident stride making her impossible to ignore.

They took a seat, Diane staring down the tourists who were nosing at her until they became uncomfortable and returned their attention to map reading.

'The weapon was the same as Sonja McBride, but the angle of the wound was different.'

'What does that mean?'

'Well, given the bruising on Sonja McBride, I would suggest the body was suspended before she was killed. This would mean the killer could strike the blow from underneath. We also know she was probably drugged because of the needle mark on her neck. In the Parks' case, there was no bruising or needle mark. It's likely he was just walking by when someone jumped him.'

'Did forensics find anything else at the scene that could identify the killer?'

Diane shook her head.

'No. All the blood in the forest was the victims. The fingerprint was incomplete -didn't yield any hits.'

'I bet Ross didn't like hearing any of that. He seems frustrated about the lack of progress.'

'Ross hates to lose. But he's like a dog with a bone. He'll get the bastard in the end.'

For a moment, they sat in silence, Chrissy feeling uncomfortable under the pressure of Diane's stare.

'Are you fucking my husband?'

Chrissy coughed, her latest swallow of Glenmorangie catching in her throat before splattering all over the table.

'What?'

'Are you shagging my husband? It's a simple question?'

'I thought he was your ex-husband?' Chrissy said, mopping up the whisky with a tattered tissue she'd found in her pocket.

'He is. But I still like to know who he's doing.'

'Would it matter if I was?'

Diane sat back against the bench, crossing her legs, flicking her beaded braids back over her shoulder.

'No. I came here to tell you I approve. You'd be good for him.'

'You think so?'

'I do. He's been alone too long.'

'Well, thanks for the vote of confidence but I can assure you, Ross and I aren't sleeping together.'

'Why not? He's a good-looking guy, you're a good-looking girl. What's the problem?'

Chrissy's insides whirled at Diane's compliment.

'Ross has had the unfortunate experience of seeing me at my best.'

Diane's brow furrowed.

'A few nights ago, Ross came to the cottage. He brought me a case file. I'd been drinking, a lot, and didn't stop when he arrived. I was so plastered, he had to put me to bed. At which point, I tried to seduce him.'

Diane laughed.

'Ross is made of sterner stuff than that. A pissed woman making a play for him wouldn't be that big of a deal.'

'That's not the worst of it. He gallantly stayed on

the sofa to make sure I was all right. The next morning, I woke up with a raging hangover, vomited all over the bed, all over Ross and all over the bathroom. He cleaned up my sick! He even stripped the bed and washed my spew-covered clothes for Christ's sake! Kind of puts a dampener on any romantic interest.'

Diane threw her head back and laughed raucously so that everyone in the bar looked in their direction. Chrissy rested her forehead on the table, reliving her embarrassment. Controlling herself, Diane placed her hand on Chrissy's head, stroking her hair.

'You underestimate Ross. I bet he stayed and made you coffee and a full Scottish breakfast, didn't he?'

Chrissy sat up, laughing at herself as she nodded.

'Why did you and Ross split up?'

It was out of her mouth before she could engage her brain.

'Sorry, you don't have to answer that.'

'You don't want to know?' Diane said, a smile curling her lips.

'I really, really want to know. I've been dying to ask Ross, but you know... he seems so private.'

'It's simple really. I wasn't the marrying type. I like sex, lots of sex with lots of people. I couldn't stay faithful. Ross forgave me over and over, but I just went out and did it again. Eventually, we decided we shouldn't be married.'

'But you stayed friends?'

'The best of friends. I think Ross always knew I

209

wouldn't be a good wife. There was no point falling out over it. We loved each other. Still do. Just not in the way he wanted. He's the loyal type. I'm not.'

The door to the bar opened again and DCI Ross Fraser came in, folding up his umbrella and stowing it in the coat stand.

'Speak of the devil. Were your ears burning?' Diane asked Ross as he joined them at the table.

'Should they have been?'

'I was just telling Chrissy why we are no longer man and wife.'

Chrissy felt her cheeks flush as Ross turned his hazel eyes towards her. She sensed his annoyance. But at what she wasn't sure. That she had asked or that Diane had told?

'I'm sure it was an illuminating story,' he said, his face giving nothing away.

'Can I get you a drink?' Chrissy asked tentatively.

'No. I just came to see if you wanted to come with me?'

'Where to?'

'We've been trying to find something, anything, that can link the victims together. We haven't had much luck. The only commonality is that all bar one were found on land belonging to a Ged Hughes. Calvin Parks was found less than half a mile beyond the edge of his land too. It's a long shot, but I thought I'd go and talk to him. See if he recognises any of the victims.'

Chrissy nodded, glad to have something to extract her from the awkward moment.

'I'll come.'

'Drink up then. What about you Diane? Fancy a field trip?'

'I'll pass. I'm heading to Dundee this afternoon. Another case has come in from Tayside. I'm not just at your beck and call husband.'

'Ex-husband.'

Ross smiled, any irritation about her blabbing their past forgotten. Diane raised her beer bottle and nodded to them both. Chrissy downed the rest of her whisky then followed Ross out into the rain.

Mirren Doyle waited until the woman called Diane finished her beer, pulled on her coat and left the bar. Only the hikers remained now, and they were still pouring over their latest route. She slipped into the back and pulled her mobile phone from her handbag. Scrolling through the contact list, she stopped at the number she was looking for.

She tapped her foot impatiently while the call connected, waiting for the click that told her she had been put through. Quickly, Mirren leaned out of the door, checking the bar was still empty, the hikers still engaged. Eight rings, then nine.

She was about to hang up when the ringtone cut off halfway through ring ten.

'Hello?'

Mirren took a deep breath. No need for pleasantries.

'Chrissy's here. She's asking questions about Bonnie Harrison.'

18

THE RAIN HAD STOPPED by the time Ross turned into the drive of McKinley House, the October sun peaking intermittently through grey clouds. The sandstone building stood back from the road, its imposing baronial-style façade hidden by large pine trees standing inside a five-foot wall that circled the entire property. Wrought iron gates over six feet tall barred their entry. Privacy was important here.

Ross wound down the window and pressed the button on the intercom.

'What is this place? Chrissy asked.

'It's a refuge for women and children.'

A stern voice blared out of the speaker.

'What's your business here?'

Ross raised his eyebrows.

'DCI Ross Fraser. I need to speak to Ged Hughes.'

They heard a metallic click as the gate began to swing open.

'Friendly bunch,' Ross said, pulling the car slowly into the drive.

The gates clunked shut behind them, keeping everyone out, or everyone in. The house had a 'new build' look about it, even though it had been sympathetically designed. A large porch wrapped around half the extensive exterior, gables extending upwards to three stories giving the building a castle-like feel. The many windows shimmered as the light caught raindrops leaving trails on each pane as they drifted away. It was a beautiful house.

'Nice place,' Chrissy said as they stepped out of the car, her gaze travelling up to the pitched roof and down again.

There were a few women out in the grounds, each wearing rubber gloves and carrying garden tools.

'They must be bloody dedicated,' Ross said, shivering as he pulled his jacket closer around his body, the filtering sun having no effect on the temperature.

With the break in the rain, the women were cutting back spent plants, raising some from the ground and throwing them into an old metal wheelbarrow. None of them spoke, not even to each other, their attention fixated on their task. Chrissy found their silence unnerving. Pulling her coat around her body, she folded her arms before following Ross towards the front door. When they moved, the women stopped their work, all eyes tracking them as they climbed up the three steps onto the porch. Their scrutiny was uncomfortable. Visitors were obviously unwelcome.

A small brass sign announcing all callers must report to reception glinted in the sun above the bell. Ross pressed it, fidgeting from foot to foot as he waited for the door to be released by someone on the inside.

Granted admittance, they entered a bright and airy hallway, with pale yellow walls, a thick grey tartan carpet and copious amounts of art adorning the walls. Unlike the atmosphere, the decor was warm and welcoming.

Ross strode over to the desk where an austere woman with an ample bosom, half-moon spectacles perched on her beaky nose and long grey hair twisted into a bun at the nape of her neck, stood waiting for them to speak.

'Hi, I'm DCI Ross Fraser,' Ross said, flashing his badge. 'And this is Dr Chrissy Ferguson. We need to speak to Ged Hughes about some of the farm buildings on his land.'

The beaky woman pursed her lips, emphasising the lines around her mouth, making her look even more formidable.

'Do you have an appointment?'

Chrissy saw a tick start in Ross's cheek and knew he was irritated by their reception.

'I need to talk to Mr Hughes about an ongoing

murder investigation. I think an appointment is unnec-
essary, don't you?'

Beaky looked away and began to straighten the
papers on her desk.

'I'm afraid Mr Hughes isn't here.'

'Can you tell me where he is? When he'll be back?'

Ross fixed Beaky with his most determined glare,
hands pushed into his hips on the inside of his jacket.

'I'm afraid I don't know DCI Fraser,' she said,
straightening up and challenging Ross's stare.

Ross opened his mouth to retaliate but was cut off
by the appearance of a man, somewhere in his late
forties, entering through the door to the right of the
desk. He was focused on a paper in his hand, oblivious
to the presence of a police officer in the hallway.

'Agatha, do you know where....'

The man looked up, noticing Ross and Chrissy for
the first time. He was tall, just shy of six feet, and well-
built. He was wearing baggy grey trousers held up with
striped braces, and no shirt. His body was toned with
no visible fat giving him a wiry appearance, like
someone who could hold their own in a fight. He fixed
steely grey eyes on Ross, then Chrissy, a broad smile
revealing crooked teeth as he stretched out a hand.

'Sorry, I didn't know we had company. I'm Ged
Hughes.'

His accent was strange, a mild Scottish lilt mixed
with a hint of a New York twang. Ross took his hand,
shooting the beaky Agatha an angry glare.

'Mr Hughes. I'm DCI Ross Fraser and this is Dr Chrissy Ferguson. We were just telling your assistant here that we needed to speak to you about the buildings on your land.'

Beaky glared at Ross over her half-moon spectacles, unappreciative of being called 'an assistant'.

'You mean the building where that poor girl was found? I'm not sure what I can tell you. We only farm about three acres around the house. I don't think I've even been out to that part of the land.'

'Still, we'd like to ask you a few questions.'

'Of course. Come through to the office.'

Ged indicated the door he had come through.

'Agatha, could you bring us some coffee?'

Beaky was still unimpressed, an audible sniff accompanying a curt nod before she disappeared through a different door. Ged led them into another pastel-coloured room, green this time, a large desk with a computer and piles of paperwork dominating the centre. Ged indicated they should sit on the leather corner sofa, taking a seat at the other end himself. Chrissy wished he would put on a shirt. His grey chest hair was too long, curling around his braces.

'Mr Hughes, do you recognise this girl?'

Ross took a stack of pictures from the inside pocket of his jacket. He pushed an image of Sonja McBride across the coffee table to Ged. He rubbed his bearded chin, the salt and pepper bristles covering all but a ragged scar on the lower part of his cheek.

'This is the girl who's been in the news. Sonja something? She's the one who was found on my land isn't she?'

'Yes. Did you ever see her before?'

'No. I'm afraid not. We're pretty self-sufficient here, so I don't go into the village often. It's better that way. The women feel safer if we keep the outside world out as much as possible.'

'What about either of these girls?'

Ross placed Bonnie Harrison and Ciara Campbell on the table. Chrissy noticed Ged was shaking his head even before he looked at the pictures. He made a cursory glance at the girl's images, the head shakes becoming more intentional as he looked down.

'I saw this girl in the news. About four years ago, wasn't it?'

He was pointing to Ciara Campbell.

'I didn't know her. And I've never seen the other one.'

Ross left the images lined up on the table, shuffling back on the sofa so he could survey Ged Hughes more easily. The bare-chested man was perched on the edge of the seat, his spine lamppost straight, knees pressed together, his feet, ensconced in lilac Crocs with no socks, pressed into the floor.

'Mr Hughes, all these girls were murdered, their bodies found in farm buildings on your land. That seems like a hell of a coincidence don't you think?'

Ged's jaw tightened, all pretence at pleasantries

sliding from his face. Anger flared in his eyes, quickly subdued to become a fixed, emotionless glare. He shifted slightly as if recognising his stoic body language was inappropriate for an innocent person being interrogated by the police. Letting his shoulders relax, he shuffled his feet into a wider position, letting the knees fall casually open. Leaning forwards, he ran a hand through his grey-streaked hair, the relaxed curls falling back to frame his weathered face. Strands of hair caught in a sovereign ring on his right hand. He pulled them out absently and dropped them to the floor. Fixing his steely eyes deliberately on Ross, he held eye contact, attempting to support his sincerity.

'Surely you don't think I had anything to do with any of this DCI Fraser?'

He waved his hand across the images staring up from the table. Ross didn't answer because Beaky arrived carrying a tray with three mugs of coffee and a milk jug. She set it down giving Ross a vicious look, then exited the room.

Ged picked up the milk jug.

'Do you take milk?'

Chrissy shook her head, but Ross nodded. Ged poured milk into one mug and handed it to Ross.

'Sorry, Agatha hasn't brought any sugar. I can go get some,' Ged said, passing Chrissy the other mug.

'Not for me,' Chrissy replied, her voice sounding unused.

'It's fine thank you,' Ross said, eager to get the

conversation back on track. 'Mr Hughes, can you think of any reason why all these bodies would be left on your land specifically?'

Ged re-established his helpful demeanour, his brief animosity dispelled with the arrival of the coffee.

'I really have no idea. But I do technically own a good portion of the land around here. It came with the farm when I bought it. The law of averages would mean a body found anywhere near Kinloch Rannoch would be on land I owned. I don't even know exactly what does belong to me. Like I said, we only work the area immediately around the house.'

Ross placed the picture of Calvin Parks in the gallery of dead people.

'What about him? Do you recognise him?'

Ged leant over to look at the image, shaking his head slowly as he looked back up at Ross.

'No. I don't. Is he dead too?'

For the first time, Ged's tone was genuine, unforced.

'Yes. He was found about half a mile outside the perimeter of your land.'

Leaning back, Ged folded his arms stubbornly across his naked chest, closing himself off from any more questions.

'Look, I'm really sorry I can't be of more help. But like I said, I don't know any of these people. We keep to ourselves here. I don't really know anyone in the village.'

Ged's grey eyes hardened again, his face tense.

'Calvin wasn't from Kinloch Rannoch. He was staying here with some friends.'

Ross was looking pointedly at Ged who remained tightly folded opposite him.

'DCI Fraser, I don't know anything about these murders. So, unless there's anything else, I need to get back to work.'

Ged stood up, making it clear Ross and Chrissy were no longer welcome. Ross put down his mug and stood up, taking a step towards Ged Hughes. They were the same height, their eyes level as they glowered at each other. For a moment, their silent stand-off filled the room. Ross broke away, walking towards the door, Chrissy going after him as Ged ushered them both out.

In the reception, Ross turned towards Ged, Beaky coming around to stand by her boss in a show of solidarity.

'Thank you for your time, Mr Hughes. We may have more questions so please make sure you're available.'

Ged didn't respond.

Ross marched out the door, waiting for Chrissy to join him on the porch. As they walked down the steps, Chrissy's attention was caught by a face peering at them from around the side of the house. A woman was staring, her skinny body half concealed by the angle of the wall. Chrissy touched Ross gently on the arm to slow him down, then took a step towards where the woman was hiding.

Seeing Chrissy come towards her, she disappeared, her fingers still curling around the stone to show she was still there.

'Hello? Did you want to talk to us?' Chrissy asked, tentatively taking a few more steps forward.

A protuberant eye reappeared around the wall.

'My name's Chrissy. If you need to tell us something, please come out. I won't hurt you.'

The woman leaned out a little further, both eyes staring at Chrissy. Her straggly brown hair was pulled back into nothing more than a rat's tail, pale skin pinched and taut across her pointed cheeks. The thin lips drew back in a childish smile, making the bird-like face seem unhinged.

'Please, talk to me,' Chrissy tried again.

The woman continued to grimace, then turned on her heel and ran across the gardens. Chrissy watched her disappear into a clump of trees, then headed back to Ross.

'What was all that about?'

'I don't know. There was a woman watching us. She seemed to want to talk to us but as soon as I got near, she took off.'

'Just something else to add to the weirdness of this visit,' Ross said, heading back towards the car.

Settled in the passenger seat, Chrissy watched Ross rub his eyes. He looked tired, probably wasn't sleeping. He turned towards her, frustration etched in the lines on his forehead.

'What did you think of Ged Hughes?' he asked, starting the car and sliding it into gear.

'I'm not sure. On the surface, he seems like a good guy, offering these women somewhere to go. But I'm a pessimist and don't believe anyone is completely self-less. It all felt a bit fake. He was obviously angry we were there despite his best efforts to appear helpful. He got a bit weird when you showed him the pictures.'

'Yeah . . . he was very quick to dismiss knowing any of the victims. But there's absolutely nothing to tie him to any of the crimes. I've got Jason doing a background check on him, so we might unearth something.'

'I don't know why, but something felt strange about the place, sort of cult-like,' Chrissy said, her skin rising in goosebumps. 'And why couldn't he put a bloody shirt on!'

Ross laughed. It was good to see the tension fall from his face for a moment.

'Seriously though, that woman who wanted to talk to us, she seemed odd too, like she was afraid to get too near.'

'I think she was afraid to get too near *me*,' Ross said, turning out of the drive and back onto the main road. 'I felt like a pariah. I don't think those of the male persuasion are welcome at McKinley House.'

19

THE OFFICE WAS quiet when Ross came in the following morning. He was later than usual, needing to spend some time pounding the pavements to clear his head. It was almost ten now, and there was no sign of anyone. The coffee machine was on though. Ross collected his Highland cow mug from the sink and poured himself a cup. There was no milk. Black and bitter it was then.

He had just sat down at his desk and taken a mouthful of coffee when DI Hugh McCann blustered in followed by DS Jason Moore. The two men couldn't be more different. Hugh, short, round and irritated, Jason, tall, muscular and smiling. They were clutching paper bags from the Waterside Café, grease seeping through suggesting Hugh was not on his diet today.

'Morning sir,' Jason said, throwing his bacon sandwich onto Hugh's desk. 'We weren't sure what time you'd get here so we didn't get you anything. I can nip back out though?'

Jason had been overly attentive since he had got up Ross's nose by flirting with Chrissy.

'I'm fine thanks. I made apple Danishes at Mirren's last night,' Ross replied, pointing to the Tupperware box sitting on the table in the make-shift interview room.

Hugh followed his gesture then shuffled out, coming back seconds later, his face full of apple pastry, his cream shirt covered in flaky crumbs and the Tupperware clutched in his other hand.

'Not on a diet today then?' Ross asked, his eyes crinkling at the corner.

Hugh hmphed, his mouth bulging.

'I've done the background check on Ged Hughes,' Jason said, picking up some handwritten notes from Hugh's desk.

'Anything interesting?'

'Not really. Nothing that seems relevant anyway. He was born here in Kinloch Rannoch but left when he was eighteen to live in the USA – New York I think – yes. His mother was Scottish, but his father was an American. Seems he moved over there with his father after his mother was killed in a car accident. He did well for himself. Got into property development. Made a fortune.'

'What brought him back here?' Ross asked,

retrieving an apple Danish from the box before Hugh's hand went back in for a second.

'Not sure. He came back about fifteen years ago and bought a whole raft of land around Kinloch Rannoch and set up the refuge. His father died in a care home in New York state about six years ago, but he didn't go back for the funeral. Probably didn't get on.'

'Anything we should know about since he's been here?'

'Nothing. He's clean as a whistle. Keeps himself to himself and stays out of everyone's way.'

'Nothing to connect him to any of the victims?'

'Not that I can find.'

Ross sighed. Why couldn't he catch a break on this case?

'If there's nothing else, I'll get going.'

'What? Oh no. I don't need anything else.'

Jason nodded, collected his bacon sandwich and headed towards the door.

'Wait, where are you going?' Ross asked, calling Jason back.

'I've been assigned as family liaison for Calvin Parks' family. I promised I would update them on the investigation this afternoon.'

Ross looked preoccupied.

'I wish I could give you something positive to tell them.'

Jason nodded in acknowledgement before disappearing out the door.

Hugh wiped a dollop of apple filling off his spotty tie shoving it into his mouth from a sticky finger, then rustled in his paper bag from the café and pulled out a sausage roll. Ross leaned forward, resting his head on his hands, running them up through his carefully styled hair.

'If Hughes only came back here fifteen years ago, he wasn't even in the country when Bonnie Harrison was killed.'

Hugh wiped his mouth with his shirt sleeve.

'Looks like another dead end.'

Ross watched him toss the remains of the sausage roll into the bin.

'Too full on your baking,' Hugh said, smiling guiltily.

'There's nothing to connect him to any of the victims. I can't believe we've got four murders in a dead-end village like this and haven't turned up a single lead!'

Hugh didn't have a response. There was nothing he could say to make the truth sound better. They were no nearer solving any of these murders than they had been the day they arrived in Kinloch Rannoch.

The uniformed officer drafted in from Pitlochry to help with the investigation pushed open the door to the incident room.

'DCI Fraser? There's a chap out here who wants to

speak to you about a missing woman. Says his name is Ged Hughes.'

Ross and Hugh looked at each other.

'You'd better show him in.'

The officer led Ged into the interview room where Hugh and Ross waited. He looked gaunt, his assertiveness from the previous day, gone.

'Please sit down Mr Hughes.' Ross indicated the chair opposite. 'What can we do for you?'

'I need to report a missing person.'

Ged ferreted in his pocket and withdrew a dog-eared picture of a skinny woman with staring eyes. She looked terrified. The image looked like a mugshot but without the identification number. Ross took it from him.

'Her name's Aisha Flannigan. She's one of the women who lives at the house.'

'How long has she been missing?' Hugh asked, flicking to an empty page in his notebook.

'It's hard to say. She wasn't at dinner last night, but that's not unusual. I wasn't worried until she didn't come down for breakfast. She never misses breakfast. I went to see if she was in her room and that's when I discovered her bed hadn't been slept in.'

'When was the last time you saw her?' Ross asked.

'Breakfast yesterday. But one of the women said she was in the house early afternoon.'

'When we were there?'

Ged nodded and Hugh scribbled some notes on the page.

'Is it like Aisha to disappear without telling anyone where she was going?' Hugh asked, pen poised to write.

'No. Aisha never left the grounds. She had a particularly traumatic journey to us. Her husband was vicious. Tried to kill her. It left her mentally scarred. She was afraid of everything and everyone. It was difficult enough to get her out of her room, never mind out of the building.'

'Did anyone have a reason to want to hurt Aisha?' Ross asked.

'I can't see it. Aisha hardly ever spoke to anyone.'

'Could her husband have found out where she was? Maybe taken her home?'

Ged looked at Hugh as he spoke.

'It's possible I suppose, but not very likely. She came to me from Ireland about six years ago. We're very clear that the women mustn't make any contact with their past for everyone's safety. Aisha was so afraid. I can't imagine she would have told anyone where she was. I don't see how he could have found her if she didn't tell him.'

'Do you have a name or address for her husband?' Hugh asked.

'No. We don't collect any information from the women. That's the point. McKinley House is a safe place. They can tell us as much or as little as they want.

We offer a refuge for them with no questions asked.
Aisha Flannigan might not even be her real name.'

Ged ran a hand through his hair, his grey eyes filled
with genuine tears.

'Were you close to Aisha?' Ross asked.

Ged looked affronted.

'If you're asking me if I was abusing my position
and sleeping with her, then no. Most definitely not.
But I did want to protect her. I want to protect them
all.'

Tears escaped now and Ged wiped a hand under
his eyes.

'Mr Hughes, can I ask you why you opened the
refuge?'

Ged stared at Ross, seeming to debate his answer.

'My mother died in a car crash over thirty years
ago. She was trying to escape an abusive relationship
when she was killed. I was in the car with her, but I
was thrown free before it exploded. I survived, she
didn't.'

Unconsciously, he rubbed his fingers across his
bearded chin.

'My father moved us to America soon afterwards,
but when I turned eighteen, I left him to make my own
way. I always wanted to do something to honour my
mother's memory and so when I was able, I came back
to Scotland and bought the old McKinley farm.
McKinley House was built within a year and unfortu-
nately, we've been full ever since.'

Ross turned to Hugh.

'Have you got everything you need DI McCann?'

'Think so. For now anyway. Can we keep the picture Mr Hughes?'

Ged handed it over.

'You will look for her, won't you?'

Ross stood up, Ged following his lead.

'We'll do everything we can. We'll be in touch if we have any news. DI McCann will show you out.'

Ross felt like he had been dismissive, but he wasn't in the mood for babysitting Ged Hughes. His story fitted with the information Jason had dug up, but there was something he couldn't put his finger on. Something in his panicked look made Ross think he was holding something back.

Hugh bundled back in, scratching his head as he plonked down at his desk.

'What do you think Hugh?'

Ross had always trusted Hugh McCann's instincts.

'Well, he seems on the straight. His story checks out but he was defensive when you asked about his relationship with Aisha.'

Ross's phone started to ring. He looked around for his jacket and withdrew his mobile from the inside pocket.

'It's Chrissy.'

He put the phone to his ear but didn't get a chance to say hello. It was a minute before he spoke.

'Calm down Chrissy. Slow down and tell me again.'

Ross listened intently, grabbing a pen and scribbling something down on the edge of a stack of papers on his desk.

'OK. I just need to alert the Crime Scene Investigators and then I'll pick you up.'

Hugh leaned forward as the call ended, Ross staring at the phone as if waiting for it to tell him what to do.

'What is it?' Hugh asked.

'It's Chrissy. She's had another dream. A woman being beaten to death then buried.'

'Did she see who the victim was?'

'No. But she thinks she knows where the body is.'

20

TAKING his coffee from the counter, he nodded at the young girl in the tight t-shirt, enjoying the flush of her cheeks as he flashed her a smile. The café was busy. He managed to find a table in the far corner that gave him a good view of the patrons coming and going. People-watching was a favourite pastime, imagining their deep dark secrets, what they got up to in the privacy of their own homes, what they dreamed about at night.

He spent some time watching a woman opposite using her toes to pleasure her man under the table. The display was common and uncouth. His game was to use his imagination to create a private life for the people he saw. No imagination was needed with this pair.

His attention switched to a family with a couple of kids, one still in nappies, the other building Lego bricks on the table. His mother was helping him build a coloured blob that he seemed to think was a car, while his father bottle-fed the baby. A twitch of jealousy reared at the sight of a functional family, doing normal things on a normal day.

Today, he felt calmer, his problem was solved. Aisha Flannigan's cold broken body was in the ground. He smiled as he remembered her tiny face, blood streaming from her pointed little nose, tears streaming down her hollow cheeks as she begged him to stop.

Aisha had been different. He hadn't wanted to enjoy her death. He just wanted her gone. The stirring in his groin as her bones broke had been a surprise, unexpected. The sight of her cowering on the floor, whimpering as her internal organs bled, had aroused him. It was the one part of the proceedings he didn't look back on with relish. He should never have let himself get excited. But it was done now. The power he had over her was thrilling. The urge to stick his cock inside her bleeding body had been overwhelming.

Still, he was confident they would never find her. After all, they had never found him.

August 1994

He watched as the nurse disconnected the respirator
that had been breathing for his mother for the last two
days. It made a wheezing sound as the oxygen keeping
her body alive escaped into the sterile atmosphere.

More tubes were removed and placed in the clinical
waste until only the lead connecting her to the heart
monitor remained.

'I'm going to turn the monitor off now. You can sit
with her until the end.'

'How long will it take?' he asked, red eyes looking
up at the white-coated doctor who was fidgeting from
foot to foot. He probably had somewhere else to be. Was
needed by someone who could be saved.

'It's hard to say, son. Sometimes it can be just
minutes, at other times, longer.'

He didn't want to tell the boy who had sat at his
mother's side for days that it could be hours.

The doctor nodded to the nurse who reached for the switch and silenced the slow rhythmic beep that told him his mother's heart was still beating. She tidied the sheets and backed out of the room, leaving him with the fidgeting doctor and the brain-dead body in the bed. All that remained of his mother.

The doctor's hand came to rest briefly on his shoulder.

'I'll leave you to be with her. The nurses are just outside if you need anything. They'll be in to check on you.'

The weight of the hand lifted, the sound of the sliding glass door telling him he was alone.

He had been avoiding looking at his mother since they moved her from ICU into this private room where she would die. When she had been hooked up to tubes and monitors, with medical staff bustling around, it had felt like there was hope. People were trying to save her. She would wake up at any second. But now, in the silence of this place, hope was gone.

Slowly, he took her greying hand in his own, the purple bruises from the IV drip livid on her papery skin. He ran a thumb tenderly across the back of her hand, hoping to wipe away the signs of damage, wanting to see her hands as he remembered them. Beautiful and soft.

He let his eyes wander across her body, watching her chest as it rose and fell. She was breathing on her own. It was hard for him to understand. The doctors had warned that this might happen. That her heart might struggle for life, for a while. But she was breathing. Surely this meant she could wake up. No. The doctors had told him she would never regain consciousness. The injuries to her brain were too severe. The brain stem had ceased to function. She was effectively, dead.

He couldn't see much of her face. Her head was swathed in a turban of bandages, her beautiful hair shaved off in the three surgeries she had endured to try and fix the damage. One eye was swallowed up in a dark red swelling, the other patched to cover the laceration that would have cost his mother her sight. Her jaw was broken, finger-shaped bruises starting to yellow around the edges marked her throat.

Tears began to run down his hollow cheeks, his hatred for the man who had done this confused with his grief. He was glad the nurse had pulled the sheet high up under her arms so he couldn't see any more of the trauma she had suffered at Father's hand.

The movement of her chest began to slow, the breaths coming intermittently, the intervals in between getting longer and longer. He wanted to shout at her. Tell her to fight. Tell her to come back to him. But that was selfish. Even if she continued to breathe, her head was so mashed up she would never be the mother he knew. He had to let her go.

What would happen now? So far, the hospital staff had accepted his lies, the hopelessness of his mother's *condition keeping their questions at bay. He had driven her here in the smashed-up truck Father kept for hauling pig feed around the farm, telling them she had been in a road traffic accident. But they weren't fooled. Once his mother was gone, they would push him for more information. Demand details of where they lived. Who had done this to her. An explanation for the injuries old and new. The police were probably lurking somewhere now, waiting for his mother to die.*

An hour passed, the puny chest still making an occasional effort. Now, he just wanted it to end. The nurse had been in three times, checking her pulse, bestowing a faltering smile before leaving without a word. The shallow breaths were accompanied by a rattling sound now as fluid built up in the weakened lungs. His eyes were sore, arid with no more tears left to shed.

He was finding it too difficult to look at his mother's face, focusing instead on the small hand, the hospital blankets, his own breathing. It was a few minutes before he realised the chest was still, the room silent again. He watched for a few more minutes. No rise and fall. No death rattle. She was gone.

Looking around, he stared out of the glass door, searching for someone to confirm what he already knew. The nurse spotted his panic and came hurrying in. She felt his mother's wrist then called in the fidgeting doctor who placed a stethoscope on her chest and shook his head solemnly.

'She's gone son. Would you like a few moments.'

He shook his head. He wanted to be as far away from here as possible.

The doctor nodded.

'Time of death, 18:24.'

21

CHRISSY SNORED HERSELF AWAKE, catching the drool escaping down her chin. Fidgeting in the passenger seat, she pulled her coat tighter around her body. It was bloody freezing. She had no idea how long she had been asleep. It was dark outside now. But then it had hardly gotten light all day.

Sitting up, she unscrewed the top from the water Ross had insisted she drunk. When Hugh and Ross had picked her up, she had still been three parts cut having downed most of a bottle of whisky during her insomnia last night. She had only been asleep for a little over two hours when the dream yanked her awake. If Ross hadn't needed her to show them the place, he would have made her stay at home to sober up.

Fumbling with her coat sleeve, she uncovered her watch face. Her eyes wouldn't focus on the small dial, so she looked around for her phone. It was nowhere to be seen and all her pockets came up empty. Then she remembered it had been in her hand when she got in the car, irritably trying to force it to get an internet signal in the middle of nowhere. It must have fallen on the floor when she fell asleep.

Chrissy opened the door, her feet squelching in the muddy tyre tracks as she got out. The wind was vicious, howling across the open field, threatening a stormy squall at any minute. That wouldn't help the excavation.

She felt around under the seat, her fingertips catching a corner of the gel case, pushing it further under the seat.

'Fuck! Fuck! Fuck!'

Chrissy was in no mood for groping around Ross's Freelander, her feet freezing as the mud seeped into her very inappropriate fabric trainers. Her head was starting to thump, her stomach doing somersaults, the bottle of whisky threatening to reverse its journey and reappear all over the cream leather. She sat on the sill, reaching as far as she could until her hand closed around the phone. Pulling it out, she looked at the screen. Still no signal. It was five o'clock. They had been here almost six hours.

Chrissy hopped back into the passenger seat, closing the door and kicking off her shoes. Her socks were wet and brown where mud had invaded. Pulling them off, she placed them over the heating vents, then searched her pockets for Ross's keys. She slid across to the driver's side so she could depress the brake and make the car come to life when she pressed the ignition. Turning up the heat, she huddled back into the seat waiting for the warmth to permeate the chilly interior.

She felt like shit. Her hands were shaking and not only from the cold. Her stomach growled, needing food to sop up the lake of whisky gurgling around the pit of her belly. If it wasn't so God damn nippy, she would have gone to find out what was happening, see if she could get someone to take her home.

The Freelander's headlamps bathed the empty field in light, silvery droplets shining in the beams as the rain began to fall. She definitely wasn't getting out of the car now. Her socks were starting to smell, the aroma of warm sweat mixed with fusty dampness. She wanted to glug down the rest of the water but already needed to pee.

The headlights seemed to flicker as someone walked across the front of the car. Chrissy looked up to see Ross coming around to the passenger side, a plastic mac zipped over his clothes. He opened the door and climbed in, undoing the coat, his hair dripping wet despite the hood. He looked reproachfully at the socks stiffening up on his car's heating vents.

'Sorry,' Chrissy said, pulling them down and balling them up in her hands.

'Are you feeling better?'

Ross was looking at her like a matron treating a child who had stuck a toy soldier up their nose, the ensuing consequences being entirely their own fault.

'To be honest, no. I feel worse. I'm cold, hungry and I need to pee.'

'I'm sure you don't feel as bad as the woman we've just dug out of a hole in the ground must have done before she died.'

'You found her?'

'Yes, buried deep, exactly where you said she'd be.'

'Oh God. I didn't think... I hoped it was just a run-of-the-mill dream.'

'If you can stop feeling sorry for yourself, I'd like you to come up, see if you recognise her.'

Chrissy wanted to be angry at his patronising, but she couldn't be. She was wallowing when a woman was dead. Nodding sheepishly, she unrolled her stiff socks and pulled them onto her feet.

'Wait a minute,' Ross said, jumping out of the car and opening the boot. He was back a minute later clutching a clean pair of white sports socks that he handed to Chrissy.

'They might be a bit big, but at least they'll be clean and dry.'

'Thank you. They'll probably fit. I've got big feet.'

He waited while she pulled on the socks and tied up her filthy trainers.

'Ready?'

Chrissy nodded and stepped out into the rain that

had upped its game from pouring to lashing. Her coat wasn't made for this weather, the wool soaking up every drop, feeling heavy on her shoulders as she followed Ross into the darkness. By the time they saw floodlights filtering between the trees, her hair was plastered to her face, rainwater running off the end of her nose.

The Scene of Crime Officers had erected a tent, providing some protection from the pouring rain as well as privacy for the morbid task of digging up a dead body. Chrissy and Ross huddled inside the door, keeping out of the worst of the weather but staying as far away as possible from the hole in the ground.

Diane Fraser saw them standing there and came over, her eyes glittering as they caught the light. It was the first time Chrissy had seen her unnerved, teary even, and it took her by surprise. Ross placed his hand on Diane's arm, patting it affectionately. His show of concern caused a tear to escape from the corner of Diane's eye that she quickly brushed away, pulling herself together and getting her pathologist head on.

'They're just about to bring her up. Are you sure you're up for this Chrissy?' Diane asked, her brow furrowed as she took in Chrissy's drenched state, rainwater running down from her forehead as she nodded.

'Do you have any idea who she is?' Chrissy asked.

'No, she's been undressed so there's nothing to identify her. All I can tell you now is that she looks in her late thirties or early forties, and she was severely beaten before she died.'

Chrissy looked over Diane's shoulder to see four paper suits lifting someone easily from the hole in the ground. She could see arms and legs barely larger than those of a child sticking out from beneath a sheet draped over the body. Diane turned to follow Chrissy's line of vision, watching as they laid the woman's corpse on the plastic sheeting on the floor.

'Are you ready?' she asked Chrissy who nodded again, wiping the water running down her face with a sodden sleeve.

Diane led her forwards, bending down to pull the sheet away. Chrissy's breath felt sharp in her chest as she inhaled, her hand spontaneously reaching up to cover her mouth in shock. The body was barely recognisable as a woman, nearly all the bones of her tiny frame, twisted and broken. Her face was a mask of dried blood caked in dirt. The naked breasts were childlike and bruised, her backside and inside thighs, marred by finger-nail-shaped welts.

Chrissy tried to see through the mess of swollen skin and congealed blood, ignoring the desire to turn away from the horrendous sight. Whoever had done this was an animal. It was the woman she had dreamed about, and now they were staring at her, she knew who it was.

'It's the woman from McKinley House. The one who tried to talk to us.'

She looked up at Ross, waiting for him to remember.

'The one who ran off when you approached her?'

'Yes. I'm certain.'

Ross stepped forward and bent down to look at the woman's face, determinedly keeping his eyes away from her battered bare skin.

'Ged Hughes came into the station this morning saying one of the women hadn't been seen since yesterday. He gave me a photograph. Her name's Aisha Flannigan. Or that's the name she goes by at the refuge. I think it's her.'

Everyone stared at the broken body, a moment of silence for Aisha Flannigan. Diane gave a nod to the waiting paper suits who covered her over and began to bundle the corpse into a black body bag.

'What about the other one?' Ross asked.

'Other one?' Chrissy questioned, eyebrows raised.

Diane, still watching the progress of her team as they dealt with Aisha, replied absently.

'We found another body buried beneath this victim.'

'Another body? Who?'

Diane noticed something she didn't like and strode across to the paper suits, shaking a finger, shouting instructions that got lost as she moved away.

'We don't know,' Ross said. 'So far, we've only found bone fragments. The body's been underground for a long time.'

Chrissy noticed how tired he looked as he spoke, weariness dripping from every word.

'Come on, we might as well leave them to it. It'll be a while before they bring up the rest of the second body and Diane won't have any other information until she gets them back to the mortuary. They're taking them to Bell Street so I'll head down to Dundee tomorrow. I'll have to go and see Ged Hughes now. He'll need to come and identify her.'

Ross headed out of the tent, taking a small flashlight from his pocket. It was fully dark now and beyond the ring of floodlights, the landscape looked ominous.

'Thank God it's stopped bloody raining,' he said, looking skyward, checking for errant flecks of rain. 'I'll drop you off at home on the way to McKinley House.'

Chrissy trotted after him, struggling to keep pace with his long strides as always.

'Can I come with you? To see Ged Hughes I mean.'

Ross paused and turned to look at her.

'You're drenched Chrissy. You should go home, take a hot bath and get some sleep.'

'I will. I'll do all those things after we see Ged.'

He cocked his head, brow wrinkling as he considered her. She must have looked dreadful. Hair starting to dry at the ends into a frizzy mess. Face gaunt and makeup-less, probably with a hint of green given the sloshing of whisky mixed with visions of Aisha's dead body playing havoc with her insides.

'OK. But you take off that wet coat when we get to the car. I've got a sweatshirt in the back. You can put that on.'

'Have you got your whole wardrobe in the back of that car?'

Ross grinned wearily.

'No. But in this line of work, it always pays to have a set of clean clothes in the boot. You never know whether you'll be pulling an all-nighter, rolling about in squalor or standing in the middle of a muddy field for hours in the pissing-down rain.'

'Good point,' Chrissy said, looking down at her sodden clothes.

They walked at pace across the field, Ross passing her a clean, dry sweatshirt from a bag in the boot of the car that Chrissy quickly exchanged for her wet woollen coat.

'Didn't you need to pee?' Ross asked as she moved back towards the passenger door.

She nodded, her bladder pushing uncomfortably against her waistband.

'Me too. You take the left side and I'll take the right.'

He went around the far side of the Freelander. She heard him unzip his flies and a steady stream of man-pee hit the grass, steam rising in a small flurry as his warm wee hit the cold air. Hearing him relieve himself increased the urgency of her bladder and she quickly dropped her pants and squatted over the ground. It was the longest pee she had ever done. Ross having finished waited patiently on the other side of the car until he heard her do up her zip.

Relieved, they both climbed into the Freelander. She felt marginally warmer and more comfortable now, but her jeans were still stuck to her skin, the shoulders of her t-shirt, cold and slightly damp against her body. Ross must have noticed her shivering because he turned the heat up full as the Freelander buffeted across the uneven field. The swaying did nothing for Chrissy's nausea and she was glad when they turned onto the flat, tarmacked road.

They drove in companionable silence, each lost in their own thoughts. The roads were dark, bereft of streetlights until the gates to McKinley House came into view. Here, lamps had been lit to illuminate the intercom, the button to gain entry shining red. Ross pressed it and waited until Ged Hughes's voice rang out asking for their identity.

'Mr Hughes, it's DCI Fraser. I need to speak to you.'

'About Aisha?' he asked, something between hope and mania emanating from the intercom.

'I think it's best we talk inside.'

They heard a click and the gates swung open. Ross drove the remaining distance, their way guided by the bright lights shining from almost every window of McKinley House. Ged was on the porch, still in grey trousers and braces, but tonight, thankfully, wearing a round-necked blue jumper tucked in way too tightly. He was fidgeting as they pulled up, his body language willing them to move faster.

Ross had only just planted his feet on the gravel when Ged rushed forward, words tumbling from his mouth.

'Did you find her? Is she all right? Where is she?'

Ross placed his hands on the top of Ged's arms, stopping him from peering into the back of the car looking for evidence of Aisha Flannigan.

'Mr Hughes, let's go inside and talk.'

Ged's cheek muscles lost their tension, his jowls dropping as he read between the lines. His steely grey eyes sparkled with tears gathering across their surface, ready for the words he knew would come out of Ross's mouth. He nodded tightly, lips pressed together, then led them into the house.

Ross and Chrissy followed him into a different room than before. This one was set out as a lounge with floral sofas and rattan furniture facing out to a large window that looked like a black hole now, but probably gave a good view of the hills in the daylight. The room was filled with amateur paintings, likely done by the residents of McKinley House, an abundance of plants and numerous vases of cut flowers. It was an oasis of summer in the dour October landscape. It was the most inappropriate environment to deliver news about the shattered body of Aisha Flannigan.

Ged motioned for them to sit, taking a position opposite, his body rigid. No pleasantries or coffee on offer today. Only his intense stare as he willed Ross to speak.

'Mr Hughes, I'm afraid I have some bad news. We have located the body of a woman that, based on the photograph and description you gave us, we believe to be Aisha Flannigan.'

Ross paused, giving Ged time to process. He didn't blink, eyes glazed, tears spilling over leaving small rivers down his lined cheeks that disappeared into the bristles of his beard.

'How did she die?'

His voice was stoic, flat as he asked the question Ross didn't want to answer.

'We don't have a formal cause of death yet, but it seems she was badly beaten.'

Ged bowed his head, the tears changing direction and dripping off the end of his misshapen nose.

'Are you all right Mr Hughes?' Chrissy asked, leaning forwards, lowering her head to try and gauge his expression.

Ged raised his head, tears still flowing, but his face impassive.

'Do you know who did this?'

'Not yet, but I'm going to do my best to find out,' Ross replied.

Another slow nod from Ged.

'Where did you find her?'

'She was buried on the south side of the loch, in a small patch of forest that was well off the beaten track.'

Ged snapped his head to look at Ross as he spoke, a twitch visible in his cheek.

'You know this place?' Chrissy asked seeing his reaction.

He turned to look at her.

'What? No, no. I just can't think what she'd be doing so far away from the house.'

'We don't know if she was killed there or taken there to be buried after she died,' Ross said. 'It was a very remote place. It's possible it was deliberately chosen by someone who knows the landscape.'

Ged's mouth tensed into a pencil-thin line. Ross shifted forwards so his buttocks were perched on the edge of the sofa, elbows resting on his knees, hands clasped together.

'Mr Hughes, there's something else. When we found Aisha, we also found evidence of another body buried beneath her. Do you have any idea who that might be?'

Ged got to his feet and began pacing around the room, his eyes darting from Ross to Chrissy and back again.

'Why would I? Why would I know anything about this?'

His movement became more frantic, his fingers running repeatedly through his wavy hair.

'I don't know anything about dead bodies buried on

the south side of the loch, or bodies dumped on my land. I don't know anything.'

He was rambling, his voice becoming louder, higher pitched.

'Calm down Mr Hughes. Come and sit down.'

Reluctantly, Ged returned to the sofa, his eyes still flitting between Chrissy and Ross like a prey animal waiting to see which predator would strike. It was Ross.

'Mr Hughes, can you think of anyone, other than her husband, who would want to hurt Aisha? Anyone she might have met outside of McKinley House?'

'I already told you, Aisha was a sweet woman. No one would want to hurt her. As for meeting someone outside of here, I doubt it. She never left the grounds.'

'But she did, didn't she?' Chrissy asked. 'She must have left unless she was killed here, by someone at McKinley House.'

'Impossible! No one here would hurt her. No one here would hurt anyone!'

Ross took up the thread.

'In that case, she must have ventured outside Mr Hughes. Is there anyone she would have gone outside to meet?'

'She wouldn't . . . she would never go outside. I'm sure of it.'

'That leaves us with a dilemma then. If you're certain she wasn't killed here, and she wouldn't go out of the grounds, where does that leave us?'

'I . . . I don't know. I just can't believe . . .'

Ged's words petered out, his whole body sagging. Ross sensed it wasn't worth pushing further now. Ged was closed for business.

'We'll need you to come down to the mortuary to make a formal identification. I can take you tomorrow if that suits you? And I'll need to ask you more questions down at the station.'

Ged sat motionless, the only sign he was still with them was the repeated blinking of his eyes.

'Mr Hughes? Did you hear me?'

Turning his head towards Ross, Ged nodded slowly.

'Where is she?' he asked tonelessly.

'She'll be taken to the police mortuary on Bell Street in Dundee.'

'I'll drive myself there. What time should I go?'

'If you're sure. I'll leave you the phone number of Diane Fraser who's the pathologist on the case. If you call her in the morning, she'll arrange a time with you.'

Ross slid Diane's card over the table towards Ged. He looked at it but didn't pick it up.

'We'll need to talk to you again Mr Hughes, once you've had time to process your loss. I'll also need to come back and speak to the women here who knew her.'

Ged sat up straighter, suddenly waking up and fidgeting in his seat.

'Is that really necessary? This is a safe place for

these women. They've all been through hell. Being grilled by a police officer is not in their best interests.'

'I appreciate it might be difficult for them, but a woman has been brutally murdered. I'm sure they'll understand the need to talk to me.'

'They won't know anything. Aisha kept to herself.'

'That might be how you see it Mr Hughes, but she may have confided in someone. It's obvious you didn't know everything about Aisha given she likely did leave the grounds with someone, or to meet someone. The women may have information that could help us iden-tify her killer.'

Ged flashed Ross a hostile glare, his words becoming clipped as he spoke.

'All right. But someone they know should be with them. And you should give me chance to explain before you turn up.'

'That seems reasonable Mr Hughes. We won't come back until tomorrow afternoon. You can arrange for someone to support them, but we won't allow them in the interviews. We need to speak to each of them alone. I'll bring Dr Ferguson with me. Hopefully, the presence of a woman will make them more at ease.'

With this, Ross stood up and headed towards the door. Ged did not get up, his fingers pressing into the sofa cushion as he gripped the edge, his hardened stare fixed on the place Ross had just vacated.

'We'll see ourselves out Mr Hughes,' Chrissy said, getting to her feet. 'I'm so sorry for your loss.'

. . .

Back in the car, Ross banged his hands on the steering wheel, exhaling deeply, pushing his head back against the headrest.

'What did you think of that?' Chrissy asked.

'He's hiding something.'

'I thought so too. The location of the body seemed to rattle him.'

'And the discovery of the other remains. Sorry I roped you in to coming to the women's interviews without asking first. I needed him to agree to it.'

'It's OK. I would have wanted to come along anyway.'

Ross started the car and pulled away from McKinley House.

I'm too tired to try and think it through tonight. Hopefully, it will seem clearer tomorrow. Diane might turn something up on the bodies. We could use a break.'

'Can I come with you to Dundee?'

'You can provided you stay off the booze tonight. I'm not nursing you through another hangover.'

It was the first time he had referred to her drinking too much. Chrissy's cheeks flushed as she swallowed hard. He made her feel like a child caught with her hand in the cookie jar. When she didn't answer, he took his eyes off the road for a moment, glancing in her direction, his eyebrows raised in a silent gesture of 'well?'

'OK,' she said sheepishly. 'No booze.'

He returned his eyes to the road.

'I'll pick you up in the morning at eight.'

22

Ross had been early, arriving on her doorstep looking collected and well-rested at 7.30 am. In contrast, Chrissy had still been in her cat pyjamas, eyes stuck together with sleep, black coffee barely touched. She suspected he had tried to catch her out, expecting to find empty whisky bottles and other evidence of a night on the booze. She smiled smugly to herself. Last night, she had done as she was told and had gone to bed after a long hot bath, sober as a judge.

The smugness faded rapidly, her pounding head and shaking hands making it difficult to be too pleased she had behaved herself. Even though she hadn't had a drink, she felt like shit. Trying to stop herself picking at her fingernails, Chrissy pushed her hands between her knees, then pulled them out again, raising her thumb to her mouth and chewing off more skin.

'Stop biting your nails.'

Ross didn't take his eyes off the road as he spoke. Chrissy gnawed off a strip of flesh, then folded her arms, shuffling in her seat.

'How much further is it?'

'About twenty minutes.'

It felt like they had been travelling for days, rather than an hour and a half. Chrissy stared out of the window, her eyes trying to focus on trees flashing past. Her stomach growled, protesting at the lack of breakfast. She'd been banking on Ross's muffins, but he hadn't brought any today.

'At least the weather's better,' she muttered, looking up at the blue patches peeking out between rolling, grey clouds.

'How are things going between you and Martin Doyle?'

Chrissy spun her head to stare incredulously at Ross.

'What? What did you say?'

'I was just wondering how things were going with Martin?'

Ross's elbows were locked as he pushed against the steering wheel.

'What do you mean, 'going'? Going where?'

'I thought there was a budding romance there.'

'Why the hell would you think that?'

'Mirren mentioned it. She said you two had always been fond of each other and that now you were back, sparks were flying.'

Chrissy choked on her own laughter, collapsing into a coughing fit as she looked at Ross. His eyes stayed fixed on the road, his face showing no signs of teasing.

'You're serious?' she asked.

He glanced quickly in her direction, then back at the road.

'It's none of my business. Sorry I asked.'

Once her cough subsided, Chrissy cleared her throat.

'There's nothing between me and Martin Doyle! Never has been and never will be. I've seen him in the hotel bar a couple of times, but never by arrangement. If Mirren thinks there's something more to it, that's all in her head.'

Ross smiled but said nothing.

Traffic was picking up as they came into Dundee, the built-up cityscape looking dour and uninviting after the rolling hills and glens of rural Perthshire. They turned into the police station on Bell Street and parked in one of the reserved spots. Chrissy climbed out of the car, pulling her coat tighter, the air cold despite the sun peeking through the clouds. She followed Ross in through the rear door, smiling nervously at everyone who acknowledged them as they passed.

'Diane's probably downstairs. Just wait here while I call down.'

Chrissy pressed her back against the wall in the

corridor while Ross entered an office on the left to use the phone. He was back in seconds and they loitered around the glass door leading to the bowels of the building that was opened moments later by Diane Fraser appeared wearing blue scrubs and a plastic apron. Today was all business. No polite chat. No riling her ex-husband.

'Come on down. I've finished the preliminary autopsy. Ged Hughes is coming by in about an hour to make the formal identification so we need to be quick so I can get her ready.'

They followed Diane down a flight of stairs into a brightly lit room dominated by two silver mortuary tables. Aisha Flannigan lay prone on the one nearest to them. Her feeble body was covered up to the chin by a thin white sheet, the muscles of her battered face sagging, making the skin drag across her broken bones.

Chrissy didn't want to look at the misshapen body but couldn't seem to tear her eyes away. The sound of Diane snapping on a pair of latex gloves finally drew her attention from Aisha's corpse.

'Female, forty-two years of age, killed around thirty-six hours ago.'

'So that puts time of death around 10 pm on Tuesday?' Ross confirmed.

Diane nodded, then pulled back the sheet. Chrissy gasped, the brutality of what Aisha had suffered laid bare.

'Cause of death was this blow to the side of the head.'

Diane pulled back a few strands of thin, blood-stained hair to reveal a tennis ball-sized depression in the skull.

'Looks like it was probably done with a rock.'

'Could she have fallen?' Ross asked.

'No. The force of the blow came from behind. Someone hit her as she was turned away from them.'

'What about all these other injuries.'

'Some were done before the fatal blow. She was still alive when she got these on the torso and face.'

Diane was pointing to boot-shaped bruises down Aisha's sides, purple rings around her eyes, two gashes across her cheek, and the unnatural angle of her broken nose.

'You can clearly see the ones on the body are boot marks. She was given a series of kicks to the ribs, most likely when she was lying on the ground. The facial injuries are from someone's fists. The tears in her cheek were done by something sharp, possibly a ring.'

Chrissy could feel bile rising in her throat as empathy for what Aisha had endured played with the smell of thirty-six hours of decay.

'These other injuries, the broken leg bones, broken arms and fingers, they were done post-mortem. Whoever did this stomped on her limbs for the hell of it.'

Ross didn't speak. He stood looking at the broken

body of Aisha Flannigan. No one felt like rushing the moment. They let the silence hang, shocked at the atrocity before them.

Diane covered the body, tucking the sheet down Aisha's sides like a mother tucking in their child.

'There is some good news - well, potentially good news,' she said, picking up a sealed bag containing swabs sealed in plastic tubes.

'We found traces of semen in her vagina.'

Ross was staring at the plastic bags.

'Was there any sign of sexual assault?' Ross asked, traces of hope flickering in his hazel eyes.

'Nothing definitive. There was some bruising on her buttocks and legs as well as nail marks, but she's so skinny, it wouldn't take much to damage her. There's nothing else to suggest the sex was forced. It could have been from a consensual sexual encounter.'

'Maybe she was in a sexual relationship with someone who turned on her?' Chrissy said.

'It's possible. If I was testifying in court, I couldn't swear whether she was a willing participant in the sex, or not.'

'When will you get DNA results?' Ross asked.

'I'll send it up to the lab as soon as we're done here and try and get a rush on it. Twenty-four hours, forty-eight at most.'

Ross sighed heavily. Patience was in short supply.

'What about the other body?' he asked, pointing to the second mortuary slab.

Diane walked over to where various bones were laid out in an approximation of a human skeleton. Chrissy and Ross followed her, standing on the opposite side of the table. The bones were clean, flesh long since devoured by decomposers in the earth.

'Can't tell you much yet. We recovered all the remains we could as well as some fragments of fabric that are with forensics. He was buried about a foot below Aisha's body. The victim is male, approximately six feet tall and around fifty years of age at the time of death.'

'Cause?'

'Unknown. Nothing on the bones to give us a clue.'

'Any estimate on when he died?'

'Best I can do for now is to say he's been in the ground at least ten years, but it could be a lot longer. Forensics should have a better estimate for you in a few days.'

Ross rubbed his brow, his jawline tense, eyes fixed on the man's remains.

'We've no idea who he is then?'

'Not yet, but I did manage to extract some DNA. Might get something from that.'

'Is there anything else you can tell us?' Ross asked, desperation in his tone.

'Sorry, nothing else I can be sure of.'

Diane looked at her watch.

'I need to get going. Ged Hughes will be here any minute and I need to move Aisha's body upstairs.'

'Let me know when we have the formal identification.'

'Will do.'

Ross turned towards the door, Chrissy following, her legs almost running to escape the stale air.

'Ross?'

'Yes?' he said, turning back to face his ex-wife.

'How did you know where to look for Aisha? That place was so remote, no one without insider knowledge would have come across the burial site.'

Ross shot Chrissy a conspiratorial glance.

'We got a tip-off.'

'That was lucky,' Diane replied raising her eyebrow. 'Who from?'

'Anonymous. Ring me as soon as you get the DNA results.'

Chrissy met Diane's unconvinced gaze, smiled guiltily and then followed Ross out the door.

23

THE WOMAN FACING them folded her arms tightly across her chest, communicating her obstinance non-verbally.

'Donna isn't it?' Ross asked, the open smile he had given the last nineteen women starting to set around the edges.

She nodded grudgingly, chin pulled back, lips set in a thin, taut line.

'You know why we're here Donna. We want to ask you some questions about Aisha Flannigan.'

The woman's stoic expression didn't change, her hard blue eyes narrowing, the lines on her face set like a formidable maiden aunt. Chrissy felt Ross sink a little in the chair next to her. He already knew they would get nowhere.

'How well did you know Aisha?'

His standard opener got the standard response

they had heard from the lips of every woman interviewed that day.

'I didn't. She kept to herself for the most part,' Donna said, crossing her legs so her body was folded away like a closed concertina.

Ross nodded, waiting for Chrissy to follow up as she had in every meeting so far.

'Donna, it's important you tell us anything you can, no matter how small. Aisha is dead. The victim of a brutal assault. We need to find out who did this to her.'

Blinks told Chrissy the woman had heard although no response was forthcoming. Ross leaned forward, his elbows resting on the rickety table Ged Hughes had set up in the reception area of McKinley House, positioned as close as possible to the front door. He didn't want to allow them to contaminate the inner sanctum of the refuge with their questions about murder.

The women had been parading through the 'interview room' for the last four hours. Donna Taylor was the last one and wasn't going to be any more use than any of the others.

'Donna, I'll ask you again. How well did you know Aisha Flannigan?'

'I already told you, I didn't.'

The woman's arms curled more tightly around her broad torso, her foot clad in a sensible shoe on the end of American tan tights, jiggling as she waited for Ross's next move.

'When did you last see Aisha?'

Donna raised her eyes to the ceiling, chewing on the inside of her lip.

'It would have been Sunday morning, at breakfast.'

Exactly what everyone else had told him.

'I understand there is a tradition here that you all take meals together. A way for you to check in on each other?'

Donna nodded, still chewing her lip.

'Wasn't anyone concerned when Aisha missed dinner on Sunday night?'

'If it had been anyone else, we would have been. But it was normal for Aisha to miss at least one dinner every week.'

'Why was that?' Ross asked. 'Why did she regularly miss dinner?'

'Don't know. Anxiety got the better of her on some days I suppose.'

'Aisha was anxious?'

Donna unfolded her arms, letting her clasped hands fall into the well her flowered skirt made over her crossed knees.

'Yes, I would describe her as anxious. Jumped at everything. But that's not surprising, is it?'

'What do you mean Donna?' Chrissy asked as she leaned in.

'Well, you'd be jumpy too if you'd been through what she had.'

Donna's gaze shifted between Chrissy and Ross.

'And what was that?' he probed.

'Well, I don't know exactly. It's not the kind of thing you ask, is it? But it couldn't have been pleasant for her to end up here. And judging by her behaviour, she was pretty messed up about it.'

'What behaviour?' Ross followed.

A flush radiated across Donna's sagging cheeks as she began to fidget on the uncomfortable wooden dining chair.

'Aisha was a bit odd. Strange like.'

'What made her strange?'

Donna's voice ratcheted up a notch.

'I don't know, do I? She just was.'

Chrissy gave her a moment to calm down, then spoke gently to her.

'Donna, I know this is difficult, and that you don't want to speak ill of someone who is gone. But can you give us an example of something Aisha did that was strange?'

Donna relaxed back in the chair, folding her limbs again, hoping the tightness of her body would offer protection from their questions and from her own words.

'It's difficult to say just one thing.'

Chrissy and Ross waited, their gaze fixed on her, the silence becoming uncomfortable for Donna.

'She would just laugh sometimes. Be sitting on her own, then laugh, as if someone told her something funny. She had a weird look about her, big eyes sticking

out and her lips curled in when she smiled. I don't
know. She was just weird.'

'You didn't like Aisha?' Ross asked, not wanting to
lose the momentum Donna's outburst had created.

'It's not that I didn't like her. I just didn't
encourage a friendship with her. No one did. She
didn't seem to care. She never sought any of us out
either.'

Donna seemed to deflate, her arms dropping back
into her lap again, her shoulders drooping as she gazed
at the floor. Ross let her words hang in the air for a
while before changing direction.

'Do you think Aisha may have made friends with
someone outside of McKinlay House? A lover maybe?'

Donna's eyes snapped back to Ross, a humph
escaping her thin lips.

'A lover? Never. She was terrified of any man who
came here. If a delivery man came, she'd hightail it
back to her room and lock the door. Only Ged could
get near her.'

'Why do you think she wasn't afraid of Ged?'

Donna looked affronted.

'I hope you're not insinuating there was anything
improper going on between Ged and Aisha? Ged's a
good man. One of the best. He would never do
anything like that.'

They'd heard this a million times today. *'Ged is a
good man, salt of the earth, blah blah.'*

'Is there anything else you can tell us Donna?' Ross

asked, his body language collapsing under the weight of the nothing they had learned today.

Donna shook her head.

'Can I go now?'

'Yes. Thank you for your time. And if you do think of anything else, Ged knows how to contact me.'

Donna was on her feet like a gazelle given a reprieve from the hunt. No sooner had she disappeared into the day room that had served as today's police waiting room, when Agatha, the beaky receptionist appeared and began to drag the recently vacated chair across the reception back into the dining room.

'I assume you don't need to speak to anyone else?' she asked, making sure they felt as unwelcome as snow in summer.

Ross stood up, shuffling his notes that had become progressively briefer as they listened to the same responses over and over again.

'I don't think there's any point talking to anyone else given that I'm just going to hear the same story.'

Ross challenged Beaky's hostile stare with the militancy of his own.

'You'll be going then?' she spat, no sign of cowing.

'Yes, we'll be going.'

'You can let yourselves out.'

With that, she turned and continued to drag the chair out of reception.

Ross didn't speak until they got to the car. He opened the back and threw the notes inside. They scattered across the seat, some wafting to the floor as he slammed the door. Chrissy climbed in the passenger seat, letting him work off some steam as he paced around the Freelander for a few minutes.

'Sorry,' he said, getting into the driver's seat, closing his eyes and deliberately controlling his breathing as he forced himself to calm down.

'That was a complete waste of time,' Ross said, turning to look at Chrissy. 'The whole thing was so bloody contrived. I'm sure they'd been coached in what to say. Every interview – Aisha was weird, she'd never take a lover, and Ged is wonderful. That's too much of a coincidence. He told them what to say.'

'Ged?'

'Who bloody else!'

Ross's shoulders sagged.

'Chrissy, this whole thing is a mess. We've got three murders now, not to mention two unsolved cold cases, at least three different MOs suggesting at least three different killers – maybe four if you're right Bonnie Harrison, and no leads.'

Chrissy let him rant. He needed it. And she didn't have anything useful to contribute. They were at another dead end. Ross's anger seemed to have burnt itself out as he sat slumped in the driver's seat, his hand reaching for the start button. The car sprang into life at the same time his phone started to vibrate in his pocket. He fished it out, turning the screen towards Chrissy to show her Diane's name under a thumbnail picture of his stunning ex-wife. He pressed the answer button.

'Just a minute while I put you on speaker. I'm in the car with Chrissy.'

He fumbled with Bluetooth until the car audio crackled announcing the connection had been made.

'Please tell me you've got some good news for me.'

Diane's voice came loud and clear across the Freelander's speakers.

'Hello to you too husband! Hi Chrissy.'

'Hi Dianne.'

'He's in a grump.'

Chrissy could hear the cock of her head towards Ross in her tone.

'What have you done to him?'

Chrissy laughed.

'Not me I'm afraid. Bad day on the case.'

'What's happened Ross?'

'I've been interviewing the women at Ged Hughes' refuge. Got nothing.'

'Well, that's probably not surprising. I would imagine those women have lived some pretty harsh realities that the police weren't able to save them from. Talking to you would have dug up painful memories.'

'You've got a lot to say on the subject,' Ross chided.

'You know me lover. I've got a lot to say about everything.'

Chrissy was relieved to see a smile creep across Ross's lips.

'What have you got for me Diane?'

'I'm not sure it's going to make things any clearer for you. Remember the blood we pulled from Sonja McBride's crime scene?'

'Pig's blood?'

'We also found a small amount of human blood, remember?'

'Go on.'

'I had forensics run it against the DNA profile I got from the male remains at Aisha's burial site on a hunch. We found similarities.'

'What does that mean?' Chrissy asked.

'It's not a hundred per cent conclusive because we only got a partial profile from the blood sample, but it looks like our mystery bones could belong to whoever bled in that pig shed.'

'Any idea who he is?'

'Still waiting on the results. The samples are being run as we speak. But I wouldn't get your hopes up. Our latest estimate suggests he was killed over twenty years ago.'

'Great. Just another layer of crap to add on top of what I'm already ploughing through.'

'You are crabby today Ross. I'll leave Chrissy to handle your sulk. I'll be in touch as soon as I have more.'

The receiver went down, and Ross drew in a long, deep breath.

· · ·

The journey back to Chrissy's cottage had been silent, Ross wading through a pile of thoughts and a sour mood. She invited him in, but he offered some excuse that really meant he wanted to be on his own. She understood. Sometimes people were draining.

Chrissy watched him drive off, pulling her coat in against the bitter wind whistling across the loch, hurrying inside once his taillights disappeared. She hadn't left any lights on inside, her hip banging into the table as she lurched around in the dark. She swore loudly, hopping a few steps until the pain subsided.

The lamp flooded the kitchen with a warm glow, giving a false impression of cosy. It was freezing inside, the stone walls keeping out the wind chill, but also the weak autumn sun that had warmed up the day. In the living room, she threw some kindling and logs on top of last night's ash, lighting firelighters and watching the flames dance into life.

Back in the kitchen, she pulled whisky and a glass from the cupboard, downing her first pour in one, then topping it up. The warmth trickled down her throat, leaving her brave enough to take off her coat. Ross had asked her not to drink last night and she had been good. But one night without the comfort of the bottle was enough. Besides, he hadn't told her to lay off the booze tonight.

The crackle of the fire was building, an orange glimmer filtering through the living room door. Chrissy opened the freezer and took out a chicken pasta bake.

She tossed it into the microwave, watching it revolve around inside for a few moments.

The ding of readiness came as she downed the last of her second whisky. The tray burned her hands as she tried to get it onto a plate without using the oven mitts. Refilling her glass, she picked up her mediocre dinner and headed towards the promising warmth of the living room.

A knock on the door halted her. Swearing under her breath, she put down the pasta and whisky. Whoever was knocking was impatient, giving her no time to answer before rapping again.

'I'm coming! I'm coming!'

Chrissy pulled open the door and came face to face with Mirren Doyle, Ness on a lead straining to get inside.

'Mirren, what can I do for you? Come in. It's bloody freezing out here.'

Mirren did not move. She looked strange to Chrissy, in her 'mum' jeans and pink cashmere twinset rather than her hotel tartan. Her face was red from the buffeting wind, her expression making Chrissy's stomach twist.

'Mirren? What is it?'

The words came tumbling out of Mirren's mouth like only the act of keeping her lips closed had contained them.

'Chrissy you must try and understand, give us chance to explain. Hear us out before you fly off the handle, which you have got every right to do of course. But please, listen to us, try and put yourself in our shoes.'

'Mirren, what the hell are you talking about? Listen to you about what?'

Mirren's face contorted with worry lines, her lips pressed together in an apologetic smile.

'What's going on?' Chrissy asked, her brows furrowed, the knot in her stomach tightening by the second.

Mirren turned her body sideways, leaving the doorway vacant. Someone stepped forward, their face obscured by dark shadows and a voluminous hood. Chrissy squinted, trying to focus her eyes in the limited light.

'Hello Chrissy.'

The hood lowered, but she knew who it was even before their features came into view. The world stopped and all Chrissy could hear was the rush of blood over her eardrums, her heart racing, the last four years dissolving in seconds.

'Mum?'

24

Ross TRUNDLED across the uneven ground, grateful for the added traction the Freelander offered. A lesser vehicle would have stranded him in the muddy field with an unpleasant hike in the bitter wind. He could see activity up ahead, silhouettes moving around in torchlight brightening the near darkness.

He parked by the side of the Scenes of Crime van, mud slopping over his pointed shoes as he stepped out of the car.

'Bastard! Shit!'

Ross heard someone laughing as they emerged from the darkness ahead of him.

'I always told you those shoes were ridiculous.'

DI Hugh McCann came into view wearing sensible wellies with his grey suit trousers tucked in snuggly up to the knees.

'Why can't I ever get a case where the victim is killed in a five-star hotel?' Ross grumbled.

'Don't suppose you've got any cake in that silver truck of yours?' Hugh asked, straining his head to peer into the front seat of Ross's car. 'I'm bloody starving.'

'Sorry, no. I came straight from the McKinley House interviews.'

'Did you shake anything lose?'

'Not a bloody thing. All the women told me the same tale. Completely contrived. I think Hughes coached them before we got there.'

'We?'

'Chrissy was with me. I thought it might help, having a woman there.'

Hugh smiled in an infuriatingly knowing way.

'We do have women on the force you know.'

Ross didn't acknowledge the sarcasm.

'I know. I just thought someone who wasn't in the police might put them at ease.'

'Why can't you just admit it? You like our weird Dr Ferguson.'

'What? Yes. Of course I like her. What's not to like?'

Hugh shook his head.

'You're bloody hopeless Ross. And a bloody useless liar.'

Ross fidgeted, attempting to scrape mud off his shoes but making the whole thing worse.

'Did you invite me to this mud pit just to grill me

about Chrissy or is there a reason I'm stood ankle-deep in sludge?'

Hugh knew when to leave it.

'Come on, it's just up here.'

Ross followed the circle of light coming from Hugh's torch, the sodden ground threatening to steal his shoes with every step. He wasn't dressed for a trek through rural Perthshire on a raw October night. Every gust of wind penetrated the weave of his well-cut suit, nipples so prominent they were chaffing on his poly-cotton shirt. This had better be worth it. He was tired, hungry and now, freezing.

Hugh stopped a little way ahead, pointing his torchlight off into the distance. Ross caught him up, his gaze following the beam of illumination towards the ruins of what used to be an old barn.

'Why am I looking at a derelict heap of stone?' Ross asked, temper fraying as another gust of wind reached his bones.

'Not the barn. Look on the floor.'

Ross narrowed his eyes, taking a few steps forwards.

'Is that a cellar?'

'It certainly is.'

'Is it *the* cellar?'

'It could well be. I told uniform to focus the cellar search on land owned by Ged Hughes. I can't help thinking whoever is doing this is making a point, planting all the victims around McKinley House.

Anyway, I got a call about an hour ago saying I needed to get over here.'

'Is it the kill site?'

'I don't know. You'd better come and look.'

Ross was grateful to pull on the paper suit. It gave the wind an extra layer to penetrate. He followed Hugh through the storm cellar doors, padding down the slatted stairs in his blue shoe covers.

The whiteness of the room scarred his retinas after the darkness outside temporarily blurred his vision. When his focus returned, the cellar Chrissy had described spread out before him. All the walls were tiled in white, every inch shining like a brand-new bathroom. The floor was the same, white tiles gleaming in the brightness coming from eight strip lights secured to the white-painted ceiling.

'What the hell...' Ross muttered.

'I know. It's just like Chrissy described, isn't it?'

'How could she know? How could she know the specifics?'

'I hope you're not even contemplating the idea that she's somehow involved?' Hugh said incredulously.

'I . . . I don't know. No, of course not. Well, I don't think so. But maybe she's been here before? Otherwise, how could she know?'

'Look Ross. I've no idea what's going on with Chrissy. But I do know that these dreams of hers helped us find that poor beaten woman . . . '

'Aisha.'

'. . . helped us find Aisha, and she knew Sonja McBride was dead before we did.'

'Both of which could be considered suspicious.'

'Come on Ross. You can't seriously believe she's hiding some deep dark secret?'

Ross didn't answer. He stared around the room, taking in the iron chains strung up across the ceiling, the ominous shackles hanging down.

'Have forensics found anything?' Ross asked, ignoring Hugh's questioning stare.

'Nothing. This place is cleaner than an operating room. It looks like everything's been disinfected with bleach.'

Hugh pointed over to the right-hand wall where shelves of bleach stood above a shining sink.

'Have they checked the drains?'

'Yep. Nothing. If this is where Sonja McBride was killed, whoever cleaned up did a thorough job of it. Heather and her team are outside now. Maybe something will turn up that can point to who's been coming here.'

Ross didn't relish the idea of going back outside, his feet now turning to blocks of ice as the mud congealed in his socks.

'We'd better go and talk to her,' Ross said, his trudge up the stairs as leaden as his mood.

Heather Stone saw them emerge from the cellar. She came over, looking more rotund than usual. As she approached, Ross noticed her paper suit was stretched over an Aran jumper and a zip-up bomber jacket. The fact she was probably warm irritated him more.

'DCI Fraser,' she said, her face wearing the usual sour expression.

Ross had been working with Heather Stone for ten years, but she still refused to call him Ross.

'Any good news for me Heather?'

'There's what look like footprints around the building, but no one's been here since the rains, so they're too degraded to be of use. We have found something around the back. There's a large incinerator bin that's been very well used. Most of what's been burned in there is just ash, but we've found small pieces of what looks like rubber that escaped the flames. Could be from trainers or boots.'

'Sonja McBride's shoes?'

'Maybe. There's not enough for us to give you anything accurate. We should be able to confirm the rubber's consistent with the sole of a shoe, but that's about it.'

Ross sighed heavily. Another titbit of evidence that wouldn't give them anything concrete.

'Anything else?' he asked, his own face as sour as Heather's.

'Tyre tracks coming up from the road on the opposite side. It's easier going cutting through the wood than the way we came,' Heather said, pointing to where the van and Ross's Freelander stood. 'There's an old logging trail that goes down to a dirt track, well hidden from the main road. If you didn't know it was there, you'd never stumble across it. Looks like whoever's been coming here came up that way because the tyre tracks come right up to the back of the cellar.'

'I suppose that would be helpful if you wanted to move a body. I wouldn't have fancied carrying Sonja McBride down to the field where we're parked.'

'Probably means whoever this belongs to is local,' Hugh said. 'Someone who knew about the old logging road.'

Ross nodded, rubbing the tiredness from his eyes.

'Thanks Heather. You'd better get back to it.'

Heather left abruptly, her usual lack of social protocol upheld.

'Are you going to head back to the hotel?' Hugh asked. 'You look dead on your feet.'

'No, I'll hang around. See if they turn up anything else. Think I might try and get my head down in the car. You can go if you like, but leave me those boots,' Ross said pointing to Hugh's feet.

'I'll nip off for an hour, get something to eat. Then I'll be back. Do you want me to bring you a sandwich?'

'Yes, that'd be great.'

'Shall I bring you Chrissy?'

No answer.

August 1994

The bus dropped him at the main road, the brightness of the day incongruent with his mood. It felt disrespectful for the sun to shine on the day his mother died. Slowly, he trudged up the dirt track, the farmhouse basking in the morning sun. Numbness pervaded every inch of his body, breathing in and out and forcing his legs to take ungainly steps forward as much as he could manage.

The walk from the road took longer than usual, the weight of his grief pressing down hard. The door to the house stood ajar, but no one was home. He didn't want to go inside. Didn't want to see his mother's blood smeared all over the living room.

He scanned the yard, not expecting to see anyone. He was alone. More alone than ever before. The feeling of loss surprised him. Not the loss of his mother. The loss of everything that had tethered his life here. He was free.

The urge to look around the place where he had

grown overwhelmed him. It would be the last summer day he ever spent here. It was like he was seeing it for the first time, with new eyes. Eyes not perpetually scanning for signs of impending pain and violence.

He was shocked by the shoddiness of the house, the dark green paintwork peeling away, tiles missing from the roof and weeds overrunning the neglected gardens. The barn had so many loose panels a determined pig could have pushed their way out. The killing shed roof was beginning to sag, the bolted door barely hanging on its hinges. Until today, this had just been 'home', somewhere he lived but never noticed.

He walked over to the killing shed, the place that had witnessed his greatest humiliations. Sliding open the locking bar, he went inside, his eyes taking a moment to become accustomed to the gloom. Missing panels on the roof let in a stream of sunlight, illuminating the dead body of Father swinging from the roof like a morbid, inverted holy idol.

The buzz of flies filled the silence as they flitted between the decaying flesh and drying blood pool beneath the body. Maggots squirmed in the gaping neck wound, the occasional one falling to the ground as gravity worked against them.

Slowly, he walked towards the carcass that had been Father. The sweet, sickly stench of death washed over him but did not turn his hardened stomach. He had spent too many years in this place of slaughter to be phased by rotting meat.

Father's eye sockets were a mass of writhing larvae, his skin putrefying, body bloating as bacteria decimated his dead tissues. As he stared at the decaying flesh, the numbness subsided, leaving in its wake an intense fury so great he couldn't control it. His lungs filled with air, exhaling in a battle cry as he launched a fist at Father's body.

The corpse swung around, a flesh and bone punchbag that he pummelled with every ounce of strength he possessed, the force of his blows fuelled by the rage searing through him. He didn't stop until his muscles could take no more. Sinking to the floor, his knuckles bruised, inhuman cries wracked his young body.

He didn't know how long he sat there, spent, emotions gone, the corpse of Father swinging back and forth above his head. Clambering to his feet, pain seared through his hands as they began to swell. The cerebral paralysis had returned, his next move, opaque. For so long he had dreamed of escape. Planned it. Now, he could just go. Walk out the door. Yet something held him in this stinking shed, listening to the rafter's creak as they bore the weight of the Father's corpse.

It was him. Father. Dead as a doornail but still threatening to ruin everything. If anyone found him, there was only one person who would be under suspicion. He needed to bury him somewhere no one would find him.

The chains clunked as he released the brake, bracing

Father's descent with his own body weight. His muscles trembled as he steadily lowered the corpse to the floor, his hands slipping, the body crashing the last few feet. With nervous fingers, he undid the shackles, desperately trying not to touch the putrefying skin.

There were plastic sheets in the cold room that Father used to cover the bottom of the van when he transported the butchered meat. He took two, laying them out, edges overlapping on the floor. On his knees, he rolled Father's dead body onto the sheets, careful not to touch the disintegrating flesh.

Tucking one end over the body, he continued to push until the corpse was rolled in numerous layers of white plastic. With the features of Father concealed, his mind came back to life. He knew a place. A place where he would never be found.

25

HER FACE WAS MARKED with more lines of life. Her hair, once an unruly frizz streaked with grey but now entirely silver, was cut into a sleek, shoulder-length bob. Other than that, the woman on Chrissy's doorstep was unmistakably her mother, Neve Ferguson. Dead for four years.

'Are you going to let me in?'

Her mother's voice was softer than she remembered. More like the distant memories of her childhood, before their life had fallen apart. Chrissy couldn't speak. Could hardly move. She shuffled her feet backwards, opening the door fully, allowing her mother and Mirren Doyle in.

Chrissy closed the back door, her mind vacant, incapable of processing what was happening. Panic started to grip her. This was her brain playing tricks again. When she turned around, she would be alone in the dimly lit kitchen, her ready meal going cold on the end of the table.

Deep down, she knew this wasn't how it would be. She could sense people behind her. Ness was whimpering, straining to get to Chrissy to say hello. Slowly she turned around to see her mother unbuttoning her coat as if she had just returned from shopping in the village.

'How are you here?' Chrissy asked, finding a thready voice.

Her mother stopped fiddling with the buttons and stared at her daughter.

'I'll explain everything, I promise. Shall we go and sit down? Maybe have some tea?'

Anger flared in Chrissy. Her mother, bold as brass, talking like she was going to explain the facts of life rather than where the hell she'd been for the last four years.

'Tea! You want tea like you just popped in for a gossip and a slice of cake?'

Neve prickled glaring at Chrissy, the glare of a parent about to chastise their child for rudeness.

Mirren had been standing quietly by the door, Ness still tethered and very unhappy about it. She took a tentative step towards them, positioning herself in the middle of their standoff.

'Chrissy, this is bound to be difficult for you. Your mother understands that,' Mirren said, casting a look in Neve's direction. 'But getting angry at each other won't help. Why don't you and your mother go into the living room to talk? I'll make some tea.'

Neither mother nor daughter moved, each continuing to glower at the other.

'Please Neve? Chrissy?' Mirren begged. 'Go and talk to each other!'

It was Neve who gave way, breaking focus by dropping her gaze, her face softer as she looked back at her daughter.

'Please Chrissy, let's go and sit down where it's warm. I've got a lot to tell you.'

'You don't say?'

Mirren sighed in relief as Chrissy stomped past her mother, grabbing the whisky bottle and glass as she went into the living room, leaving the pasta to congeal in its tray. Neve took off her coat, hanging it over the back of a kitchen chair, then followed her daughter.

Chrissy threw herself down onto the sofa, arms tightly hugged around her body, legs crossed. She looked up at her mother from under hooded eyelids, her jaw set. Neve went over to the fire, throwing two more logs onto the dying flames, nudging them with the poker until they began to char.

Chrissy never took her eyes from her mother, holding her silence until Neve perched on the edge of the armchair.

'So, explain,' Chrissy spat, her arms tightening further around her body.

Mirren came in carrying a tray with three mugs of

tea, Ness trotting behind her. She handed one to
Chrissy who ignored it, snatching up her whisky glass,
topping it up to almost overflowing before resuming
her barrier position sat back against the sofa. Mirren
put the mug back on the tray, placed it on the table,
and sat in the last remaining chair, dragging Ness by
the collar to stop her launching at Chrissy for some
attention.

'This is a difficult story to tell,' Neve began.

Chrissy smirked, a disbelieving humph escaping
her tight lips.

'More difficult than grieving for a mother?
Grieving for the loss of the only family member I had
left? Being left totally alone?'

A tear ran down Chrissy's cheek. She brushed
it away irritably taking a large swallow of whisky,
determined not to break down. Neve looked down,
closing her eyes in an extended blink, her shoulders rising as she took a deep breath to compose
herself.

'I know how difficult it must have been for you
Chrissy . . .'

Chrissy slammed her glass on the table leaning
towards her mother, fists clenched, every muscle and
sinew tensed.

'How can you know? You left me. Left me to deal
with all this. Let me think you were dead! Swanned off
to God knows where, never thinking about what losing
you would put me through!'

Chrissy's voice broke up, tears free-flowing despite her best efforts.

'That's not true Chrissy! I thought about you every day. Worried about you constantly!'

Chrissy felt the tension wilt, leaving only a small girl devastated by her mother's death all over again.

'Then why? Why did you do it? Why did you leave me?'

Neve was on her feet coming to sit beside Chrissy, taking her daughter's cold hand in her warm ones.

'I had no choice, Chrissy. Or at least, it felt like I didn't. I thought I was doing the best thing for you. I know now it was wrong. I was stupid, not thinking clearly. But I'm here to put things right.'

Weeping uncontrollably, Chrissy collapsed into her mother's arms, tears and snot mingling as she clutched onto Neve. She felt the gentle caress of her mother's hand on the back of her head, feeling safe in the gentle rocking of her embrace. She cried inconsolably. Cried four years' worth of grief held in the arms of the woman she was grieving for.

As the tears subsided, Chrissy pulled away from her mother, accepting the box of tissues Mirren held out, feeling the weight of Ness's head on her lap. The dog seemed to judge the situation well, her natural exuberance replaced by supportive calm.

Chrissy blew her nose loudly, taking a second tissue to dry her eyes. She began to stroke Ness's furry face, the repetitive action calming her. More in control, she shuffled down the sofa, the closeness of Neve now stifling.

Sensing the shift in Chrissy's need, her mother returned to the armchair, her position immediately taken by Ness who curled up against Chrissy's thigh. She could feel the anger stirring again, her emotions flip-flopping, making her head spin.

'You'd better get on with it,' Chrissy said, her voice spiky, her eyes stinging and raw. 'Then I want you to go.'

She reached for the glass and took two healthy swigs while she watched Neve cross her legs, clasping both hands over her kneecap.

'Do you remember how things were after your father and sister died? Do you remember how I was?'

'Some of it. I was only six years old.'

Neve nodded.

'It was very difficult for me. I couldn't come to terms with their loss. My grief was overwhelming. I turned to my faith, hoping God would explain why he had taken them away. Of course, he didn't. I started to drink too much - way too much and I wasn't looking after myself, or you.'

'That I do remember,' Chrissy chipped in testily.

Neve continued, ignoring Chrissy's hostility.

'For a year, I more or less held things together. But then, my health began to suffer. I was spiralling out of control, losing my grip on reality. That's when I met him.'

Chrissy's brow furrowed.

'Met who?'

'You've got to understand, I was alone, mentally ill, becoming increasingly paranoid about the possibility of losing you.'

She paused, gazing at her clasped hands, her cheeks colouring.

'I met a man who offered me a way out. A way I could protect you. Make sure you were always safe.'

'That's impossible. No one can make that kind of promise.'

'I know that now Chrissy. But at the time, I believed him. He was kind to me, made me feel like I wasn't crazy. That my irrational paranoia was justified. He was tender, kind, very patient with me.'

'You were in love with him?' Chrissy asked, eyebrows raised.

'I thought so, at the time. But you must understand, I wasn't in my right mind. I was ill. Very ill. I just didn't realise it.'

Her mother was watching her, looking for some indication of what was going on behind Chrissy's eyes. But she gave nothing away. Neve sighed and began picking at her fingers. Chrissy registered it must be a hereditary habit.

'He convinced me God spoke to him. That God told him how I could protect you.'

'And you believed this nutter?'

Chrissy was on her feet, pacing around the coffee table, Ness indignant at being left.

'I know it seems crazy to you now. It does to me! But back then, it didn't. He was telling me exactly what my ill mind wanted to hear. I was an easy target.'

Chrissy stopped hands on hips, staring down at her mother. How could she be so stupid?

'Please Chrissy. Sit down. Let me tell you the rest.'

Reluctantly, Chrissy flopped back onto the sofa, snatching up the whisky glass and draining it.

'Go on then,' she said, sitting back, wrapping herself up in her limbs again.

'He was an expert manipulator. He knew exactly how to handle me, how to make me do what he wanted.'

'And what was that?' Chrissy snipped.

'He convinced me God wanted me to help him. He wanted me to help him rid the world of bad girls, promiscuous or criminal young women who would contaminate the purity of humanity. He told me that if I . . . if I killed a bad girl, bathed you in their blood, God would keep you safe forever.'

Chrissy leapt up again.

'And you believed that shit? Please tell me you didn't believe that!'

Neve stared up at her daughter, waiting for the realisation to seep in. Chrissy's face dropped, the bottom falling out of her stomach as she caught up. Her lips began to tremble, her legs in severe danger of giving way.

'You did it . . . you really did it. My dream . . . my dream, it was all true. You killed Bonnie Harrison!'

'Please, try and understand. I was convinced Bonnie was evil, that God wanted me to rid the world of a bad person.'

'How could you believe that? How could you be so stupid!'

Chrissy was shouting now, her pacing frantic.

'I was stupid. Very stupid. There's no excuse, I know that. But I was ill, so very ill.'

Neve's tears spilled over, but Chrissy could feel no empathy. Her mother had killed someone. Killed an innocent girl on the word of a psychopath. And then left her daughter to question her own sanity for the next twenty years!

'I was there, wasn't I? I was there, in that cellar when you drove a knife through Bonnie Harrison's neck?'

Her mother flinched but knew there was no going back now. She had to tell it all.

'Yes, you were there. It was all part of the ritual. I was to kill the girl . . .'

'Bonnie!' Chrissy interrupted.

'Yes, I was to kill Bonnie and then bathe you in her blood. That would keep you safe, protected forever.'

Chrissy shook her head in disbelief, biting her

bottom lip as she stared at the family portrait on the mantelpiece.

'I can't believe it. I can't understand . . .'

Neve got to her feet and reached out towards Chrissy who shied away.

'Don't touch me! I don't know who you are!'

'I'm your mother Chrissy. Your mother who made a mistake . . .'

'A mistake! A mistake is when you buy the wrong kind of tea or get the train times wrong. Killing someone is a lot more than a mistake!'

'You're right. Of course you are. But I didn't understand what I was doing! I truly believed it was the right thing. The right thing to keep you safe!'

Mirren came towards Chrissy, placing a hand on her shoulder.

'Chrissy, I know this must be a shock . . .'

'A shock? Are you kidding me?'

'Sorry, inappropriate words. I know this must be devastating for you. But there's more if you'll hear it?'

Chrissy stared at her, then at Neve. She wanted to flee, to get far away from here. She needed time to think. Yet at the same time, she wanted to listen, to understand. She let Mirren steer her back towards the sofa, lowering herself onto the seat, every muscle tense. Ness's tail gave a few dull thuds as Chrissy sat beside her again. Neve followed her lead, returning to her position in the armchair.

'After I killed Bonnie, I seemed to come around. I'd been totally absorbed by what I was being told, lost in the world he was constructing for me. When I saw you covered in the blood of a girl I had killed, that world dissolved instantly, and I was left facing what I'd done. My mind couldn't cope. I broke down, sealing myself in a private space in my head where I wouldn't have to deal with any of it. He took us to an abandoned building outside Kinloch Rannoch where he dumped Bonnie's body. She was wrapped in plastic, discarded like rubbish. Then he brought us here, back to the cottage. I never saw him again.'

'So, you just thought, '*OK, I killed someone, now let's make dinner*'?'

Tears were streaming down Neve's cheeks.

'Of course not. I didn't know what to do. That night, I went back to where Bonnie had been left. I couldn't stand to see her like that. I took the plastic off her body and covered her over with a blanket.'

'Nice. That made up for the killing thing,' Chrissy said sarcastically.

Neve ignored her jibe.

'I came home and woke you up, told you we were going for a walk. I intended to kill both of us that night. To walk out into the loch, to end it all.'

'Well, that's great. Why stop at one murder? Finish off your daughter too!'

'I couldn't do it Chrissy. I didn't care about me, but I couldn't end your life. I lay down on the shores of the loch, thinking I would never get up again. Then Mirren found us.'

Neve looked towards Mirren who was leaning against the wall by the mantelpiece, trying to dissolve into the background. She came forwards, perching on the coffee table in front of Chrissy, placing her perfectly manicured hands on her knees. Ness stirred, shuffling around so her front paws were hanging over the edge of the seat, seeming poised to listen to what Mirren was about to say.

'Chrissy, your mother was in a bad way when I found her. She was rambling words that I thought were nonsense at the time. I got you both back to the cottage, warmed you up and got you back to bed. Your mother was broken, incapable of anything. I stayed until she calmed down. Then she told me what happened.'

'You knew? You knew she'd killed someone and didn't do anything about it?' Chrissy spat.

'I didn't believe her then. She was out of her mind. I thought she was having a psychotic break, that it was all in her head. It wasn't until they found Bonnie's body a week later that I realised she was telling the truth.'

'And you didn't think that was a good time to tell the police?'

'I had my reasons for not wanting the police snooping around here. But I did tell your mother she needed to get help. She wasn't coping well, drinking too much, slipping in and out of reality.'

'Well, that makes the whole murder thing all right then, doesn't it?'

'Chrissy, don't blame Mirren. She did everything she could to help me. It was her who convinced me to go to the hospital.'

Mirren moved away, allowing Chrissy to glare directly at her mother.

'You mean you got yourself committed to keep her silent!' she yelled, cocking her head towards Mirren who had retreated to the fireside.

'I suppose it could seem like that. But that's not why I went. I knew I needed to get well. For you.'

'For me? For me! Don't try and say any of this was for me! You kept quiet so you wouldn't have to pay for what you did! You spent four years in and out of a secure hospital rather than go to prison! And because you were a coward and didn't own up to what you did, two other girls have died!'

Chrissy couldn't stay sat down. She was pacing the room again. Silence weighted the air, her accusations hanging like dark clouds filled with lead rain.

'You're right. I am responsible. I know and I will pay for that. But I wasn't well . . .'

Her mother's voice wavered, tears dripping from her nose as she fixed her eyes on her hands.

'Stop blaming all this on being ill! You knew what you'd done!'

'Chrissy, stop!' Mirren said. 'Your mother knows

what she did was wrong, and she is going to go to the police. Screaming at her isn't helping!'

Chrissy flashed rage-filled eyes in Mirren's direction.

'Stay out of this Mirren! This is nothing to do with you!'

'But it has Chrissy! I'm involved in this as well. Do you think the police will just let my part in this go?'

Chrissy held her tongue. Mirren was right. She wasn't helping.

'Were you involved in Ciara Campbell's death?' Chrissy asked, staring at her mother, her voice more even.

'Of course not. After I was discharged from the hospital, I tried to put it behind me. Then Ciara Campbell's body was found. The similarities with what I'd done to Bonnie were too much of a coincidence. I thought he must have done it again, got some other vulnerable person to commit murder for him. I panicked, sure they would link Ciara's death to Bonnie's, and then to me.'

Neve collapsed, unable to speak through the sobs wracking her body.

'We made a plan,' Mirren continued, 'for your mother to disappear. You were set up in Edinburgh. You hadn't been back home in years and Neve didn't think you wanted to know her anymore.'

'How could you think that?' Chrissy asked, staring

at her mother's bent head. Neve looked up, her red-rimmed eyes still overflowing with tears.

'I thought you hated me.'

'You're my mother! Of course I didn't hate you!'

'I'm so sorry Chrissy, so sorry.'

The sobs renewed. Mirren moved over to place a hand on Neve's back.

'We thought it better for everyone if your mother disappeared. She was too afraid to own up to what she'd done, for herself and for what it would do to you. You were just getting your life together. So, we decided to make it look like she had drowned in the loch,' Mirren said quietly. 'I told the police I saw her out in the water, that I'd tried to swim out to her, but it was so cold. I couldn't save her and she was lost below the surface. Given your mother's history, it was easy to convince the authorities she'd killed herself. They were convinced enough to release the death certificate soon after so we could hold the funeral even without recovering a body.'

'You faked your own death so I wouldn't have the inconvenience of dealing with a mother who is a murderer? Chrissy snarked. 'Well, it didn't work because I did have to deal with it! All of it! Practically every night since I was nine years old! You know that! Every time I came into your room mum, crying that I'd seen a girl killed. You always said it was just a dream.'

She stared at her mother, her eyes wide.

'I'm sorry Chrissy. I didn't think you'd remember. I

thought the dreams would stop.'

'They never stopped. I just stopped telling *you* about them.'

Chrissy sat back down, resting her elbows on her knees, running her hands through her hair. She was lost, flailing about in the sess pool of her mother's lies. Ness slid off the sofa, annoyed at all the getting up and down, throwing herself down on the floor in the kitchen.

'What am I supposed to do with all this?' Chrissy asked, her eyes stinging, no tears left to shed.

'You don't have to do anything Chrissy. I'm going to the police station. I'll tell them everything.'

'You'll go to jail.'

'I know. It's what I deserve. I'm ready to pay my dues.'

'And what about this man? The one who managed to brainwash you into becoming an idiot? A killer?'

Neve winced at the venom in Chrissy's last word.

'I'll tell them everything I know. I can't be sure he was involved in the deaths of these other girls, but maybe something I know will help them find out who was responsible.'

'Who was it Mother?'

Neve fidgeted, the pressure to say the words she had buried so deep for over twenty years becoming uncomfortable. The words that would now seem so stupid.

'I never knew his name.'

26

'WHAT THE HELL IS THIS PLACE?'

Ross turned away from Hugh to see Diane Fraser striding across the field towards the cellar.

'Could be the kill site for Sonja McBride.'

'Really? Have you found trace?'

'Not yet. But Scenes of Crime hasn't quite finished. We didn't find anything inside. The whole place has been bleached. But they're still looking around out here.'

Diane pulled her black trench coat tightly around her body, tucking her hands into the folds.

'Bloody freezing!'

'Yep. Joys of a murder case in the Scottish glens.'

'What the hell happened to your feet?' she asked, looking down at Ross's pointed shoes, once black, now mud-brown along with his socks and the bottom of his black suit pants.

'In case you haven't noticed, we're standing in the middle of a bloody field that's been pelted with rain for the last forty-eight hours.'

She looked down at her own feet, cosily ensconced in black Hunter wellies, then glanced across to where Hugh was talking to Heather Stone, both also wearing rubber boots.

'It didn't occur to you to put your boots on before you came then?'

'Of course it bloody occurred to me! I came straight here from the interviews at Ged Hughes's place. I didn't have time to pick them up.'

'Tetchy! Who's rattled your cage?'

'Sorry. It's this case. Every time we find a new piece of evidence, it just seems to muddy the water even more.'

'Nothing came of any information from the women at McKinley House?'

Ross shook his head.

'What are you doing here anyway?' he asked. 'Not like you to venture out into the sticks after dark.'

'Too right. I came to give you a bit more confusing evidence. Can we go and sit in your car though? I can't feel my hands.'

Ross was happy to oblige, needing to get reacquainted with his toes that had been wet for almost an hour now. They headed down the hill, Ross slipping on the uneven mud, Diane walking like it was a summer's day on the Royal Mile. He suddenly decided he hated these shoes.

Once in the Freelander, Ross started the engine, whacking the heaters to full as they both rubbed their reddened hands in front of the vents. Neither spoke until faint traces of warmth filled the car.

'So, what's this evidence that dragged you out here?'

Diane relaxed back in the passenger seat, still rubbing her hands together.

'You know we found similarities between the DNA profile of the recovered bones and the blood where we found Sonja's body?'

'Yes.'

'Well, we've also found shared markers between the bones and the semen we recovered from Aisha Flannigan.'

'What? What the hell does that mean?'

'The profile we got from the semen was more conclusive than from the blood at the shed. We can be pretty sure that whoever had sex with Aisha was related to our dead man's bones from beside the loch.'

'But we still don't know who either he or the mystery sperm donor is?'

'Not yet. I'm waiting for forensics to call. They might come back with a hit.'

'Let's bloody hope so.'

Ross was staring out of the window, watching the distant figures milling around the cellar.

'I had Heather get a DNA sample from Ged Hughes,' Ross said, turning his attention back to his ex-wife.

'You think he might be the one sleeping with Aisha?'

'I don't know. But there was something strange going on when we told him Aisha was dead. And the bodies have all turned up on, or very near his land. That can't all be a coincidence. Make sure you run the DNA samples from Aisha and the bones against him.'

Diane nodded.

'I need to get Chrissy here to take a look at the cellar,' Ross said absently.

'Chrissy? Why on earth would you want to drag the poor girl out here in the dark and cold?'

'I doubt you'd believe me if I told you.'

'Try me.'

He sighed, his shoulders sinking with fatigue.

'Chrissy sees things.'

'Don't we all?'

'I mean things we don't see.'

'What do you mean? Like ghosts?' Diane asked, smirking.

'No, not ghosts. At least I don't think so.'

'God, you're serious. I was taking the piss. I thought you meant she was ultra-observant.'

'She is pretty observant. But that's not what I meant. She has these dreams. Dreams about murders. I don't understand it. But she knew Sonja McBride was dead before we did and described this bloody cellar to me in perfect detail. And she knew exactly where to find Aisha Flannigan's body. And from what I can gather, she's been dreaming about Bonnie Harrison's murder since she was a kid!'

'Bonnie Harrison?'

'One of the cold cases.'

Ross grabbed hold of the steering wheel, resting his forehead on his hands. Diane let him have his moment, then placed a hand on his arm.

'Ross, what's going on? Something more than just a lack of evidence or Chrissy having weird dreams is bothering you.'

'Diane, what if Chrissy's involved? What if she's the killer?'

'Are you serious?'

'I don't know. I don't know what I am. My head's up my arse. I want to believe her. But having dreams about real murders is less plausible than her knowing these details because she was there.'

'Ross, Chrissy isn't a killer.'

'How do you know? How can you be sure?'

'Didn't you check out her alibi for the first murder? She was in Edinburgh when Sonja McBride was killed wasn't she?'

Ross paused.

'Yes, she was. But she could have come here to Kinloch Rannoch without anyone knowing. It's not that far. There and back could be done in one night.'

'Ross, you're being insane. You're suggesting Chrissy Ferguson taught a day's classes at the University, drove to Kinloch Rannoch, abducted Sonja McBride on her own, drugged her, took her to this cellar, somehow managed to hoist a none-too-slim dead weight to the ceiling and drove a knife through her neck? Then after all that, took her down, wrapped her body in plastic, carried her to the car, drove to the middle of nowhere to deposit her in a shed, then calmly drove back to Edinburgh to teach the next morning?'

'Well . . . when you put it like that. But it's not impossible. She could have had help.'

'Ross be serious. What about the other killings? Where was Chrissy when Aisha was killed? Or Calvin Parks? She was only nine years old when Bonnie Harrison was killed.'

A smile spread across Ross's face.

'Chrissy was with me. She was with me when Aisha died!'

Diane laughed, her logic banishing his fears about Chrissy.

'I knew you liked her.'

'I do. But she can't be entirely sane. Dreaming about death and murder.'

'Probably not. But who is? I don't know how Chrissy sees these things in her sleep, but I do know that we're only scratching the surface of what we know about the human brain. Maybe she really is tapping into . . . something. Something we can't understand.'

'Hugh said the same thing.'

'So, Hugh doesn't think Chrissy is your prime suspect?'

'No.'

'Well, you've always trusted Hugh.'

Ross nodded, pulling his phone out of his pocket and waiting while it connected to the Bluetooth.

'I'm not tromping back up that hill. Let me call Hugh. Tell him we're going to pick up Chrissy.'

'We?'

'Yes, you're coming with me. I need a chaperone.'

Diane laughed, settling back into the passenger seat.

'OK. I always knew Chrissy was going to be interesting.'

27

CHRISSY FLED FROM THE COTTAGE, running down the pot-holed lane away from the ruins of her life. She needed to get to him. Ross would know what to do. The night was tar black, not even the moon to light her way. She yelled as her ankle twisted on the uneven surface, her hands and knees crashing into the gravel, the skin scraping off as she tried to stop her face planting into the floor.

Winded, she rolled over, laying on her back, staring up at the starless sky. Water seeped through to her skin, the day's rain still collected in puddles where small craters dented the road. She had to get up, had to keep going.

Painfully, Chrissy got to her feet, her ankle protesting as she tried to bear weight. The wind gusted around her body, bringing up goosebumps as the chill penetrated her denim shirt. In her haste to be away, she

hadn't picked up her coat, running out into the cold
night completely ill-prepared.

She felt stupid now, standing in the pitch dark.
Her car keys were still in the glass bowl by the
kitchen door. She had considered driving as she fled
the house but then remembered how much whisky
she'd drunk and so left on foot. As if that mattered
now! She should have gotten in the car. Her mother's
revelations had driven away any trace of alcohol
anyway.

Going back was the sensible thing to do. Go back,
get your keys and your coat, then drive like a sensible
person to the station to see Ross. But her mother was
there. At the cottage. Going back meant seeing her
again and she couldn't take that. Not yet.

Limping on her sore ankle, Chrissy continued in
the direction of the main road, her arms wrapped
tightly around her body to try and ward off the cold.
The headlights coming towards her were dazzling. Her
heart soared. It must be Ross.

Waving as the car slowed down, red and white
spots danced before her eyes. She heard the car door
open and then close as someone got out.

'Ross? Ross, is that you?'

No answer. Chrissy's heart began to pound. Something was wrong. The gravel crunched under booted
feet coming towards her.

'Who is it? Who's there?'

Chrissy raised her open hand trying to shield her

eyes from the light. A silhouette moved through the headlight beam, closer and closer.

'Hi.'

'Oh my God! It's you! You scared me half to death!'

'Sorry. What the hell are you doing out here with no coat on a night like this?'

'It's a long story. Can you give me a lift? I need to get to the station, but I've hurt my ankle.'

'Sure. Take my arm.'

Chrissy hooked her arm through his, using his strength as a crutch, hopping towards the car. He opened the back door.

'I can manage the front seat,' she said, placing her hand on the handle.

'I'm sure you can. But that's not what I'm offering.'

His hand closed over hers, pulling it away from the handle. Quickly, he twisted around, wrenching her arm behind her back. She felt the needle puncture the side of her neck, the world blurring in seconds. Her head lolled forward, the muscles useless, like warm putty.

'Come now. There's a good girl.'

His hand bent her head forward as he bundled her onto the back seat. She heard him go around to the other side, the door opening, two hands sliding under her shoulders to pull her further across the seat. Chrissy tried to push herself up, thinking she could escape through the open door. It was futile. There was no strength in her limbs. Her arms flopped like bone-less chicken wings.

The door behind her head slammed shut, then she felt her legs being pushed so her knees bent upwards. Her shoe caught on the leather trim of the seat coming off at the heel. The rear door closed and she sensed him get into the driver's seat. The engine was still running. Through the haze in her head, she felt the car turn around, bouncing over the potholes, heading back towards the main road.

The motion of the car began to smooth. They were almost at the end of the lane. She watched the shadows lengthen on the roof as he turned left. Streetlamps filled the car with transient yellow light, each one they passed dimmer than the last as her mind struggled to stay conscious.

In minutes, they were travelling through blackness, the light pollution of the village left behind. With nothing to keep her focus, Chrissy succumbed to the darkness.

When Chrissy came to, he had turned off the main road again, the car struggling over uneven ground, branches bashing against the windows and doors. She had no idea how long they had been travelling. The car stopped, plunging everything into complete darkness as the headlights flicked off.

She tried to sit up again, this time managing to get

her feeble arms to raise her enough to see out of the window. Squinting, she could make out lights in the distance, artificial lights illuminating the remains of an old barn, people in white suits moving around.

'Ross,' she croaked weakly, her arms giving way, leaving her prostrate across the back seat.

Her kidnapper banged his hands on the steering wheel, swearing under his breath. Chrissy squirmed in the back seat, trying to make her body move.

'Be a good girl Chrissy and keep still. I need to think. It seems we need a change of plan.'

Silence now except for the drumming of his thumbs on the steering wheel as his mind whirred. She wanted to scream, make the white suits hear her. Make Ross hear her. But she could make no sound.

He was fumbling in the pocket of his jeans. Chrissy heard key tones as he dialled a number on his mobile phone. The rings were audible in the quiet – four rings before someone answered. A male voice.

'Hello?'

Her kidnapper only spoke seven words in answer to the greeting.

'Meet me at home and bring cash.'

28

Ross PULLED up at the white cottage overlooking the loch.

'She's got visitors,' he nodded to Diane, noting the grey jeep parked beside Chrissy's blue Ford. 'I think Mirren's here.'

'Mirren from the pub?'

'Yeah.'

They climbed out of the car, a gust of wind billowing Diane's coat.

'Christ, it's even colder here than it was in that bloody field!' she said, pulling her clothes tightly around her.

Ross knocked on the back door of the cottage, waiting as a light flicked on in the kitchen, keys turning in the lock. A woman answered, grey-haired, tall like Chrissy, eyes red from crying.

'Oh, hello. I'm DCI Ross Fraser and this is Dr

Diane Fraser,' Ross said, instinctively flashing his badge. 'I need to talk to Chrissy.'

'Ross, is that you?'

Mirren appeared behind the mystery woman, Ness flying out of the door, jumping ecstatically at her master. Ross bent down, letting her plant wet, slobbery kisses all over his face until she calmed down.

'Hi Mirren. I need to speak with Chrissy.'

'She's not here Ross. She left about thirty minutes ago. She went looking for you.'

The woman in the doorway stood aside.

'You'd better come in DCI Fraser.'

Ross, closely followed by Ness and Diane, followed them into the kitchen, closing the door on the blustery night. The unknown woman was eyeing them with something between wariness and interest.

'You both look freezing. Come through to the living room. The fires on in there,' she said, extending an arm to indicate the way.

Diane didn't need asking twice, heading straight for the fire, showing the palms of her hands to the heat. Ross followed on, standing by Diane's side but facing into the room, the heat warming his back. Ness jumped up on the sofa returning to a dent in the cushions indicating that was the spot she had vacated when he knocked on the door.

'I'm sorry to intrude on your evening,' Ross said, his bones starting to thaw in the warmth of the room.

'That's quite all right DCI Fraser. I needed to talk to you anyway.'

'Neve, you're going to do this now?' Mirren said, coming to the woman's side.

'No time like the present,' she replied. 'Won't you please sit down?'

Lines furrowed Ross's forehead as he and Diane took a seat on the sofa, Diane leaving the fire somewhat reluctantly. The woman remained standing, Mirren dropping into one of the armchairs.

'My name is Neve Ferguson. I'm Chrissy's mother.'

'What?' Ross said, turning his head towards her as if he hadn't quite heard her correctly.

'I'm Chrissy's mother,' she repeated.

'Forgive me Mrs Ferguson. But aren't you supposed to be dead?'

'I am. But as you can see, I'm very much alive. And please call me Neve.'

'I don't understand. Does Chrissy know?'

'Given that we are standing in her house, I think she knows,' Neve replied, a wry smile so like Chrissy's, curling her lip.

'Yes, obviously. I mean, did she always know?'

'Chrissy had no idea until tonight. She held a funeral for me DCI Fraser. As you can imagine, it came as quite a shock.'

Ross knew he should have been asking more questions about why Neve Ferguson was standing here in the cottage, very much alive. But right now, all he could think of was Chrissy and what she must be going through.

'Where is she now? Is she OK?'

'I told you, she ran out of here looking for you,' Mirren said.

'I'm going to call her. Get her back here.'

Pulling his phone out of his pocket, he dialled Chrissy's number. A phone began to ring in the kitchen. He followed the sound, returning to the living room holding Chrissy's mobile.

'She didn't take her phone.'

'Nor her coat or her keys,' Neve said. 'I'm starting to get worried.'

Ross noticed the half-empty whisky bottle on the table. Only one glass so Chrissy was drinking alone.

'I'll call the station. If she was looking for me, that's where she'll have gone.'

Hugh McCann answered the station phone.

'Hugh, it's Ross. Is Chrissy at the station?'

He paused while Hugh spoke. Everyone in the room listened to the one-sided conversation.

'OK. If she turns up, make sure she stays put and ring me straight away . . . I don't know. She left the cottage about half an hour ago but she wasn't wearing a coat and didn't take her phone. She was coming to find me . . . On foot, I think. Her car's still here . . . Thanks Hugh.'

'She's not there?' Diane asked, getting to her feet.

'No. No one's seen her.'

'Is there anywhere else she might go?' Diane asked, looking at everyone in the room.

'I'll ring the pub,' Mirren said, already scrolling down her mobile phone.

She wandered into the kitchen while she made the call, coming back a minute later shaking her head.

'She's not there either.'

Neve sank slowly into the armchair vacated by Mirren.

'Oh God. What have I done?' she murmured.

'What do you mean Mrs Ferguson . . . Neve?' Ross asked, sitting on the coffee table in front of her. 'What do you know about Chrissy's disappearance?'

She looked at him with furrowed brows, tears beginning to gather in the corners of her hazel eyes, lighter than Chrissy's but with the same doleful look. Her mouth opened to speak just as a mobile phone began to ring. Everyone looked around, questioning the source of the ringtone.

'Sorry,' said Diane, fishing the ringing phone from deep inside her trench coat.

She was already placing the phone to her ear as she went into the kitchen, speaking quietly to whoever was at the other end. Ross turned back to Neve.

'Neve, tell me if you know something?'

Diane came hurriedly back into the living room.

'Ross, I need to speak to you now.'

The assertiveness in Diane's command made him turn around.

'What is it?'

Diane looked pale, her face stony.

'Diane?'

Ross left Neve and came towards his ex-wife.

'We got a hit on the DNA from the semen.'

'Who? Diane, who is it?'

Diane turned her mobile phone towards him, the forensic report squashed into the tiny screen. Ross squinted to make it out. His face fell, all words abandoning him.

Snatching the phone, he scrolled down the pages.

'Shit! What if he's got Chrissy? I need to go.'

He turned agitatedly towards Neve, pushing the phone back towards Diane.

'I'm sorry, I've got to go. If there's anything you know that can help us find Chrissy, tell Diane and she'll contact me. I'll be back soon.'

Ross's heart was beating frantically as he turned back to Diane.

'Are you OK staying here? I can get someone to come and collect you.'

'It's fine. You go. I'll stay here with Mrs Ferguson and Mirren.'

'Thank you.'

He squeezed Diane's hand briefly before racing back out into the cold night.

29

'Is he there?' Ross snarled down the phone without preamble.

'No. The delightful lady who opened the door, Agatha I think she said her name was, told me after some persuasion that he left about half an hour ago,' Hugh McCann replied down the phone.

'Did he take a car?'

'Yes, a green pick-up with McKinley House on the side. I've spoken to a few of the women. No-one knows where he was going or which way he went.'

'What a surprise!' Ross said sarcastically. 'Stay there in case he comes back. I'm going to have a drive round, see if I can spot him.'

'Fine but be careful Ross. Call for backup if you need it. A couple of uniforms are heading over from Pitlochry. They should be in Kinloch Rannoch in about twenty minutes.'

'Hugh, if he hurts her . . .'

'Don't think like that. You don't even know for sure that he's got her. Now go and find Ged. Get some answers.'

The receiver went dead leaving Ross alone with his thoughts. How did he not see it? He must be losing his touch. Or maybe Chrissy with her weird dreams and drinking problem had messed with his head. And now her mother?

Ross put his foot down, speeding along the dark country road, eyes scanning the few cars he passed. He drove through the village, turning down every side road, carrying on east for about five miles before turning round and re-tracing his route back towards Kinloch Rannoch.

The pick-up truck came into view as he passed the Rannoch Arms hotel, heading west. He dropped back wanting to see where Ged Hughes was going. He didn't seem to be in a rush, driving twenty miles an hour below the speed limit.

Ross followed him out towards the west end of the loch, staying on the main road when Ged turned off so as not to alert him to being followed. He pulled up just past the turning, waiting for the pickup to disappear up the single-track lane. There was no hurry to follow. Ross knew where the road led.

He dialled Hugh McCann again.

'I've found him. I followed him to the killing shed

where we found Sonja McBride. Meet me here with backup as soon as you can. And call Diane.'

Ross reversed the Freelander, turning up the track to follow Ged Hughes. He stopped before the car cleared the trees, getting out to make the rest of the journey on foot. He didn't notice the cold now, his way guided by shafts of moonlight that had appeared through the broken clouds.

Ged was out of the pickup using a torch to light his way to the killing shed door. Once he was inside, Ross crept around the walls, peering through a crack in the wooden panels. He couldn't see anything other than the pool of light moving as Ged crossed the shed, before disappearing on the far side. Ross remembered there was another room out back, some kind of old storage barn.

He inched around the shed, keeping his back pressed against the wood, checking inside whenever the dilapidated walls gapped enough for him to see. At the back of the building, light filtered through the panels, a small bulb dangling from the ceiling draped in cobwebs but still working. Ged was sitting in the centre of the room on an upturned crate, like an actor under the spotlight about to deliver the scene of his life.

Ross strained to look around the room. Ged seemed to be alone. Edging closer, he moved towards a door hanging from its hinges. From here he had a better view, sure now there was no one else inside. The floor creaked as he entered. Ged didn't acknowledge him but remained seated, head buried in his hands.

'Mr Hughes? Ged?'

Ged looked up, eyes brimming with tears. He looked completely forlorn, his knees bent at right angles, his cream chinos and half-laced boots caked in mud.

'What are you doing here Ged?' Ross asked, approaching closer.

He didn't answer, tears escaping as he blinked. Ross noticed he looked drawn, black rings accentuating the hollows around his steely grey eyes. The wavy hair was parting all over his head, unwashed and unkempt. Grime marred his beige shirt, smears where he had wiped his hands repeatedly down the front. This was not the same man that had challenged him at McKinley House.

Ross tried again.

'Ged, what are you doing here? Where is he?'

'I don't know,' Ged replied, his voice barely audible. 'He rang me. Told me to meet him at home and to bring money. This is the only part of the old farm still standing so I assumed he meant here.'

'How long ago?'

'About half an hour. I wasn't going to come. I didn't want to get involved, but . . .'

'Ged, he's taken Chrissy – Dr Ferguson. Do you have any idea where they would go?'

Ged's face went even paler.

'Oh God, Oh God, Oh God! This is all my fault! I should have said something. But I didn't want to believe it. I just thought he would never go that far. When that first girl died, I had my suspicions, but convinced myself it couldn't be him. Then nothing happened. No one was caught and no one else died. I thought I was right. He couldn't have done it. Then there was another, then another . . .'

Ged's spine seemed to crumble as he leaned forward to curl up in a foetal position, his body shaking as he cried into his knees. Ross needed him to focus. Now wasn't the time for his guilt to overwhelm him.

'Ged! Ged! I need you to think. I need you to help me!'

Ged continued to sob, gently rocking back and forth. Ross lurched forward, dragging him to his feet.

'Ged, listen to me! Where would they have gone?'

August 1994

*They had been digging for three hours, rain impeding
their task as a summer storm thundered overhead. Wet
clothes stuck to their thin bodies, hair flecked with dirt
plastered to their heads.*

'That's deep enough. Come on, let's get him.'

*Together, they went over to the pickup truck, sliding
on the mud where temporary rivers of rainwater flowed
between the trees. He had driven here even though he
had no licence, hoping the late hour and cover of darkness would prevent them from being seen. So far, it had
gone to plan. They had met no one as they drove away
from the village.*

*He flipped open the tailgate, heaving Father's body
towards him.*

'Help me will you!'

*With both pulling, they managed to slide the rotting
corpse off the truck bed. It crashed to the floor, a putre-*

fying grey foot protruding from the plastic sheet. He had removed Father's boots, afraid the thick rubber soles would take too long to decay beneath the ground.

'You get his feet.'

'I'm not touching that!' he said, pointing at the exposed flesh.

'Fine. I'll go at that end.'

He came around and hoisted Father's feet from the ground, waiting for his brother to lift the head. Slowly, they edged closer to the grave, both bent over with the weight of their burden.

'Lay him down here,' he instructed, placing the feet on the edge of the hole.

His back ached as he straightened up. His brother felt the same pain as he let their Father's shoulders go and rubbed his sore back. The brothers stared at each other then down at the corpse of the man who raised them.

'Should we unwrap him? Won't he, you know, rot faster?'

'Probably. Come on then.'

They pulled the sheet away, the stench making them both shy away covering their noses.

'He stinks!'

'That's what happens when you die, imbecile!'

'Is that it then? Can we put him in now?' his brother asked.

He looked around, checking for he knew not what.

'I guess so. On the count of three. One . . . two . . . three!'

Together, they pushed the body of Father into the grave. It made a dull thud as it hit the bottom. They peered over, no signs of sadness on either face. He thrust a shovel at his brother.

'Let's get this done quickly. It'll start getting light soon.'

They worked in silence, earth building up quickly, the desire to be done fuelling their tired muscles. With the ground level again, they tromped it down, kicking leaves and detritus over the edges to disguise the obvious shape of the disturbed earth.

'That's it then?' his brother asked.

'I suppose so.'

He stared at the grave for a few moments longer, making sure there were no obvious signs that Father lay beneath. He knew it was unlikely anyone would come out here, and no one would ever come looking for Jock McKinley.

30

GED HUGHES WAS LOST in his own world of memories. He looked around the shed, taking in the cobwebs strewn across every corner, the sagging roof and the failing walls.

'I grew up here,' he said, his eyes rolling towards the ceiling of the shed. 'This was where we slaughtered the pigs.'

Ross fidgeted from foot to foot, running one hand through his hair, the other pressed into his waist.

'Ged, do you know where they might have gone?'

'Who?'

Ross sighed heavily, his eyes rolling in frustration.

'Do you know where your brother might have gone with Chrissy?'

Ged looked at him, hearing the words but not the question.

'My brother? My brother used to love coming here.

To this shed. He would hide outside, peering through the cracks. Watching me and my father killing the pigs. I hated it. But he . . . he seemed to have a fascination with it.'

It was obvious Ged was going down memory lane with or without Ross.

'I never understood why my father didn't make him come in here with us. He dragged me in when I was ten years old. Put me to work as soon as I was strong enough to hold the knife. Yet he never made my brother do it. I resented him for that. But I think Father knew. Knew he wasn't . . .'

'Wasn't what?'

Ross was in the story now. Maybe it would take him somewhere he would find Chrissy. Ged's eyes glazed over, staring out at nothing, replaying images and memories in his mind.

'My father found him one day – he was about nine years old – laying in here. He'd stripped naked and covered himself in the entrails. He was laughing as he rolled about in the blood. My father leathered him for that. And me for not keeping a better eye on him. After that, he never let him near the killing shed. My father was a bastard, but I think he knew there was something wrong with my brother.'

Ged focused on Ross, his hands folded in his lap, spine lamppost straight.

'You know it was my father you found with Aisha don't you?'

'I assumed so. We knew the remains were a relative after you came in and gave a DNA sample. The approximate age and time suggested someone at around fifty years old. That fits with him being your father or brother. Father seemed more likely.'

Ged nodded.

'Jock McKinley. He died a week after his fiftieth birthday.'

'Did you kill him?'

'No. I wanted to. Probably would have. But I didn't do it.'

Ged fixed his gaze on Ross.

'DCI Fraser, do you know anything about my father?'

'Not much. We only got the DNA results an hour ago.'

'Let me save you some time. Jock McKinley was a drunk and a bully who solved everything with his fists. I hated him. Not only because he beat me, but because he beat my mother.'

Venom burned behind Ged's steely eyes as he spoke, his jaw set in a hard line. Ross felt his own anger stir at the thought of Jock McKinley hitting his wife and son.

'My brother was the only one who escaped his temper, mainly because my mother protected him, stepping in between them, taking the beatings instead of him.'

'She didn't do that for you?'

Ged averted his eyes, picking at the nail on his thumb.

'No. Things were different for me. I went to school, came home, worked in the killing shed and dealt with my father's temper. When my brother came along, my mother clung to him, much more than she ever did with me. She couldn't bear to let him out of her sight. He was home-schooled, never left the farm. I don't even think anyone on the outside knew he existed.'

'That must have been hard for you.'

'Not really. I had my own problems. My brother and I were never close. He only wanted to be with our mother and that suited me. I was making plans to get away. But all that changed . . .'

Ged floated off again, his moment of lucidity gone. Ross let him wander down the alleys of his mind for a moment, then hauled him back.

'Ged, why did it change?

Blinking, Ged turned his attention back to Ross.

'It changed when Father beat my mother to death.'

It was such a matter-of-fact statement, Ross raised his brows, pulling his chin back to look at Ged from below hooded eyelids.

'I don't know what sparked it. I wasn't here. But something set my father off. He beat my mother so severely she ended up on life support. I sat holding her hand for two days in the hospital before they turned off the machines.'

A lone tear streaked its way down Ged's lined face,

catching at the top of his beard, hovering there like a sparkling diamond. He let it sit for a moment, then wiped it away.

'When I came home from the hospital, I found my father hanging in here, like a slaughtered pig.'

'Ged, do you know who killed him?'

Ross needed him to say the words.

'Yes. Don't you?'

31

CHRISSY MANAGED to roll onto her side in the back seat of the car, some strength slowly seeping back into her leaden limbs. They were moving again. She fought to raise her head and peer out of the window, trying to recognise where they were going but seeing only blackness and trees fleeting in and out of the headlights' beam.

The small show of strength was exhausting, her arms crumpling to leave her neck wedged uncomfortably against the door. Her lids drooped, threatening to send her back to unconsciousness. With an almighty effort, she opened them again, focusing on the back of his dark head.

'Why are you doing this? What do you want with me?' she croaked, only the silence of the night making her audible.

'Ah Chrissy! You're back in the land of the living. Good. I was getting bored here with no one to talk to.'

He flicked his head around briefly, flashing her his debonair smile that had once made her giggle girlishly.

'Why am I doing this you say? Because I need to frame my dear brother and you will make the perfect victim.'

'Your brother?'

'Yes, you've met him. Strange man who runs a women's refuge on the edge of the village.'

Chrissy blinked, forcing her brain to process. The inside of the car seemed to swirl in front of her eyes as she fought against the need to slide back into oblivion.

'Ged. Ged Hughes is your brother?'

'Hard to believe isn't it? How can someone so dashing be related to a bore like him? But there it is. You can't pick your family. You should know with that mother of yours.'

DS Jason Moore smirked, his slight on her mother jarring her awake.

'I knew your mother you know. Crazy women. Believed she could appease God and keep you safe if she rid the world of one bad girl. I was sorry to hear of her death though. I know what it's like to be an orphan.'

Chrissy wanted to scream. Wanted to shout that he was to blame, not her mother. Even if she wasn't sure she really believed that. But she didn't have the strength.

The car began to slow, Jason's attention distracted. He pulled off the road and cut the engine, turning off the lights and plunging them back into total darkness. Jason slid down in his seat as headlights approached. Making her arms push her high enough to see over the window ledge, Chrissy could make out a pickup turning off the main road and disappearing up a single-track lane to the left of them. A second car came past, stopping further up the road, a few yards after the turning.

Jason waited, watching. Chrissy tried to pull herself higher, turning her head to squint at the car that had pulled up and stopped. It was square, tall, a silvery colour reflecting in the glow of its headlights.

'Ross,' Chrissy murmured. 'Ross.'

'Now don't do anything stupid Dr Ferguson.'

Chrissy tried to make her fingers grip the door handle, feebly pulling the black plastic towards her.

'Don't waste your time Chrissy. Child locks are a wonderful thing.'

Buoyed by Ross's nearness, she called out his name. Putting the flat of her hand against the window, she banged as hard as she could. Her effort was pathetic, making no more than a muted thud that would never be heard across the road.

Jason stretched back, grabbing her arm and pulling her easily until she was pressed against the driver's seat, her face inches away from his. Placing a hand across her mouth, he silenced her.

'Behave yourself Chrissy.'

His breath was minty, fresh like he'd not long since cleaned his teeth. His hand smelled of medicated soap, the kind that reminded Chrissy of hospitals. He was sporting a day's worth of designer stubble on his chiselled chin, heavily lashed eyes finishing off his handsomeness.

Chrissy struggled for breath, his hand stifling her nostrils. He wasn't paying attention to her lack of air. Jason was staring out of the window at Ross's car. Chrissy heard an engine rev, headlights washing over where they hid. Ross must have turned around and come back towards them. Before the Freelander passed them, its lights disappeared, the sound of tyres crackling on the gravel telling Chrissy he must have followed where the truck had turned up the track.

'Fuck! Fuck, fuck, fuck!'

Jason let her go, turning round and slamming his hands repeatedly onto the steering wheel. She watched him grab the sides of his head, twisting his hands angrily into his movie star hair. He was breathing heavily, teeth clenched together, making every exhale rasp. Chrissy flopped back against the back seat, the frustration at her situation preventing her from succumbing to the desire to drift into sleep. Jason was agitated, angry, and that made him more dangerous. Quietly, she waited for him to make a move, afraid of what that move might be.

As fast as his anger reared, it abated, leaving ominous calm in the car.

'I think we will have to change our plans Chrissy. It seems your DCI Fraser has finally had a breakthrough. No matter. I can always adapt. Your role in this game has changed my dear, and who knows, you might even live through it.'

'My role?' Chrissy asked, the muscles in her arms recovered enough to allow her to pull herself into a sitting position. 'What am I doing here Jason?'

He turned around to look at her, resting his arm casually across the back of his seat.

'Tell me Chrissy, how did you know where Aisha Flannigan was buried?'

'What?'

'You heard me. Tell me how you knew, and I'll think about letting you in on my plan.'

Chrissy's head ached, whatever he had given her leaving her mouth so parched she wasn't sure the words would form.

'I . . . I don't know.'

'You're lying. I think you do know.'

Chrissy swallowed hard, her foggy head slowing her thoughts. It was no use lying.

'I saw it in my dreams.'

'Your dreams? Now that is interesting.'

Jason rested his chin on his hand, brows coming together as he pondered her.

'Do you see other things? Other murders?'

'No!' Chrissy snapped. She didn't want him to know about Bonnie. 'Just Aisha and I've no idea why.'

'Hm, that's a shame. You would have been very useful to DCI Fraser if seeing murder victims in your sleep was a regular occurrence.'

He seemed completely accepting, not in the least sceptical about her visiting Aisha's murder scene while she slept. She would have been. She was! She had no idea how to explain it. At least with Bonnie, she had been there, the dream her repressed memory's way of stretching its legs. But Sonja? Aisha? It was just plain weird.

'What are you going to do with me Jason?' Chrissy asked tentatively.

'Well, we're going to get my money and then you are going to make sure I get out of here to spend it.'

'How do you expect me to do that? Ross probably knows by now it was you who killed Sonja, Ciara, Bonnie and . . .'

'No need to revisit my greatest hits, Chrissy. Anyway, I didn't kill those girls. It wasn't me who thrust a knife into Bonnie's throat. That was your mother.'

Jason sneered at Chrissy, waiting for a reaction that didn't come. The smug expression slipped off his good-looking face.

'You knew that didn't you?'

She needed to be careful. Didn't want to let slip that her mother was alive, that she was here in Kinloch

Rannoch. Chrissy's head was getting clearer, but her mind was still muddy.

'I suspected. When she was ill, she rambled about it. I was young and didn't want to think about it. I guess I blocked it all out.'

'Who can blame you? No one wants to think their parent is a killer, do they?'

Chrissy wanted to know more now, wanted to get inside his head. She wanted to understand what had happened, how her mother had got mixed up in all this.

'What about Ciara, Sonja and that boy who was killed in the woods?'

'You mean Calvin Parks? Nope, none of those deaths can be laid at my door either. Aisha was the murderer you see. I am more innocent than you want to believe Chrissy.'

If Chrissy had all her faculties, his condescension would have enraged her. But now, all she could manage was mild irritation.

'But you did kill Aisha?'

'Sadly yes. You see, I'm not averse to killing if the person concerned deserves it. I've killed twice in my life Chrissy. Aisha, who was going around killing innocent young people, and my father who beat my mother to death when I was sixteen. I just don't enjoy the kill. Murder is dirty, uncontrolled. Not my thing at all.'

'Then why? Why coerce Aisha, my mother, into killing for you?'

'Coerce? Who said anything about coercion? Is that what the police are saying?'

Chrissy sensed danger. His eyes blazed even in the darkness, a tick pulsing in his cheek.

'I don't know. Maybe. But *I* need to believe my mother wouldn't have killed anyone without someone in her ear telling her to do it.'

The tension left his face.

'Your mother wasn't in her right mind Chrissy. She did have someone in her ear guiding her behaviour. God. She wholeheartedly believed she was acting on God's will.'

He absolutely didn't see himself as responsible for the deaths committed by her mother and Aisha. In his mind, he had painted himself as some kind of hero, doing the right thing in killing only those who caused harm.

'So, what about me? What are you going to do with me.'

'Yes, yes, we digress here. It's time we got on with it.'

'With what?'

'Well, as I'm sure you can see, I'm not the villain here, but I think your DCI Fraser may take some convincing of that. You're how I'm going to convince him.'

'Me? Why do you think I could convince him that you're innocent?'

'I don't think you'll manage that Chrissy. After all,

as far as the police are concerned, I did murder two people and that's generally frowned upon, even if it was for the greater good. No, my dear Chrissy. Your DCI Fraser is going to let me go to save you.'

'Save me? From what?'

'I don't like killing unless it's for a good cause. And saving my own skin is the best cause I can think of.'

'You're . . . you're going to kill me?' she asked, her bottom lip trembling.

'Let's hope it doesn't come to that. If Ross chooses your life over catching me, then you'll live to see the next sunrise.'

'You're crazy if you think Ross would let you get away for any reason, especially for me.'

'Dr Ferguson, I never took you for a fool. Don't disappoint me now. Ross Fraser would do anything to keep you safe. And now, I'm going to prove it.'

32

Ross let Ged go, watching as he sunk back down onto the upturned crate.

'It was your brother who killed your father?'

'Yes, my wonderful brother,' Ged spat, hatred burning in his grey eyes. 'Jason was very close to our mother. Too close. While I was at the hospital waiting for Mother to die, he rammed a knife through Father's neck and strung him up in here. I thought it was an act of revenge – revenge for what he'd done to our mother. I never thought Jason was a killer. Never imagined he would kill again . . .'

Ged's mind wandered, his gaze fixed on the blank wall.

'What happened after you found your father?'

Ged got up, running a hand through his dirty hair.

'We buried him. I wanted to protect Jason. No one would miss Jock McKinley. His death wasn't upsetting anyone. And with Mother gone, I just wanted to end it, get us both out of here. We buried Father out at Annat Burn, somewhere we thought no one would ever find him.'

'And then you left?' Ross prompted.

'Not straight away. I was almost eighteen then, a man. I'd been planning my escape for years. I'd only stayed because I was afraid of what would happen to my mother if I left. I'd gotten to know a guy who came here every year on holiday. He said he could help me get away. He arranged a new identity for me, got me a passport, driving licence and so on, for a hefty price mind. Getting the money was easy. My father didn't believe in banks. He kept all his money here, at the farm. I'd been stealing from him for years, bits at a time so he wouldn't notice. I had enough to pay for my papers and for the fare to America. After he died, I took the rest. I wanted Jason to leave with me. I thought we could just disappear, put it all behind us.'

'But Jason didn't go?'

'No. He didn't want to. He asked me to get him papers, make him a new person.'

'Jason Moore?'

Ged nodded.

'I tried to convince him to come with me, but he was adamant. So, I got him what he asked for, gave him half the money and he left Kinloch Rannoch. I don't know where he went. We agreed on that day we would never see each other again, never acknowledge we were brothers. After Jason left, I went back to my plan. Jack McKinley ceased to exist, and Ged Hughes, real estate entrepreneur working out of New York, was born.'

'Why on earth did you come back here?' Ross asked, pacing back and forth, partly because he was restless, partly because it was freezing in the shed.

'McKinley Farm was eventually repossessed when the mortgage wasn't paid. I was doing well for myself in the States. When I heard the bank was going to auction it off a year later, I bought it. I had no idea what I was going to do with it. I just couldn't bear the thought of someone else living here. I tried to get on with my life in America, but once I owned the farm, I couldn't stop thinking about my home, my mother and what she went through. McKinley House seemed like the right thing to do to honour her memory. So, fifteen years ago, I came home.'

Ross wrapped his arms around his body, rubbing his biceps, his shoulders creeping upwards.

'And Jason? Did you see him?'

'Not until that girl was found, Ciara Campbell. It crossed my mind Jason could have been involved when I heard about how she died and with the body being found on McKinley land. But he came here with the investigation. He was in uniform then. I convinced myself it couldn't have been him, that he really had moved on, got himself together.'

'And what about when Sonja McBride was killed? You didn't think to mention anything then?'

Ross's temper was igniting at Ged's inaction – inaction that could cost him Chrissy.

'I don't know what I thought. I just wanted to stay out of it. I didn't want my past raked over. I have a good life now DCI Fraser. I sacrificed a lot to get it. It may sound selfish, but I wasn't eager to lose it. Jason was working for you! How could he be involved if he was a police officer?'

The sound of footsteps coming from the main shed spun Ross and Ged around. Jason Moore was silhouetted in the doorway, pushing Chrissy in front of him, a knife held to her throat. The light caught in his dark eyes, the pupils so large they obscured any colour surrounding them giving him a demonic appearance. He didn't speak as he moved into the room, Chrissy meekly obeying, her feet scuffing the floor as she tried to walk.

Ross could see her eyelids drooping, her head lolling intermittently before she fought to focus again. He must have given her something to keep her weak. The tip of the knife was denting her skin, a small bead of blood threatening to run down her neck.

'I see you two are having a nice, cosy chat,' Jason said, his voice sounding like something from a Jane Austen movie where the host was pleased everyone was getting along.

Ross took a step towards Chrissy.

'Ah, ah, ah, DCI Fraser. Chrissy stays with me.'

The blade pressed harder, creating a gash in Chrissy's white skin that started to bleed profusely. Ross stopped, his foot hovering mid-air for a moment before he replaced it back on the floor.

'Let her go Jason. She's hurt. Let me get her out of here. Then we can talk.'

'I don't think so. In case you haven't noticed, you're not in charge here Ross.'

Jason emphasised the use of Ross's Christian name instead of his rank. He took a few steps forward until Ged was in his line of sight.

'Hello brother,' Jason said, his black eyes filled with hatred. 'Did you bring the money?'

Ged seemed dumbstruck. He opened his mouth as if to speak, then closed it again. The words that would have greeted Jason like a long-lost family member failed to leave his throat, leaving only a weak nod behind.

'Have you been filling DCI Fraser in on our sordid past?' Jason asked, turning away from his brother to look back at Ross. 'It makes for quite an interesting tale, doesn't it?'

Chrissy's eyes opened again, her brown irises surrounded by bloodshot white.

'Ross,' she whispered. 'It was him. He killed them.'

Jason jerked her back against him, tightening his grip, pushing the knife a little further into her throat. Ross instinctively tried to reach out for her, but Jason was too quick. He pulled her close, taking a few steps away to increase the space between them.

He was shaking his head, tutting at Ross.

'Ross, you really need to stop trying to be the hero or Dr Ferguson isn't going to make it out of here.'

The nervousness that had been swirling in Ross's stomach since Jason had appeared suddenly drained away, calm and control flooding over him. If he was going to get Chrissy out of this, he needed to keep his head.

'What do you want Jason?'

'Now, let me see . . . I want to negotiate.'

'Negotiate?' Ross repeated, his eyebrows raised.

'Yes, negotiate. You see, despite what Chrissy here tried to tell you, I didn't kill Bonnie Harrison, Ciara Campbell or Sonja McBride and you have absolutely no evidence that can tie me to any of their murders.'

Ross clenched his teeth, the tendons in his neck, taut. He was right. They had nothing that would convict him in front of a jury of his peers. Jason smiled.

'I see you are with me on that Ross. And I'm afraid that boy, Calvin wasn't it? His death was not my doing either.'

'But you did kill our father.'

Ged found his voice, eyes hard as he glared at his brother.

'That would be hard to prove. I think you'll find you are more likely to be linked to his death than I am. You were the one who found him, who lowered his body onto a plastic sheet, transported him out to Annat Burn to bury him.'

'I was covering up for you!'

'Well, that would come down to your word against mine. And I'm afraid to tell you dear brother that you won't make the most believable witness. You had reason to want him dead, even more so than me. And it was you who stole all his money, changed your name and fled the country wasn't it?'

Ged looked away, his gaze dropping to the floor as Jason smiled in victory. Ross knew Ged would never testify against his brother.

'What about Aisha Flannigan?' Ross asked. 'Are you going to tell me you had nothing to do with that either?'

Jason threw back his head and laughed, his inattention nudging the knife sticking into Chrissy, dislodging a pool of blood that had been hanging on the edges of the wound.

'The only evidence you have linking me to Aisha Flannigan is the sperm that ex-wife of yours pulled from her cunt. All that shows is I had sex with her before she died. And I assure you, my sex life with Aisha Flannigan was entirely consensual.'

He leaned in closer to Chrissy's ear so that only she could hear.

'As was my sex life with your mother,' he whispered.

Ross couldn't hear what Jason said, but whatever it was made Chrissy struggle ineffectually against him.

'Are you trying to tell me you didn't kill Aisha Flannigan?'

Impatience exuded from Ross. It was taking every ounce of control he had not to charge at Jason, pummel his smug ass to a bloody pulp. But he was afraid he would pre-empt him, push the knife deeper into Chrissy before he could reach them.

'Let's not be so black and white Ross. I can tell you that Aisha Flannigan killed Ciara Campbell and Sonja McBride. She was also responsible for the death of Calvin Parks. So, whoever did kill Aisha, was doing you a favour.'

'What about Bonnie Harrison? You're not going to try and blame her death on a twelve-year-old Aisha are you?'

Jason smirked, placing his cheek against Chrissy's. Rage roared in Ross's stomach at his intimacy with her.

'Are you going to tell him or shall I?' Jason said, his lips brushing Chrissy's skin with every word.

Chrissy's tried to pull her head away, but there was nowhere to go.

'Seems Chrissy is a little shy today, so I'll fill you in. It was Chrissy's mother who killed Bonnie Harrison.'

Ross fought hard to maintain a stoic expression, hiding the turmoil Jason's words had stirred.

'It's hard to believe, isn't it? But it's true. Tell him Chrissy.'

Jason squeezed the arm he was holding painfully behind her back. Chrissy's eyes flicked fully open.

'You made them do it . . .' was all she could manage before her eyes rolled back, her head dropping again.

'That would be quite something if it were true. Of course, no one is alive who can testify to that. So, Ross, as I'm sure you're realising, you have nothing on me. Aisha and Chrissy's mother are dead. If I was somehow coercing them into killing people, which of course, I wasn't,' he said, smiling sadistically, ' . . . you still have nothing useful to prove my involvement. So, I'm going to take my brother's money so I can disappear, and you are going to let me walk out of here.'

Jason's words snapped Ross's focus away from Chrissy.

'The hell I am!'

'You are DCI Fraser, or I'm going to drive this knife right through Chrissy's neck. Are you willing to pay with her life? Is it worth it to put me in front of a jury when odds are, the case would be dismissed through lack of evidence?'

Ged was standing uselessly halfway between Ross and Jason, his head swivelling one way then the other as each took conversation turns. If he could catch his attention, maybe between them, they could overwhelm Jason before he could cause Chrissy much damage. But then, Ross wasn't even sure Ged would side with him. He seemed confused, pathetic. He was on his own until Hugh got here. Where the hell was Hugh? He should have been here by now.

With his mind reeling, Ross stared at Jason, trying to find the right words to keep Chrissy safe.

'I can't do that Jason. I can't let you go until we've questioned you more. Both of you,' he said, acknowledging Ged, still mute at their side.

'That's a shame for Chrissy here.'

Movement behind where Jason stood caught Ross's attention. Recognising Neve Ferguson, he quickly brought his gaze back hoping his distraction had gone unnoticed. The paltry light caught steel as Neve raised the barrel of a semiautomatic shotgun. She crept forward, the gun wedged against her shoulder and pointing directly at Jason's back. The floor creaked as she moved, the sound causing him to wheel around, placing Chrissy between himself and the loaded weapon. Jason's smug expression slid away as he registered the presence of the woman he thought was dead.

'Let my daughter go.'

There was no sign of nerves in Neve's voice. She was calm, collected, completely in control.

Jason's face paled in the dim light, the knife at Chrissy's throat trembling.

'Neve! You . . . You can't be here. You're dead!'

'Am I? I'm feeling pretty good for a dead woman.'

Ross recognised the panic of a cornered man, saw the danger coming.

'Now, let my daughter go!'

'Neve, Neve!' Jason said, a nervous laugh escaping his lips. 'You're not going to shoot that gun. You wouldn't hurt me. You and I, we meant something to each other. And what if you hit your daughter? Firing a gun isn't as easy as you might think.'

'Don't patronise me! You mean nothing to me. I'm here to save my daughter and to make you pay for what you did to me and to those other girls. And you're a fool if you think I'd be standing here with a gun I didn't know how to fire!'

Ross saw fury flash behind Jason's eyes. This wasn't going according to plan. He was losing control.

It all happened in slow motion. Jason spun around to face Ross, starting to push the knife further into Chrissy's neck. Chrissy slumped down, her knees buckling, her body slipping lower against Jason's body. It was what Neve needed. With his back turned and Chrissy collapsed forward, she had a clear aim.

Neve didn't hesitate. The gun blasted once, twice, three times. At close range, the shot went straight through Jason. She had targeted him high in the shoulder, the first shell bursting through his flesh above her daughter's head. The pain caused the knife to fall from Jason's grip, Chrissy crumpling in a heap on the floor.

The second and third shots hit Ged Hughes full in the face and chest as he threw himself in between Neve and his brother. His legs buckled, the crash as his body hit the floor resonating around the silent killing shed.

Time seemed to stand still. Jason clutched at his wounded shoulder, staring down at his brother lying still at his feet, pools of blood blooming from his head and chest. Neve lowered the shotgun letting the muzzle rest on the floor like a weaponised walking stick. She seemed frozen, her eyes glazing over as she looked at Chrissy lying prone in the centre of the circle of light. Ross was shellshocked, a moment of indecision seemed to last an age before he ran to where Chrissy lay.

33

Everything was silent. Chrissy could feel the floor of the shed beneath her back, the pain emanating from her neck, but she could hear nothing. She was caught in a vortex in time, waiting for the next second to happen, but it seemed in no rush to come along.

Her eyelids refused to open, keeping her apart from the rest of the world. She needed to see what was happening. Needed to see Ross, her mother. If she was going to die here, she wanted to look at them one last time.

Chrissy forced open her eyes, the world flooding in with the flare from the light. She wasn't alone. Ross was on his knees by her side, his hands pressed over the wound in her neck.

'Is she . . . is she . . .'

Her mother's voice, shaking and scared.

'No. She's still with us. It doesn't look too deep. Get my phone. It's in my pocket.'

Through the slits in her eyelids, she saw the shotgun laid on the floor, her mother's sensible shoes coming over to where Ross sat, her hands routing through his jacket pockets until she pulled out the phone.

Before Neve could do more, the sound of footsteps running across the shed turned Ross's head. Diane Fraser, flying in like a saviour on a white horse.

'Keep your hand on the wound, press harder!' she commanded.

Pain seared through Chrissy's neck as Ross increased the pressure. She heard bags being opened, packages ripped before Ross's hands were pulled away.

'Let me look.'

Diane leaned closer, tilting Chrissy's head away so she could clean the wound. The pain seemed less now, but she felt cold, shivery.

'He missed the main arteries. But we need to stem the blood loss.'

The pressure was back, softer hands and cloths soaking up the blood. Ross was still kneeling beside her, passing Diane new bandages as each became sodden.

'It's slowing down,' Diane said. 'The ambulance is on its way. I called one from the car just in case.'

'How did you know where to find us?'

Ross's voice was cracking as he spoke.

'I rang Hugh when Neve disappeared. She said she was going to make tea then did a runner in Chrissy's car. Mirren drove me here. Luckily, she had a first aid kit in the car.'

Diane took her hands away from Chrissy's throat, bending low again to examine the wound. She smelled of soap, clean and fresh. Out of place in this squalid shed. The beads in her hair felt cold as they touched Chrissy's neck, the sound as they clinked together when Diane sat up, strangely comforting.

Chrissy realised she was hearing things, smelling things. Her senses were coming back to life. Diane was putting a dressing on the wound, pulling it tight as she pressed the edges of sticking plasters across her throat. Her work finished, she laid a hand on her ex-husband's arm as the sound of sirens drifted towards the killing shed.

'She's going to be fine.'

Diane gathered up the first aid kit, then was gone. Chrissy watched her feet walk away, meeting another set wearing blue court shoes standing by the door. That must be Mirren.

'Chrissy? Chrissy? Can you hear me?'

Ross was leaning over her, his hazel eyes glistening with tears. He gathered up her hand and pulled it to his chest.

Chrissy turned her head to see him better. It hurt, a lot. A whimper escaped her lips and she laughed. It was good to feel even if it hurt like hell. Ross exhaled, his shoulders relaxing, his lips meeting her hand still clutched in his.

'Thank God!' he said, the tension visibly leaving his body at the sight of her awake. He leaned forward, placing his head against her chest.

'I thought . . . I thought I'd lost you.'

She managed to lift her arm, placing a hand on the back of his head. They stayed there for a few moments before Ross sat up, more composed but desperately reaching for her hand again.

'Jason? Where's Jason?'

Chrissy's throat was dry, her voice sounding alien to her.

'Don't worry about that,' Ross said, brushing a lock of hair away from her forehead.

'He got away didn't he?'

'For now. But he won't get far. He's wounded and Hugh has uniforms out there looking for him. They'll find him.'

'You should go after him.'

'I'm fine right here.'

Chrissy smiled weakly, her eyes struggling to focus again. She was so tired.

'He knew. He knew you'd save me rather than go after him. He was banking on it.'

'He's a smart man. Psychopathic, but smart.'

The last thing she saw was Ross's smile as he caressed her face. Then her eyelids closed, unconsciousness finding her again.

34

CHRISSY WAS BORED. Hospital stays gave you too much time to think. She had been in here four days now, the eight stitches in her neck helping the wound to heal, her liver taking an enforced holiday from alcohol.

She looked around the sterile room, the antibiotic drip fixed into her arm treating a post-surgical infection that had developed on day three. Despite the continuous dull ache in her neck and the occasional shooting pain when she moved too quickly, she felt OK - provided she stayed lashed to the bed by the tight sheets and extreme hospital corners the nurse felt necessary. She had appreciated the private room at first, probably Ross's doing. But now she felt alone.

Flowers and cards filled every available surface. A large bouquet in pinks and yellows from Professor Patricia Edgecombe and the School of Philosophy,

Psychology and Language Sciences told her to take time to recover, not to rush back. In other words, '*don't come back until the scandal of your murderous mother has died down*'. Pink and white carnations from Hugh McCann with a card apologising for not getting to the shed sooner. An ugly cactus plant from Sarah Cohen, her friend from work who had driven all the way to see her, stayed only ten minutes because hospitals made her jittery, then driven back to Edinburgh.

Diane had brought the magazines that stood dog-eared on the bedside table, and chocolates, the empty box languishing in the bin. Ross had only been to see her once, the day after she was admitted, leaving a box of blueberry muffins on her bedside table. She had been too out of it to talk much then, but now she was *compos mentis* and irritated by his absence and at the lack of information.

Chrissy climbed out of bed, holding the hospital gown closed at the back so the corridor didn't see her bare arse through the glass door. Her head swam as her equilibrium adjusted to being upright, her hands trembling as she reached for the IV pole and pushed it across the room. Her legs took some convincing to walk, shuffling slowly towards the chair where Mirren Doyle had propped a small suitcase containing some of Chrissy's belongings. It wasn't heavy but moving it onto the bed drained what little strength she had regained.

Opening it up, Chrissy took out her hideous pink

cat pyjamas that were freshly laundered and neatly folded on the top. Mirren had packed some jeans and a jumper in readiness for when she could leave the hospital, and five pairs of knickers and socks. Never had Chrissy been so grateful to see her well-worn pants.

She pulled a pair on, then sat down to slide her legs into the cat pyjama bottoms. Chrissy was breathing heavily, resting before she attempted to stand again when there was a knock on the door. She didn't have chance to answer before Ross Fraser came in. He didn't bat an eyelid that she was sitting with her trousers round her ankles, looking like she was taking a pee on the side of her bed.

'Need a hand?' he said, pointing at the wrinkled cat pyjamas.

Chrissy wanted the floor to swallow her up, but also felt unable to move. She nodded tentatively, closing her eyes to block out her embarrassment. Ross came over, taking her hands in his.

'Come on, up you come.'

He pulled her steadily to her feet, then bent down to pull up the pyjama bottoms. She rested her hands on his sturdy shoulders to keep balance, begging internally for it to be over. She collapsed back onto the bed as Ross stood up and reached for her top.

'Do you want this on as well?'

'Might as well. I already feel humiliated.'

'Don't be daft,' he said, reaching round her neck

and untying the gown. He pulled the gown down the arm without the IV. Chrissy took it out, clutching the blue fabric over her bare breasts.

'You'll have to forego your modesty if you want my help. I can't get it over the IV with you hanging on to it,' Ross said, pointing to the gown. 'I can get a nurse if you'd rather?'

Chrissy sat there, looking up at him, swithering between the intense desire to get out of the gown and into her own pyjamas without having to wait for a nurse to have the time, and her insecurity in revealing her boobs to Ross. Deciding she was being ridiculous given he had already got an eyeful when he helped her out of her vomit-stained clothes back at the cottage, she relinquished the gown, using her free arm to cover her small breasts as best she could.

Ross kept his focus on the task, sliding the gown down her arm, pulling it along the IV tubing and off over the bag he unhooked from the pole. Undoing the buttons in the cat pyjama top, he slid one sleeve over the bag, and back down the tubing, guiding it up Chrissy's arm before replacing the antibiotic drip on the pole.

'Very professional. You've done this before,' she said as he wrapped the top across her shoulders and helped her in with the other arm.

'My Dad has haemophilia. He has a lot of blood transfusions. Helping him in an out of clothes while attached to a drip is a skill learned through necessity.'

Chrissy looked at him, head cocked to one side, brows knitted together.

'I just realised, you know everything about me, but I don't know anything about you,' she said, buttoning up her top.

'I like to be a man of mystery. How are you feeling anyway?' Ross asked, taking the gown from the bed and throwing it over the back of a chair.

'Better. Much better. I'm just still so bloody weak. It's infuriating.'

'You need to rest.'

He zipped the suitcase and lifted it off the bed, placing it on the floor near the door.

'Come on, back to bed with you.'

He helped her climb back between the hospital sheets, plumping her pillow and tucking her in like a child.

'Thank you,' she whispered, her voice as small as she felt.

With her settled, he pulled up a chair, resting his forearms on her bed.

'Tell me what's been happening Ross. Have you caught Jason?'

'You shouldn't be worrying about it. Just focus on getting well. There's time for all that when you're out of here.'

'Ross, bloody tell me! It's driving me crazy being in here, not knowing anything.'

Ross looked down, suddenly fascinated by his

fingers.

'We haven't caught him yet, but we will,' he added quickly. 'There's nowhere for him to go. He didn't get the cash either. It was still in Ged's car. So, we'll find him.'

'Will you have enough evidence to convict him?'

'With the attack on you and your mother's statement, we should have.'

The sound of metal clattering to the floor made them both jump. Their eyes darted towards the glass door where a nurse was on her hands and knees in the corridor outside, picking up a kidney-shaped sliver dish, scissors and bandages she had evidently just dropped. Relaxing now the source of the noise had been identified, Ross leaned back in his chair.

'Where's my mother?' Chrissy asked, the words catching in her throat.

'On remand. When everything calmed down, she told me about Bonnie. I had to arrest her Chrissy. I had no choice.'

He looked pleadingly into her face, expecting her to be annoyed by it.

'She deserved it. She killed someone,' Chrissy replied, the anger she felt still raw.

'She's being held at Cornton Vale until the trial. I can take you to see her once you're released.'

'That won't be necessary.'

'You don't want to see her?'

'No. I don't.'

'But Chrissy, she's your mother.'

'My mother died four years ago.'

Chrissy folded her arms, her mouth set in a straight line. Ross got the message.

'What about Mirren? Did she get arrested for keeping Neve's secrets?' Chrissy asked.

'She's been charged with perverting the course of justice. She'll stand trial but she's not in jail now. She'll probably serve time though.'

Nodding, Chrissy chewed at the inside of her lip.

'When I asked Mirren why she hadn't gone to the police when she found out my mother killed Bonnie Harrison, she said she 'had her reasons'. Didn't want the police snooping around. Do you know what she meant by that?'

'Seems Mirren's got a bit of a past. She killed her husband, went to prison for seven years for it. When she got out, she came here, to Kinloch Rannoch for a new start where no one knew her or her sons.'

'She killed her husband? Mirren?'

'He was abusing her, put her in the hospital twice. She killed him in self-defence.'

'Oh God. You just never know what people are dealing with do you?'

For a moment, they sat in companionable silence, each lost in their own thoughts. Ross sat up straight, stretching his spine and rubbing his hands down his navy trousers. Chrissy noticed he was wearing new boots - black lace-ups with thick, grooved soles. She smiled inwardly. She'd hated his pointy shoes. The moustache had gone too.

'What are you going to do when you get out of here?' he asked looking around the room.

Chrissy unfurled her arms, happier now to be on a different subject.

'I'll go back to Edinburgh I suppose. Back to my life, my job.'

'What about the cottage? Will you sell it?'

'Well, it's not mine, is it? Now Neve Ferguson has come back from the dead, it belongs to her. It's up to her what she does with it.'

'I don't think your mother will be in any position to do anything with it for a long time. She's facing two murder charges and intends to plead guilty to both.'

'Two?'

'You didn't know? Ged Hughes died at the scene. When your mother shot at Jason, he threw himself in front of his brother. Took two at close range. There was no way he could survive the injuries.'

Chrissy was ashen, her eyes wide.

'But she didn't mean to kill him. She was just trying to save me!'

'I thought you didn't care?' Ross asked, a smile threatening the corners of his mouth.

'I don't! It just seems unfair under the circumstances, that's all.'

'You're right. It isn't fair, not after everything your mother went through. But even though she didn't mean to kill Ged, she did have the intent to kill when she pointed the gun at Jason.'

'You sound like a police officer . . .'

'Funny that.'

They were both smiling now. It felt nice to be able to smile in spite of everything.

'Anyway, I'm sure the judge will show some leniency. She'll go to prison, but hopefully, they'll take her mental state into account and Jason's role in it all when they set the minimum term. She could be out in a few years.'

Chrissy wasn't sure how she felt about that. Part of her wanted Neve to rot in jail because of what she'd done to Bonnie Harrison, for what she'd put her through. The other part, the little girl that still missed her mother, wanted Neve to be free. Wanted the courts to acknowledge she hadn't been in her right mind, to recognise she'd come back and done the right thing once she was well. The mixed emotions were too difficult to wrestle with now.

'What about you? What's next for Ross Fraser?'

'I'll go back home to Tayside after I leave here. Wait for the next case. Can't wait to sleep in my own bed.'

Something unspoken hung between them, neither willing to put it into words. When the silence grew awkward, Ross got to his feet.

'I better get going. You need your rest and Ness is waiting in the car.'

Chrissy nodded, unexpected tears stinging the back of her eyes.

'Oh, I brought you these.'

Ross picked up a Tupperware box he had left on the chair by the door when he arrived and handed it to Chrissy. She flipped open the lid, the sweet, sticky aroma of freshly baked chocolate chip muffins filled her nostrils.

'Fantastic! Hospital food lives up to its reputation.'

She smiled warmly at Ross who was lingering at the door.

'Thank you for everything Ross.'

He smiled back.

'Chrissy, will you do something for me?'

'If I can.'

'Get some help with the drinking.'

She lowered her eyes, fixating on the muffins, nodding uncomfortably. When she looked up, he was gone.

THE END

If you have enjoyed the Killing Shed, I would really appreciate it if you could leave a review on my Amazon page.

CARGILL'S LEAP (Chrissy Ferguson Book 2) AVAILABLE NOW IN THE AMAZON STORE!

Grab your FREE Ebook!

Thank you so much for reading The Killing Shed. I hope you enjoyed it!

You can grab your FREE Chrissy Ferguson Mystery by heading to www.cljanetauthor.com. Just tell me where to send it and I'll email it to you!

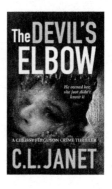

She thought she was in control. She was wrong.

When the frozen corpse of Andie Sinclair is found at Devil's Elbow in the Scottish Highlands, Forensic Psychologist Dr Chrissy Ferguson isn't surprised. She already knew the woman was dead.

Struggling with the crippling visions of death and violence that plague her sleep, Chrissy wants to flee, to find a haven where the haunting echoes of death and the weight of her mother's trial can't reach. But DCI Ross Fraser is here, asking for help. And she would do anything for Ross.

As the investigation unearths multiple suspects with motive for murder, it becomes clear that Andie wasn't the innocent she seemed. Harbouring an insatiable hunger for adoration, her every move was orchestrated to ensure love and affection from everyone around her by whatever means necessary.

Andie was good at what she did. But someone wanted something in return for their love.

Her life.

SUBSCRIBERS WILL RECEIVE OCCASIONAL EMAILS WITH NEWS, DEALS OR NEW RELEASE INFORMATION FROM C.L. JANET.

YOUR INFORMATION WILL NEVER BE PASSED ON TO THIRD PARTIES.

From the Author

I really hope you enjoyed getting to know Chrissy Ferguson in The Killing Shed! Chrissy and Ross are back in Cargill's Leap, available now on the Amazon store. See the sneak peak of Chapter 1 on the next pages.

You can sign up for my newsletter at www.cljanetauthor.com to be kept informed about future new releases, the latest book offers and even grab yourself a free Chrissy Ferguson Mystery!

The beauty and wildness of Kinloch Rannoch, a small Highland village in rural Perthshire, was the inspiration for this story. Although I was born and raised in the north of England, I have lived in Scotland for almost twenty years, the people and the dramatic landscapes completely stealing my heart. I hope to share my love for my adopted home with my readers through the lives of the characters in my novels.

The people and places in The Killing Shed are drawn from my imagination although real places in Kinloch

Rannoch did help me create the locations I used as the backdrop for Chrissy's story. For example, the Loch Rannoch Hotel, a beautiful and imposing building on the edge of the village, was the inspiration for the Rannoch Arms Hotel where Chrissy first finds out about the missing woman and reconnects with Mirren Doyle. However, the staff and patrons of the hotel are all works of fiction. Edinburgh University and the police stations at Rannoch and Dundee are also real places, but again, all characters are drawn from the depths of my mind.

I hope you have enjoyed getting to know Chrissy, Ross and the other characters who come in and out of their lives. Many will be back in the next Chrissy Ferguson mystery released soon.

Reviews are very important to me so if you have the time, I would really appreciate it if you could leave a review on my Amazon page.

If you would like to know more about me, my novels and what's coming next, head over to www.cljanetauthor.com. You can also access your reader exclusives there and get involved in the production of my next novel by becoming part of my advanced reader team.

I love to hear from my readers! Please drop me a line at clare@cljanetauthor.com with questions and comments about the book, my writing life or just to say hi! You can also contact me through my website (www.cljanetauthor.com) or through any of my social media links (see previous page or website).

I look forward to getting to know you!

C. L . Janet

Follow me on social media for regular updates on what I'm up to.

facebook.com/CLJanetAuthor

twitter.com/CLJanetAuthor

instagram.com/cljanetauthor

Sneak peak of the next Chrissy Ferguson Mystery

CARGILL'S LEAP (CHRISSY FERGUSON MYSTERIES BOOK 2)

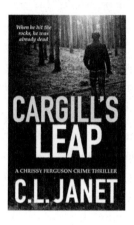

Chapter 1

Killing a man took careful planning. Killing four men felt like as much organising as sending the dam-busting 617 Squadron on Operation Chastise. Murder had never been on his bucket list. But sometimes, your life goals change.

The garden looked beautiful, the evening arriving on tiptoe, whispering secrets of summer's imminent arrival. The air was pregnant with the scent of blooming flowers and freshly mown grass that blended harmoniously with the peaty smell on his breath. Staring out across the perfectly manicured lawn, he stood motionless as daylight surrendered to dusk. He took the time to listen as the symphony of birdsong gradually quietened, the laughter of children playing in the distance fading as the darkness swallowed the sun.

The crystal tumbler clinked softly against his lips, the fiery whisky burning a path of introspection through his veins. This moment was the threshold of transformation, his conscience teetering on the precipice of an irreversible decision. A tempest of conflicted thoughts tumbled and churned around his mind like the shifting winds, always ending with the same unassailable truth. He had to do this. He needed to do this.

Everything was ready. He had been meticulous. He would leave nothing to chance. On this warm May evening, destiny was holding its breath. An ordinary man would be remade tonight as a harbinger of impending tragedy. And as much as he hated to admit it, he was looking forward to it.

AVAILABLE NOW ON THE AMAZON STORE.

Printed in Great Britain
by Amazon